JOHNNY GRAPHIC

AND THE ATTACK OF THE ZOMBIES

D. R. MARTIN

JOHNNY GRAPHIC ADVENTURES BOOK 2

CONGER ROAD PRESS
MINNEAPOLIS

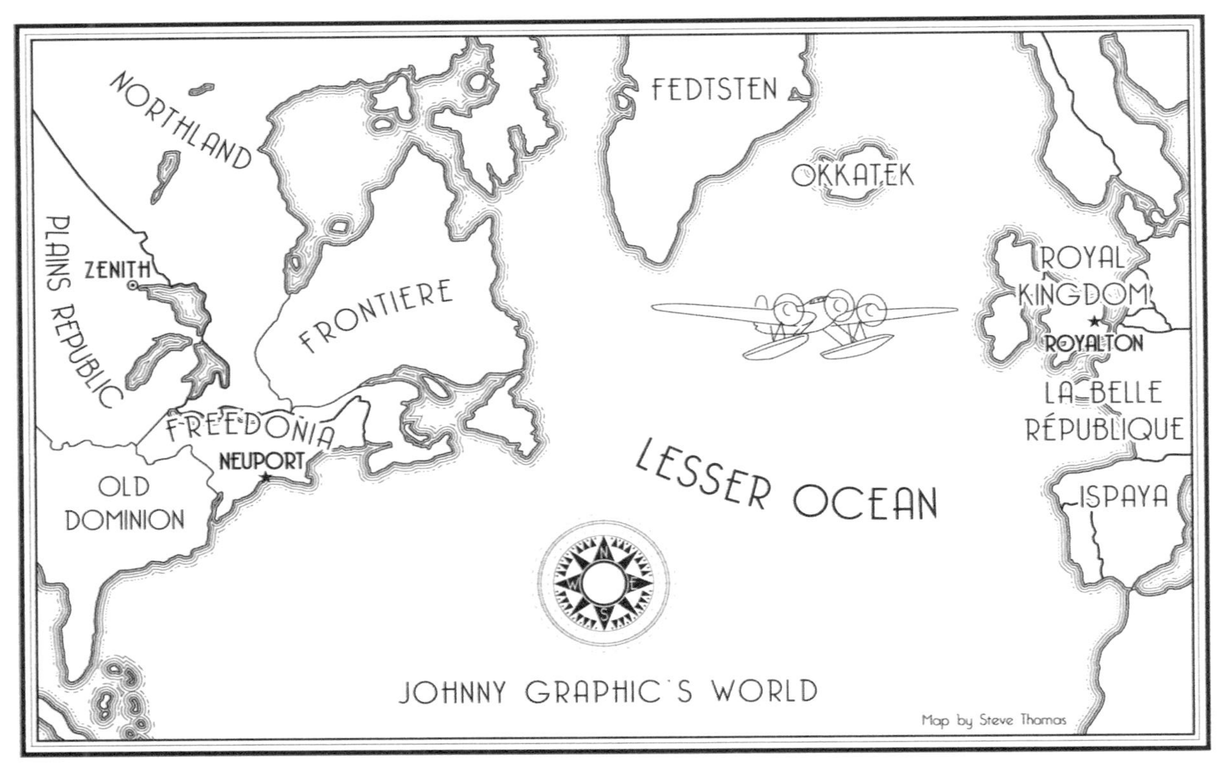

NORTHLAND
FEDTSTEN
OKKATEK
PLAINS REPUBLIC
ZENITH
FRONTIERE
ROYAL KINGDOM
ROYALTON
FREEDONIA
NEUPORT
LA-BELLE RÉPUBLIQUE
OLD DOMINION
ISPAYA
LESSER OCEAN
JOHNNY GRAPHIC'S WORLD
Map by Steve Thomas

PROLOG

BASIL HASTINGS, the third son of Lord Hurley of Evansham, slouched across the main quadrangle of St. Egbert's School, his hands thrust deeply into his pockets.

He had just taken supper in the dining hall with the two hundred and twenty other sons of nobility and wealth who populated the student body of St. Egbert's. The fare was, as usual, unappealing—some rather tough beefsteak, boiled potatoes, creamed corn, stewed prunes, and weak, tepid tea. As if the food weren't punishment enough, Basil had developed a splitting headache.

All he wanted to do was lie in his bed with a cold washcloth across his face.

Basil's dormitory was a gray, bleak pile of Gothic stonework. Drafts seemed to spill out of every chink and crack in the walls. In the depths of winter, the only real refuge from the pervasive chill was to huddle under several blankets in one's bed.

He swiftly took off his rumpled blue jacket, trousers, shirt, and tie. Then he slipped into his flannel pajamas. He padded out on bare feet to the big lavatory and soaked a washcloth in cold water. Climbing into bed, he plastered the wet rag to his forehead. As he lay on his back in the dimly lit bedroom—on one of a dozen beds—he could hear the noises coming from the common room, almost directly beneath where he rested.

Boys hollering and singing. A piano being played rather badly. Footsteps racing up and down the staircase.

Basil wished he could have been down there, enjoying himself. Well, perhaps tomorrow, after this filthy headache was gone.

The last thing he remembered before he drifted off was hearing a raucous chorus of that popular music-hall tune, "Oh, By Golly, Polly Is a Jolly Dolly."

WHEN HE STARTED to come up out of his dreamless slumber, Basil realized that his head was no longer aching. The terrible pressure around his temples and eyes had disappeared. But something very strange was going on.

Slowly waking up, he thought that he heard the sound of breaking glass. And boys shouting and screaming outside.

With a violent swing of his arm, Basil threw off his three blankets and scrambled to his feet. The bedroom seemed full of a peculiar orange, dancing light. He dashed to one of the windows and gasped in shock at what he saw.

Over on the far side of the quadrangle, the St. Egbert's School library was engulfed in soaring flames. A stone's throw away, the centuries-old chapel looked like a huge, strange lantern—full of fire. Basil saw several grown-ups sprawled on the grass, not moving. One of them looked like the headmaster.

Up and down on the muddy quadrangle, boys in bathrobes and pajamas were running about willy-nilly, howling for help. And chasing after them were weird, loping figures, tall enough to be men, wearing odd, loose-fitting tunics and coats.

A pudgy boy tried desperately to elude the lunging grasp of one of the creatures. But the boy was too slow and too clumsy. With what looked like a gentle tap of the fist, his pursuer knocked him flat to the ground, then deftly picked him up and hurried away out of the quad—the very limp lad slung over its shoulder like a sack of potatoes.

I've got to warn the other boys! Basil thought. Then he looked around the sleeping chamber.

Blast it! He was all alone.

Everyone had flown the coop. And that's exactly what Basil intended to do.

He quickly dressed, then grabbed his deluxe willow cricket bat. He rushed out into the hallway. The electricity appeared to be out, so he had to feel his way down the staircase.

Taking a deep breath, Basil—a wiry, cautious sort of boy—darted out the door and into the quad, then took a sharp right. He planned to make for the police station in Chippington-in-the-Vale, the small town a couple of miles away.

But as he ran past the infirmary, a hulking form leapt out in front of him. Basil briefly prayed that it was Angus Snodgrass, the groundskeeper, well known for his slouching posture and grimy, formless outerwear. But the boy's prayer went unanswered, as the unknown assailant lurched at him with a guttural growl and outstretched, claw-like hands.

Basil jumped backward, just avoiding the grasping, menacing fingers. Petrified right down to his bones, he swung his cricket bat and caught his attacker full on the side of the head. The hit made a horrific, sodden *thunk*.

But instead of collapsing into a heap, the thing stood there stolidly. Then it pulled aside its hood, and the glow of the burning buildings illuminated its features.

Basil's jaw dropped, and his cricket bat slipped from his grasp.

The face that regarded him looked to have been fashioned from old leather. Both cheeks and temples had been squashed inwards. The unblinking black eyes that stared at him were dull and flat and lifeless. A few snaggleteeth were all that remained in the distorted mouth.

"What do you want?" Basil asked, his voice quavering.

It seemed as if the creature tried to smile, but the corners of its mouth would not cooperate. Then it spoke.

"You."

And before Basil could move an inch, he was swept up into sinewy, powerful arms, and carried off into the night.

Basil intended to scream for help. But only one word came out of his mouth.

"Zombie!"

CHAPTER 1

JOHNNY GRAPHIC had been standing outside the jail entrance for nearly an hour. He was nervously awaiting the arrival of Harold "Mad Dog" Fleischer, the notorious bank robber.

Johnny's editor at the *Zenith Clarion* wanted a shot of Fleischer for the front page. The stickup man was a hot news item, after his daring robbery of West Zenith National Bank a few days before. A half-dozen other newspaper photographers were lined up with Johnny, all jockeying to get the perfect shot. And Johnny knew exactly how he was going to do that—even though it made him pretty anxious to think about it. If his plan didn't work, he'd be in big trouble.

He was yakking with a photographer a foot taller and ten years older than him, when a plain black van drove up to the jail entrance.

Johnny tried to relax. *Okay, this is it. Stick to the plan.*

Several cops rushed to the back door of the van and opened it. They hauled Fleischer out, his hands cuffed behind his back. He was one mean-looking guy—his long, haggard face contorted with rage.

The robber resisted the officers every inch of the way. He shouted profanities at the photographers as their flashbulbs went off. At the age of twelve and three-quarters, Johnny had never heard some of those words before. But they sure sounded bad.

With their big press cameras, the photographers had time for only one shot. Johnny waited to take his until all the others had finished. It felt like an eternity.

All of a sudden his opportunity arrived.

He rushed up toward Fleischer and yelled, "Hey, Mad Dog. Give us a big smile!"

The criminal turned in his direction, his face full of fury. At precisely that instant, Johnny mashed down the shutter button. The flashbulb flared.

Fleischer roared at Johnny and broke free of one of the cops holding him. The robber lunged, getting so close that Johnny could actually smell the criminal's sour breath.

Uh-oh, Johnny thought.

But in a wink, Fleischer's captors yanked him backward, like a calf on a lariat. They finally wrangled him, still swearing a blue streak, into the jail.

"Great move, kiddo," the other photographer laughed.

His heart racing, his hands trembling, Johnny turned to his chum. "Sure hope that shot works out."

It did.

Johnny's photo editor said it almost certainly would be on to-morrow's front page, as planned. Taking that particular shot had been a gamble, but it had paid off.

So Johnny should have felt like a million bucks. He should have had a spring in his step and a grin on his round, freckled face as he climbed off the streetcar near Grover Falkland Junior High.

Not only had he gotten the shot, he was living the life he'd dreamed about since he was little. Johnny Graphic was a genuine, bona fide news photographer. He'd achieved almost everything he had wanted to. And how many kids of twelve and three-quarters can say that?

After testing out of school last summer, Johnny had started shooting assignments for the *Clarion* right away. For a couple of months, things went swell.

Then, without warning, he got roped into investigating a ghost conspiracy that spanned the globe—with a million lives on the line, including his own and those of everyone he loved.

Along with his sister, uncle, and best friend, Johnny had traveled across the Greater Ocean, chasing ghost assassins. He had witnessed the explosion of the first etheric bomb. He had gone blind for a number of hours. He had helped to rescue his sister from the clutches of Steppe Warrior ghosts. He himself had narrowly escaped death several times. He still shuddered to think of how close the city of Zenith had come to total annihilation.

And in spite of all that, he had managed to deliver a steady stream of news photos to his boss, with his sister writing the accompanying stories. Photos and stories that were published in hundreds of newspapers around the world. He was proud of every bit of it.

A newspaperman with that kind of success should have been over the moon. But as he walked into Shep's Super Soda Shop, Johnny Graphic frowned. He was not a happy guy. Because he knew there was one thing he hadn't been able to do—maybe the biggest thing. And doing it had just gotten harder.

All around, kids from Falkland Junior were sucking on malted milks and laughing and joking with each other. As he walked past their tables, Johnny nodded to a few guys who had been in Camera Club with him before he left school. He felt a little pang of nostalgia for the many hours he had spent in the darkroom with them, talking about photo gear and sharing their plans for the future.

His best friend, Nina Bain, was waiting for him in their favorite booth at the back of the malt shop.

"I've been thinking about that rotten crumb-bum Percy Rathbone," Johnny fumed, thumping onto the seat. "He's messed up everything. *Everything.*"

Nina gave him an exasperated look. "That again?" she groaned, taking a sip of her strawberry malt. "You've been bellyaching ever since we found out the trip was postponed. I understand that you're disappointed. But what's done is done. Mel has to stay here in Zenith and help track down Percy."

"I know," Johnny said, grabbing one of the fries from Nina's plate. "I know."

It almost made Johnny go nuts to even think about it. He and his sister, Melanie, had been all set to fly across the ocean to hunt for clues about their missing parents. Nina and Uncle Louie were coming, too. All Johnny and Mel had to do was send stories and photos back to the *Clarion* about the search for Mom and Pop. The newspaper was picking up the entire tab.

And then that rodent Percy had to go and escape from the toughest jail in Zenith. And suddenly, the trip to find Johnny's parents was put off indefinitely.

They figured that one of Percy's minions had slipped into his cell and cut off his head. But it wasn't really Percy's head. Percy was a ghost. He had been residing in another person's dead body, which he had reanimated.

When the body was beheaded, his ghostly self was released. Then Percy could easily fly through the jail walls without setting off any alarms.

Nina took a bite of her Cozy Island hot dog, fixing her brown eyes on Johnny while she chewed and swallowed. "I know how much you want to find your folks. But Percy might be planning something even more dangerous than what he cooked up last year. I, for one, am glad Mel and Dame Honoria are on the case."

Johnny grumbled—the noise he made whenever anyone confronted him with common sense that he didn't like. But Nina was right about the need to find Percy, after all the terrible things he'd done.

And nobody would be better at tracking him down than Johnny's godmother, Dame Honoria, and his sister Mel. They were two of the top etherists in the world.

Etherists were professional ghost handlers. Of course, to be an etherist, you had to be able to see and hear ghosts. Mel and Dame Honoria were among the small number of living people who could. Johnny could, as well, but Nina lacked the ability. As for becoming a ghost, only two or three percent of people and animals had that rotten luck.

Etherists dedicated themselves to communicating with ghosts. They solved problems for ghosts. They enabled ghosts to interact with the real, physical world—giving them purpose and function.

Etherists found actual employment for ghosts, who were suited for certain types of jobs. Mine owners sent ghosts into the earth to locate the richest veins of ore. Government officials sought them out to clean up hazardous materials. In the dead of winter, when frigid temperatures might imperil living officers, the police hired dead cops to work the stakeouts. Deceased doctors would look inside people for illnesses.

Not all ghosts had the temperaments to associate with living beings. Many preferred to spend their days alone or with other ghosts, ruminating about the sad state of their deaths. Others acted out their anger by tormenting those who were still alive. More than a few times, Mel had been hired to evict an obnoxious wraith that was haunting a house occupied by some unfortunate family.

Mel and Dame Honoria were both authorities when it came to second-guessing rogue ghosts. But Dame Honoria had special expertise when it came to the rogue ghost Percival Rathbone. He was, after all, her dead son.

Johnny could never understand why Percy had gone so bad. The man had been given every advantage growing up.

When he was alive, Percy had been a brilliant young etherist. He had spoken passionately about helping these poor dead people who had not been able to reach their final destination after death.

Percy believed that the solution to the ghosts' plight lay in solving one of the Two Impossible Things.

The First Impossible Thing was to bring the ghosts back to life. The Second Impossible Thing was to give them a proper death by helping them escape the ether.

Johnny could kind of understand Percy's devotion to his cause. But like many fanatics, Percy took it to incredible extremes. It amazed Johnny how good intentions could go so horribly bad.

And now it seemed that Percy had figured out how to restore ghosts to "life" by possessing dead bodies. Johnny called it "zombiefication," and it gave him the chills to think about it.

"So," Nina said, interrupting his thoughts, "would you rather have Mel traipsing around the world with you, maybe on a wild goose chase, while Percy is out wreaking havoc? Or would you rather have her doing what she can to put him back behind bars?"

"What you're saying makes sense, Sparks. But I just keep thinking that a lot of bad stuff in my life seems to involve Percy. After all, he invited Mom and Pop to go on that expedition to Okkatek

Island five years ago. And that was the last time I ever saw them."

"He does seem to be a big thorn in your butt," Nina agreed. "But there's nothing you can do until he's captured again."

Out of nowhere, someone cleared his throat.

Johnny looked up. There stood Colonel Horace MacFarlane, the ghost soldier who had been a Graphic family aide since Johnny was a baby. The colonel was on foot, so apparently his ghost horse, Buck, was outside.

"What are you doing here, Colonel?" Johnny asked, surprised to see him in the malt shop.

"Commander Graphic knew you would be here and asked me to fetch you both. Something important has happened."

"What's up?"

"The commander simply said to bring you home."

Though Johnny liked flying on aircraft well enough, soaring through the sky on a ghost horse made him very nervous.

"We'd rather take the bus, Colonel, if you don't mind."

"As you will, Master Johnny. But please, don't tarry." The ghost touched an index finger to the bill of his campaign hat and floated away, out toward the street.

Johnny conveyed the colonel's words to Nina. She quickly gobbled up the last of her hot dog, left some money on the table, and then rushed out with him to catch the streetcar.

Johnny hadn't even had time to order a shake.

Maybe this was the news they'd been waiting for—a big break in the hunt for Percy Rathbone.

CHAPTER 2

FORTY-FIVE MINUTES LATER, Johnny and Nina were trudging up the serpentine driveway through the birch, poplar, and pine that sheltered the big brick house they lived in. They called it Birchwood. It was the only home Johnny had ever known. Nina lived there, too, with her guardian, Louie Hofstedter—Johnny's uncle.

Johnny sniffed the air and could smell the crisp scent of the evergreens. He knew he had the best of both worlds—the city close by, the big woods a stone's throw behind the house. Why would a fellow want to be anywhere else?

As soon as they walked in the front door, they heard a shout from the living room.

"Is that you, guys?" hollered Mel.

"Who else would it be?" Johnny hollered back.

"Get in here *right now*," his seventeen-year-old sister barked.

With Nina right behind him, Johnny trotted into the living room—anxious to find out what was going on.

Dame Honoria stood over by the bookcase, her face looking less dour than usual. In fact, the stout old lady was actually wearing a broad and very uncharacteristic grin.

Mel stood in the middle of the room, in front of the big stuffed chair Uncle Louie was sitting in. She was bent over, fussing with something on his head.

That's when Johnny realized what was going on, why the colonel had summoned Nina and him. Johnny had been waiting for this moment for weeks now.

"Holy maroley! Does this mean they're ready?"

As if to answer, Mel stepped back and Uncle Louie stood up.

Catching sight of the big man, Nina broke into a fit of giggles.

Still in the overalls he wore to work at the Babbitt aeroboat port, Uncle Louie flashed a crooked grin. Over his eyes, he had on the most remarkable pair of goggles Johnny had ever seen.

His previously gloomy mood lifted. Not just because Uncle Louie looked pretty darn comical. But because if Mel had actually succeeded, this could be big news.

Johnny had been there when the eyewear started its life as a pair of ordinary aviator goggles. Over the last few months, Mel had transformed them. She had removed the glass, replacing it with special optical lens crystal of exceeding purity. She had set the round lenses into delicate copper frames, then coated the glass with a special liquid prepared from a culture made with her own tears. Using ordinary batteries and fine copper wire, she energized the matrix of glass and dried culture. To Johnny, the goggles looked like something that belonged on the cover of a Captain Justice adventure book.

"They don't fit perfectly," Mel said. "But I think I've got the formula pretty close to optimum. The coating is delicate. I don't know what kind of endurance it has or how it will wear."

"But do they work?" Johnny asked. If they did, it meant that the ninety-seven percent of the population who couldn't see ghosts *would now be able to.* It would be an incredible achievement. And the patent would be worth millions—way more than enough to pay off the mortgage on Birchwood and provide a secure future for the whole family.

"Do they work?" Nina echoed, her own eyes wide with wonderment.

Mel and Uncle Louie could barely contain themselves. And Dame Honoria was bubbling as much as an old, plump dowager was able to bubble.

Turning to Colonel MacFarlane, who was standing at ease back by the wall of bookshelves, Mel said, "Colonel, do something unexpected for Uncle Louie."

"Such as?" the ghost officer asked.

"Something funny."

Now Johnny wanted to see this, because "funny" was not something he normally associated with the dead—and dead serious—Border War cavalryman. He understood, though, what Mel was up to. Uncle Louie didn't have etheric sight. So if he could describe what the colonel was doing, it meant the etheric goggles really did the job.

The first thing that impressed Johnny was that Uncle Louie looked right at the bookshelves, directly at the spot where the ramrod-straight ghost officer was standing.

"Holy cow!" said Uncle Louie. "There he is."

Then the colonel did indeed do something funny.

For ten seconds or so, he danced a lively little jig, his arms straight down by his sides, his legs pumping.

"The colonel is dancing!" Uncle Louie exclaimed.

Nina rushed toward Mel and grabbed her in a big hug. "You did it! You did it!" Then she turned and embraced Uncle Louie. "Now let me try them!"

Johnny was not one to normally give people hugs. So he gave Mel a pat on the shoulder. He was pretty proud of what his big sister had just accomplished.

Even the colonel was grinning as Uncle Louie took off the etheric goggles and gently rested them on the bridge of Nina's nose. Mel spent a couple of minutes adjusting them to fit her.

Then, her black corkscrew curls bouncing, Nina twisted around, holding the goggles tightly up to her eyes. "Wow!" she yelped.

Johnny watched her stare at the colonel, her mouth wide open with amazement. He could barely imagine what it must be like for someone who had never seen a ghost to catch sight of one for the first time. Maybe it was like being blind and suddenly seeing.

"I had no idea how handsome Colonel MacFarlane is," Nina said excitedly. "I am so happy to know what you look like."

Being a ghost and dead for over seventy years, the colonel lacked the capacity to blush. But Johnny suspected that's just what he wanted to do, somewhere beneath his translucent features.

"Miss Nina is too kind," the colonel said. "I'm just a plain old horse soldier."

Then Nina gazed around the room and smiled.

"Hi, Mrs. Lundgren," she said, waving at the ghost housekeeper. "And hello, Bao. You're very, very cute."

The little girl ghost giggled, her black headdress bobbing. Then she did the curtsy that Dame Honoria had taught her.

"It's just a prototype," Mel explained, taking back the goggles from Nina. "A bit rough and bulky. It needs a lot more work. But the principle is solid."

Just then, the telephone in the hallway began to ring. Uncle Louie strode off to answer it.

Johnny was giving the goggles a close inspection when his uncle returned. The big man looked worried.

"What's up, Uncle Louie?" asked Johnny.

"It was your boss, Mr. Cargill."

"Does he need me for something?" Johnny was all ears. When the editor-in-chief of the *Clarion* called you, you hopped to it.

"He said he needs to see all of us," replied Uncle Louie. "There's someone we have to meet. He didn't want to explain it over the telephone. But he said it couldn't wait. They're coming out here right away."

Something's happened, Johnny thought. If Mr. Cargill couldn't delay his news until tomorrow, it was probably something bad.

CHAPTER 3

AN HOUR LATER, the front doorbell rang. Johnny jogged out and swung the door open.

There stood his boss, Carlton Cargill, editor-in-chief of the *Zenith Clarion*. Wearing a rumpled pinstriped suit, the fireplug of a newsman looked exceptionally grim. The guy standing behind him—tall and thin, in a crisply cut, double-breasted gray suit—was a stranger.

"Howdy, Chief," Johnny said.

"Hi there, Johnny," Mr. Cargill responded, an unlit cigar jammed in the corner of his mouth. He stepped slightly aside. "I'd like you to meet Sir Colin Mariner, a diplomatic representative of the Royal Kingdom."

The Royal Kingdom was an island nation located thousands of miles east, across the Lesser Ocean. Dame Honoria was one of its most prominent citizens. She must be why this guy was here. But what was he doing with Mr. Cargill?

The tall, thin man nodded and came forward, offering his hand. "So very pleased to meet you, Master Graphic. Thank you for receiving us on such short notice."

"Nice to meet you, too, Sir Colin," Johnny said. He grabbed the hand and shook it. "Come on in."

In the living room, introductions were made again. It turned out that Dame Honoria and Sir Colin were casual acquaintances from some years before. But when Dame Honoria asked Sir Colin how a mutual friend was doing, threatening to lead into a longer conversation, Mr. Cargill interrupted.

"Excuse me," he rumbled, "but perhaps you two could discuss old pals later on. We have some serious business to conduct here."

Johnny loved how the chief always managed to cut right through the clutter and get to the point. There were no wasted words with Carlton Cargill.

"Quite right," Dame Honoria replied. "I assume that you have some news from the Royal Kingdom, Sir Colin. Shall we all be seated?"

Sir Colin lowered himself into a chair near the fireplace and began to speak.

"Within the last seventy-two hours, in two northern counties of the Royal Kingdom, a series of concerted, brutal raids were made on schools, libraries, and colleges. Many buildings were burned to the ground. Electricity is out here and there. We know that a number of people were attacked. We have no idea of actual fatalities, let alone injuries."

"That's just crazy," said Johnny, who was on the sofa with Mel and Nina. "Who would want to destroy schools and libraries?"

"Our thoughts exactly," Sir Colin answered, giving Johnny a nod. "But I'm afraid it gets worse. Well over a hundred boys and girls have vanished from their schools."

Dame Honoria looked shocked. "Students are being kidnapped? What sort of lunatics would do such a thing?"

"My superiors in the Royal Kingdom have a certain notion of who is behind these events," Sir Colin said. "And you and your friends here are the only people on earth who have thus far been able to defeat him."

Dame Honoria shut her eyes and took a deep breath. She shook her head, then pulled herself upright in her chair. Looking straight at Sir Colin, she said only one word: "Percival."

So it was starting all over again, Johnny thought. *Another horror show, orchestrated by that monster Percy Rathbone.*

"You know Percival Rathbone better than anyone on earth, Dame Honoria," Sir Colin continued. "We think that he returned to the Royal Kingdom soon after his escape here in Zenith."

"But he vamoosed only a few weeks ago," Uncle Louie pointed out. "It's hard to believe that the guy could've pulled off something like that so fast."

Dame Honoria sniffed. "My son has always taken a long view of things. He probably made plans for these atrocities some time ago. And that odious Worthington-Smythe woman almost certainly did a lot of his legwork."

Johnny knew that Dame Honoria despised Pamela Worthington-Smythe, who had been Percy's girlfriend when he was alive. Now that he was a ghost, she was probably the living person who gave him his powers.

"Sir Colin, please tell us exactly what happened," Mel said.

The diplomat took a blue folder from his briefcase, then opened it and glanced at the paper inside. "We have fairly good information from a place called Chippington-in-the-Vale," he said. "It's a little town in MacFreithshire, one of the northern counties."

"MacFreithshire?" Mel repeated. "Isn't it famous for its moors and bogs?"

"Right you are, Miss Graphic."

"In fact, I recently read an article about it," Mel recalled. "Scientists found ancient bodies in one of the bogs that were preserved almost totally intact. They're revealing all sorts of new information about life there centuries back."

Johnny looked at his sister with admiration. That girl was a walking, talking encyclopedia—she could always be counted on to know her science.

"Correct again, Miss Graphic," Sir Colin said. "The area up there remains an inhospitable landscape. But Chippington itself is a pleasant enough sort of village. A couple of miles outside of town is an institution called St. Egbert's School for Boys."

"Where the lesser sons of the nobility and the wealthy are sent for their educations," said Dame Honoria, clearly familiar with the school.

Sir Colin nodded. "Late Tuesday night, unknown individuals slipped onto the St. Egbert's campus and, using petrol bombs, set fire to the library, the chapel, and the administration building."

The diplomat described how several of the adults of the school—including the headmaster—had been knocked senseless. "But here's the odd thing. The attackers were described as strange figures wearing leather and canvas capes and tunics."

"Unusual attire, certainly," Dame Honoria observed. "Perhaps some locals had a grudge against the school, and disguised themselves, so as not to be identified."

"That might be a plausible explanation, but for one thing," Sir Colin said. "Witnesses who got good looks at these attackers claimed the skin on their faces looked like old leather, their features all squashed. Everyone who saw them swore they were not wearing masks."

The room went silent.

"According to the groundskeeper," Sir Colin continued, "the faces he saw looked remarkably like those ancient bog corpses that Miss Graphic just mentioned."

Mel gave him a puzzled look. "But that doesn't make sense.

Those bog men have been dead for ages. So they're not exactly going to swim up through the peat and muck." Her face went pale and she looked at Johnny. "Unless…"

Johnny couldn't help himself.

"They're zombies!" he blurted out. "They're bog zombies!"

"First-person accounts strongly suggest that conclusion," Sir Colin said.

This definitely sounded like Percy's handiwork, Johnny thought. *What was that weasel up to now? Was he trying to build an army of bog men? And how in heckfire did he manage to reanimate such ancient corpses?*

Dame Honoria's face showed gritty determination. "Sir Colin, I take it that Melanie and I might be more useful if we moved our operations to the Royal Kingdom."

"I gather from Mr. Cargill that you've already devoted great time and energy to the recapture of Percival Rathbone," Sir Colin said.

Mel and Dame Honoria had worked tirelessly in the days after Percy's escape. Together they had organized troops of ghost searchers to hunt for Percy and his sidekicks—Pamela, the zombie Ozzie Eccleston, and the ghost Steppe Warriors Burilgi and Checheg. They had written letters and sent telegrams to etherists around the world. They even had Nina contact people on her radio set.

"So, yes," Sir Colin confirmed. "Your help would be invaluable to us right now, closer to the problem areas. Of course, you understand we're keeping all of this under wraps. If word about bog zombies got out, there could be widespread panic."

"Sir Colin, I get why you'd want Dame Honoria and Mel over there," Johnny said. "But Mr. Cargill, why are you here?"

The gruff newsman peered at his star photographer. "Sir Colin wants you and Nina to go to the Royal Kingdom, along with Melanie and Dame Honoria, under the cover of news photographer and reporter. While they're continuing their investigation, you two will be doing secret legwork. Since you work for me, I had to okay your leave of absence from the job."

"Your part of the mission would be every bit as important as that of the two ladies," Sir Colin added. "If not more so."

Nina, almost vibrating with excitement, flashed Johnny a big grin. He was relieved that she'd be with him on this adventure. She had gotten him out of tough scrapes before. There was nobody he'd rather have watching his back than Nina Bain.

But what did Mr. Cargill mean by "secret legwork"? Sounded an awful lot like the cloak-and-dagger stories that Johnny read in the pulp magazines. Then it dawned on him.

"You mean you want us to spy for you?" he asked.

"In a manner of speaking," Sir Colin said. "You've got a newshound's nose. We want you to keep your eyes and ears open for anything that seems important up in those northern counties."

"To all appearances, you'll be over there as representatives of the *Clarion* and the World Press Association," Mr. Cargill said. "We're making up new press credentials for the both of you. Of course, we won't be able to print any of your reports right away. But once Percy is captured, and your stories are okayed by the officials over there, what you two have to say will make an incredible scoop."

"You will be provided with an escort who knows the lay of the land," Sir Colin said. "He will function as your guide and bodyguard."

Johnny thought of a big problem. "Will Uncle Louie be allowed to come, too?"

"Yes, of course. Mr. Hofstedter will be part of your entourage."

Uncle Louie laughed. "I've never been part of an entourage before. But I like to think I'm not too old to learn how."

"So what happens now?" Johnny asked.

"Even as we speak," said Mr. Cargill, "arrangements are being made to fly you to the Royal Kingdom. In the meantime, we have lots of preparations to make."

Johnny sure hadn't planned on another big adventure this soon. But if Percy Rathbone was kidnapping kids and turning bog men into zombies, who knew what kind of dreadful plan he had in mind.

Whatever it took, Johnny had to help beat him.

CHAPTER 4

BEING DEAD WAS AWFUL. In fact, for many centuries after her death, Bao hadn't felt like going anywhere or talking to anyone. The little mountain girl hid from other ghosts, and moped and pouted and felt very, *very* sorry for herself.

It was only just a few months ago that, through a strange chain of events, she had met Dame Honoria Gorton Rathbone in a dank, dark cave. At the time, Dame Honoria was being held prisoner by her wicked son, Percy.

Dame Honoria had asked Bao a question that changed the little ghost's entire existence. Would Bao help her? When Bao agreed, she suddenly had a connection with the living, real world. She could touch and hold things. She could do things—from sweeping and fetching to making beds and cooking food. She could brush Dame Honoria's hair and even give her a hug. She could, in a way, be part of a family again.

Bao had come to Birchwood with Dame Honoria, whom she called Grandmother and whom she now served. They had lived here for a few months with Johnny and Mel, and Bao had grown to love the place.

She spent a few hours every day doing chores for Grandmother. She would get the mail and make the bed and run the bathwater. But Grandmother had also ordered her to spend some time learning about her new world. Since Bao was curious by nature, this was not an unwelcome assignment.

So Bao visited each morning with Mrs. Lundgren, the ghost housekeeper, who had shown her how to do things in the kitchen. Now Bao could peel potatoes and carrots, stir pots, fry eggs, pour drinks, make sandwiches, and wash and dry dishes.

Colonel MacFarlane and his men of the ghost brigade taught her some of the games that they played when they were "at ease." The colonel said Commander Graphic—that's what he called Mel—felt it was important that ghosts stuck in the ether enjoy themselves, so she ordered them to have fun when they weren't on duty.

Bao always paid attention when the grown-up ghosts talked. And ghosts, because they didn't have much else to do, tended to gossip a lot. The colonel's men had quite a discussion one day about Percy Rathbone and how he had managed to occupy a dead body. They debated whether it was right—taking over a body that wasn't your own. The colonel thought it was absolutely wrong and unnatural. And, in the end, so did all the other ghost soldiers.

Bao was in total agreement. Ghosts couldn't be blamed for wanting to have proper bodies again. What dead person wouldn't? It was the First Impossible Thing that ghosts desired—to be in physical bodies again.

But there was something very nasty and dreadful about taking over corpses and walking about in them. Nina had a very good word to describe it. She scrunched up her face and spit it out:

"Gross!" Besides, possessing another person's body could never be as good as being in one's own body again.

The living people at Birchwood were just as nice as the ghosts. Mel had informed Bao that no one should be illiterate. Being dead was no excuse for not being able to read. So whether Bao liked it or not—and she did like it, actually, rather a lot—Mel was teaching her how to read. They'd spent dozens of hours together, and Bao could now read books with pictures and a few sentences on each page. She was incredibly proud of that.

Bao liked Johnny a lot. Maybe too much. She had gotten into trouble haunting him without him knowing it. *Big trouble.* But despite being a little peeved at the nosy ghost, Johnny was showing her how to do some basic arithmetic. She was good at adding and subtracting, but multiplication wasn't as easy. And division? Very hard.

Uncle Louie and Nina couldn't see Bao until Mel made those ghost goggles. Still, they were always polite when they knew she was around, saying, "Hi Bao, how you doing?" And things like that. Bao, though, couldn't help but feel a little jealous of Nina, who was alive and got to spend a lot of time with Johnny.

But now Dame Honoria wanted to take Bao away from Birchwood. They were going to go across another ocean, to Dame Honoria's home—a place called Wickenham. Bao's first best ghost friend, Evvie, would be coming, too. He hoped to have a reunion with his family back in the Royal Kingdom.

Bao confided to Evvie that she was sad about leaving Birchwood.

He patted her on the shoulder. "Cheer up, old girl. I've heard it said that the Royal Kingdom is quite the ghost's paradise. Lots of dead people hanging around there. Of course, I haven't been back since I drowned on my jungle expedition. I was Lord Evansham of

Hurley, you know. Would have had quite the cushy life, if I had just been able to tread water a bit longer."

IT WAS THE MIDDLE OF THE NIGHT, hours before their departure. Grandmother was asleep in bed, snoring loudly. In a corner of the bedroom sat Bao, glowing green in the dark. Bao, like all other ghosts, couldn't sleep. So night was always a good time to think about everything that had happened in her life. To ask the question that had baffled her from the start.

Why had she become a ghost?

Grandmother had explained to her that only about three people out of a hundred become ghosts when they die. Their spirits manage to get only as far as the realm that they call the ether. They are trapped there and no one knows why. No one knows how to free them. They are doomed to spend eternity as ghosts.

But why couldn't Bao have gone with her mother and father, her sisters and brothers? Were they all somewhere else, waiting for her, worrying about her? Perhaps with the great spirits up above? Or was there nothing beyond the ether but blackness and blankness?

Maybe it was a good thing that she had stayed connected to the earth. After all, Johnny had said that if she hadn't been with them on New Year's Eve, the whole town of Zenith might have been blown up. And that Grandmother seemed in much better spirits, having Bao around.

Maybe Bao needed to be here to take care of Grandmother's heart. The old lady could seem kind of gruff and unfeeling at times. But she had told Bao one day that her son Percy had broken her heart, and she didn't think it would ever mend.

Bao wondered why Percy, the son of a good mother, had done all those bad things. Why had he sent the eyeless ghost warrior

Burilgi to Zenith? To blow up the whole city and kill a million people? That awful Burilgi had hit Bao, had hurt her. She still had the cuts on her hands from his dagger.

Percy said his only goal was to help the ghosts by improving their conditions. But to do that, he was willing to kill living people. So, to do good, he would have to do evil.

Bao had to agree that ghosts had gotten a "raw deal," as Johnny liked to say. But that was no excuse for trying to murder innocent people. There had to be a better way.

Bao sighed. There were some problems that she just couldn't solve. Shaking her head, she glanced over toward the bed and saw that the glowing alarm clock was approaching the hour of four.

It was time to wake up Grandmother.

CHAPTER 5

"BUT MUST YOU GO?" Mrs. Lundgren sobbed. *"Again?"*

The Graphics' ghost housekeeper stood in front of Johnny and Mel out on the porch. It was still quite dark at five o'clock that morning, with stars twinkling above. Down on the driveway, Uncle Louie and Nina were loading up the big Morton Monarch touring car, its convertible top in upright position. Everyone was yawning and blinking.

"You've risked your lives too many times as it is," the wraith said, dabbing at her eyes with a ghostly lace handkerchief. Never mind that she couldn't cry a single drop.

Mel leaned over and hugged the ghost with the apple-doll face. She lightly kissed her on the cheek. "Of course, Mrs. Lundgren, we know. But people are under threat in the Royal Kingdom, and we might be able to help."

"Don't you worry, Mrs. Lundgren," Johnny reassured her. "We won't take any unnecessary chances."

"Oh, I wish I could believe you, Master Johnny," Mrs. Lundgren said, shaking her head. "But I know about that heroic streak of yours."

Johnny realized he'd taken a few risks in recent months that could have proven fatal. And he figured he'd caused a lot of worry for the people—and ghosts—that cared about him.

"We'll be real careful, Mrs. Lundgren," he promised solemnly. "Honest."

The ghost housekeeper grabbed him and smothered him in a hug. "You'd better be, John Joshua Graphic."

An hour later the maroon touring car was rolling west on Superior Avenue through downtown Zenith. Behind it trotted fifteen mounted ghost soldiers of the First Zenith Cavalry Brigade, led by Colonel MacFarlane and his horse, Buck. Sitting in the saddle in front of the colonel was Bao. Her friend Evvie rode with Lieutenant Finn.

Looking out the window of the car, Johnny saw a woman spot the ghost troopers, just as she came out of the Kom On Inn Diner. Too bad for her that she was one of the few living people who could see ghosts. Her mouth gaped open, and she dropped her giant raised doughnut on the sidewalk.

Johnny couldn't help himself and burst out laughing, which earned him an elbow in the ribs from his sister.

"Johnny, knock it off," Mel snapped. "It's not funny."

But it *was*. Johnny bit his tongue and tried unsuccessfully to straighten out his mouth. "Whatever you say, Sis."

The next opportunity for a good chuckle came when Danny Kailolu embraced and kissed Mel as soon as she got out of the car. They whispered in each other's ears. Sweet nothings, Johnny supposed, whatever those were. But he knew perfectly well to button up his mouth when it came to mushy matters of teenage infatuation.

Mel had known since the morning before that their floatplane would be a Gianelli and that their pilot would be her boyfriend, Danny—though she claimed they were "just friends." *Yeah, right,* thought Johnny. Anyway, she had been walking on air since then.

"Johnny," came a gruff, deep shout. "Come over here."

It was Mr. Cargill, standing at the foot of the dock that reached out into the Treport River. With the chief were Dame Honoria and Sir Colin Mariner, as well as Bao and Evvie. At the far end of the dock, a sleek, tri-motor Gianelli Z-509 floatplane gently rocked in the water. This was where they had left from when they flew to Silver City a few months ago. Maybe this was even the same Zephyr Lines airplane.

Johnny approached the group. "What is it, Chief?"

"I just want to make sure that you're going to follow the rules we set down," Mr. Cargill said, as he chewed on his unlit cigar. "You've gotta do whatever your escort says. He's the boss when it comes to keeping you and Nina safe."

"Yup, got it, Chief," Johnny replied. "And don't forget, Uncle Louie will be with us, too." The big man had been a boxer years ago, and Johnny figured any zombie who got in his uncle's way would soon regret it.

"Keep your eyes and ears open, and take a lot of notes and pictures. What you find out could be very important for the authorities. And Sir Colin here promises that as soon as the news blackout is lifted, and the censors look things over, the *Clarion* will be able to publish your accounts before anyone else."

"Don't worry, Chief. Nina's a really good writer. And with my new Ritterflex, I can shoot a lot more pictures."

Though Johnny hated to leave it behind, he clearly couldn't take his bulky Zoom 4x5 camera onto the moors of MacFreithshire. So for this expedition, he'd use his lightweight, twin-lens Ritterflex camera, which could take twelve pictures without reloading. It was a present from Uncle Louie.

Johnny was still really disappointed to have to postpone the search for his parents. But this zombie adventure was going to be a heckuva big story. He could already feel his adrenaline starting to flow.

IT WAS MID-AFTERNOON the next day when they splashed down at the vast Rowestoft Aeroboat Harbour in the Royal Kingdom. The port stretched over miles of shoreline and thousands of acres of harbor. As they headed for one of the terminals, Johnny was awed by the hundreds of aircraft—from giant Johnson Geese to small floatplanes like their Gianelli—at docks or in the taxiing lanes.

It was great to get out of the cramped quarters of the floatplane and stretch a bit on the dock. Dame Honoria looked a little crooked, as though her back had stiffened up on her. But she claimed she felt fine.

Johnny looked around. On the dock to his left, a Zephyr Lines Como Eagle was boarding its passengers. On the other side, a Moeller-Schmidt flying boat was disgorging people dressed in the turbans and robes of the desert countries.

After a while, a slight young man walked out onto the dock. He had on a brown herringbone suit and a red bow tie. He introduced himself as "Mr. Smith," bowing slightly from the waist, and said he was there to take them to the Home Office. With that, he led the weary travelers out through the bustling terminal. Danny had already made his farewells to Mel and the others, and was taxiing the Gianelli off to the Zephyr Lines base.

Back outside, they all climbed into a big, black limousine. Johnny knew that they drove on the wrong side of the road over here, but it still felt strange. More than a few times during their drive, he cringed in anticipation of a crack-up that didn't happen. They rolled through the countryside for a while, with its lovely green hills and dales. Then came interminable suburbs, with their armies of little bungalows on tiny lots.

Finally, they entered Royalton, the capital of the Royal Kingdom. The city was crammed with tall apartment buildings and townhouses. The sidewalks were crowded with people. Lots of ghosts, too. Johnny spotted a couple of mounted knights in armor, trotting up busy city streets. Medieval peasants. Soldiers from different wars. Priests. A wraith in a toga, wearing a crown of bay leaves—seventeen hundred years old at least, Johnny bet. At last, the automobile glided to a stop in front of a vast, gloomy office building, blackened by decades of sooty smog.

"Welcome to the Home Office," their young guide said, ushering them all into the ornate marble-and-granite lobby. Dame Honoria had explained that this was the ministry that dealt with internal security and law enforcement in the Royal Kingdom. They went up the grand central staircase amid scurrying workers, turned right, and were deposited in a small meeting room.

A few minutes later, Johnny saw a ghost walk through the hallway wall. A thin, aristocratic man in an officer's uniform from the Great War. But not, Johnny realized, a uniform of the Royal Army. The specter had a narrow face, clean-shaven, with dark, intelligent eyes. Over his heart was pinned a bloody cloth target, punctured by several bullet holes.

As soon as Dame Honoria saw him, she jumped up out of her chair. "Rex Ward, as I live and breathe."

"Honoria!" the ghost said with a grin.

Much to Johnny's surprise, Dame Honoria embraced the ghost. Fortunately, there was no kissing involved.

"Everyone," Dame Honoria announced, "this is Captain Rex Ward, an old family friend. He's now a liaison officer of the Special Ghost Service of the Home Office. Or the SGS, as everyone calls it. And I believe he has our marching orders."

Johnny saw Nina quickly put on the etheric goggles and carefully watch the ghost. Lucky for her, she had earned a merit badge in lip reading, as a member in good standing of the Woodland Guides, Zenith Troop 27. She couldn't hear ghosts, but with the goggles she could at least pick up some of what they said.

The ghost took a seat at the table. "The home secretary expresses his gratitude that you've offered your assistance. But I'm afraid things have gone all topsy-turvy up north. A peculiar fog has developed up there, slowing down all manner of travel. The attacks have intensified. And to make matters worse, trains sent north with army and police units have been purposely derailed. So, unfortunately, I don't know when Master Graphic and Miss Bain will be able to travel north with Mr. Hofstedter. Could be as much as a week."

Johnny sure didn't like this turn of events. If it took that long, the action might already be over by the time they got there. He scowled at Rex, knowing full well it wouldn't do any good.

"But there is an alternative," the ghost continued, "if Honoria is willing to talk to a particular old friend of hers."

"Certainly," she answered. "But to whom are you referring?"

Rex floated over and whispered in her ear. She nodded, but her expression revealed nothing.

The ghost liaison officer wafted back to his chair. "As agreed, we expect that Honoria and Miss Graphic will provide profiling information on Percival Rathbone. We want to know what makes him tick."

"Of course, Rex," Dame Honoria said. "But I must admit, right now I'm more concerned about understanding how he has managed to reanimate those ancient bog men."

"And why would he want to?" Mel added. "Can't he find fresh corpses?"

"That's what we're counting on you and Honoria to figure out," replied Rex.

"I'd like to know why these kids are being taken," said Johnny. "I mean, what does Percy want with them?"

The ghost leveled his piercing gaze at Johnny. "That, Master Graphic, is the question we hope you and Miss Bain will be able to answer."

CHAPTER 6

TUESDAY, JANUARY 28, 1936
ROYALTON, ROYAL KINGDOM

AFTER A WELL-EARNED NIGHT of rest at the Hotel Chelmsford Park, Johnny found his way down to the dining room for breakfast. He was the last to arrive at the table.

Nina and Uncle Louie were marching through plates piled high with fried eggs, bacon, sausage, and cold toast. Mel and Dame Honoria had already finished eating and were sipping tea. Johnny wasn't that hungry, so he decided to have a bowl of porridge with toast and jam.

"I have some urgent business to attend to," Dame Honoria announced. "So I will be leaving for Wickenham in a few hours. Given that the fog has stopped most travel to the north, I suggest the four of you take a day or two to enjoy the metropolis."

Nina looked as if she had died and gone to heaven. "Oh, I've wanted to visit the Queen's Library *forever*. They have the original *Carta de Iuribus* on display there. That document laid the groundwork for the beginning of all democratic government."

Chewing on a piece of toast, Johnny looked at Mel. "Did we

bring enough money to see shows and exhibits?"

"This is my treat," Dame Honoria said, removing several large banknotes from her pocketbook. "You deserve a chance to tour this great city. I'll be taking Bao and Evvie, but the colonel and his men will stay here, to keep an eye on you. And do be careful—we just don't know who or what might be lurking out there. Remember that Percy could have spies planted anywhere."

With that warning in mind, the four visitors spent the day as tourists, inspecting Royalton on a grand sightseeing excursion. Johnny felt like a millionaire riding around in the big town car from Gorton's Little Pills Limited, the company that Dame Honoria owned. They saw the King's Palace, the great Regency Park and Reflecting Pool, Dorrminster Abbey, the Queen's Library, and the vast Smithson's Department Store—where Mel and Nina both made a few purchases. At the Royal Gallery, Johnny met one of his favorite painters. Nearly four centuries dead, Antonio Cirelli haunted the museum every day, telling people who could see ghosts the story of his famous portrait of 1525, *Ragazza con una mela—Girl with an Apple.*

The great city, in fact, looked as if there was nothing badly amiss about four hundred miles to the north. People thronged the sidewalks, going about their business, carrying umbrellas to deflect the light drizzle that had come in from the west. From a second-story teashop window, Johnny took some pictures of the hundreds of water-glistened umbrellas, as they jostled this way and that.

Uncle Louie decided to stay at the hotel that evening, complaining of sore feet from all the walking they'd done. And he wanted to write a letter to his girlfriend, Flo Zuckerberg, back in Zenith.

Johnny persuaded Mel and Nina to go with him to a musical production of *Captain Justice and the Hawkmen* in Royalton's famed theater district. Watching the show from the balcony, Johnny was utterly enthralled. To see the captain and the chief of the Hawkmen flying around the stage on wires, dueling each other while singing splendid tunes—well, he'd remember it forever.

The show finally let out at eleven o'clock and the trio emerged onto the sidewalk with all the other theatergoers. The rain had stopped, but everything was glinting and glittering with the dampness. Colorful theater marquee lights blinked and winked up and down the street.

"I figured out a shortcut back to the Chelmsford," Johnny announced, when they finally escaped the crush of people.

"Well, then," Nina said, "let's go."

Mel shrugged. "Lead on, Mr. Graphic."

As Johnny set off, Mel turned and shouted back to the colonel and Sergeant Clegg, both mounted on their horses. The other troopers were back at the hotel, making sure everything was secure for the night.

Johnny led them at an energetic clip. They turned right, then left into an empty flea market. They were almost to the end of it, practically within sight of Chelmsford Park, when the slender figure of a pretty, blonde woman walked by them.

"Good evening, Mr. Graphic," she said in a very quiet voice.

And she was gone before Johnny had a chance to even say "Hello."

He had caught a brief glimpse of her face under one of the market's weak gaslights. Where had he seen her before?

He didn't have much time to think about it. Because right then, three hulking figures loomed up in front of them, blocking their passage. Johnny didn't have a good feeling about this.

"C-c-can we do something for you?" he stammered.

The three figures stood silently, not replying.

Mel stepped in front of him. "If you don't mind, gentlemen, we need to get back to our hotel."

"I sure hope this isn't a mugging," Nina whispered into Johnny's ear.

Actually, it was much worse. A point made emphatic by the rusty axes the thugs withdrew from beneath their formless coats.

That's when the colonel and the sergeant trotted up on either side of Johnny, Mel, and Nina. The horse soldiers' sabers made a metallic whishing noise as they came out of their scabbards.

"What do you want?" Johnny hoped his voice didn't give away how scared he was.

One of the interlopers threw back its hood and revealed a dark, leathery face that looked a thousand years old.

That's when it struck Johnny. *Like two hammer blows.*

The woman he'd just seen was Pamela Worthington-Smythe, Percy Rathbone's special friend and co-conspirator. The face that had briefly appeared in the floatplane door on Old Number One three months ago.

Pamela must have been spying on Johnny and his companions. Percy Rathbone might even be around here somewhere.

And these fiends blocking his way had to be bog zombies!

Johnny was jolted out of his very brief paralysis by a most welcome voice.

"Master Johnny, Commander, Miss Nina. Please move back. We'll handle these characters." Colonel MacFarlane's voice was tinged with deep contempt.

The colonel on Buck and Sergeant Clegg on his ghost horse clattered past the kids on the glistening cobblestones, toward the approaching brutes. The two cavalrymen briefly made eye contact. The colonel nodded and they charged.

In a few heartbeats, they were on top of the bog zombies, their blades flashing in the dimly lit flea market.

The zombies fought back with their axes. Johnny was horrified to hear the terrible scream of Sergeant Clegg's horse when one of those rusty weapons grazed its flank. The sergeant tumbled off his saddle and lost his saber. But he quickly pulled out what he called "my Old Equalizer," the double-barreled, sawed-off shotgun that he wore on his right hip.

As one of the three zombies charged him, Clegg hoisted the gun and fired.

The zombie's head blew to pieces. A ghost popped out of the leathery body as it sagged to the cobblestones. It was a Steppe Warrior, though not one that Johnny recognized. The ghost came at Clegg, sword drawn. The sergeant recovered his saber just in the nick of time, and the two ghosts slashed away at each other as the bog body shriveled and shrank into a pitiful pile of flattened flesh.

"We have to get out of here," Johnny yelled. "The colonel and Clegg can take care of things."

"No argument here," Mel snapped back.

Nina groaned. "That man's head exploded!" Without her ether-ic goggles, she hadn't seen what caused the ghastly sight. "Oh, maaaan… Here we go again!"

The three young people pivoted around and ran in the opposite direction from the fight. They were almost to the end of the old flea market when two more hulking figures appeared out on the cross street, blocking their way. Behind them, cackling with laughter, stood Pamela.

They were trapped.

The two monsters trotted toward them with un-zombie-like briskness, their terrible features hidden by their hoods.

Johnny desperately looked around for some kind of weapon, anything that could slow the zombies down. All he saw was a loose cobblestone by the brick wall to his left. Well, it was *something*, anyway. When he plucked it up, he noticed a nearby shop. A hardware store, its dusty windows full of implements and tools. Then he had a better idea for the cobblestone. He lifted the rough, rectangular paver and heaved it through one of the windows, making a loud percussion of shattered glass.

Nina looked shocked. "Are you nuts?"

Johnny shook his head. "Something to fight with." He pointed at tools inside the smashed window.

He darted over and grabbed a sturdy shovel with a sharpened point. Then he jumped nearly a foot in the air when the roar of another shotgun blast filled the flea market. He turned quickly and saw a second bog zombie slump to the pavement, releasing another ghost—some kind of medieval knight.

Sucking in a huge gulp of damp air, Johnny turned back to face the two zombies at his end of the flea market. Instead of waiting for them to attack, he bolted toward one of them.

He hefted the shovel and positioned it over his shoulder.

Before the bog zombie could lift its axe, Johnny swung the shovel like some big-league home-run hitter.

The edge of the shovel blade caught the creature on the left side, making a meaty *thwap*. Johnny hopped backward, thinking it best to stay out of range of that nasty-looking axe.

The zombie stood there a moment, appearing only slightly dazed. Then it threw back its hood, revealing a face out of a nightmare. As battered and tattered as old leather, oddly contorted, with a large dent above its squashed left ear. It stared at Johnny with dead black eyes. The thing seemed rather annoyed with him.

Meanwhile, out of the corner of his eye, Johnny could see that Mel was holding her own—having had the good luck to find a length of steel pipe in the shop window. She was parrying her bog zombie's blows and keeping it safely away.

For her part, Nina had simply ducked into a doorway, out of sight.

Johnny was about to take another whack at his bog zombie when someone shouted from out on the street.

"Oy there! What's this all about?"

Startled, both Johnny and his foe glanced to see who it was.

There stood a Royalton policeman, in his dark-blue uniform and peculiar high-domed helmet. The red-bearded copper had his wooden baton in hand, and he looked like he was willing to use it.

Johnny was the first to respond. "These, these…"

He shut up. He wasn't supposed to say "zombie." Rex Ward had told them so.

Instead, he hollered, "These people attacked us, officer!"

The policeman gasped, having now seen the oddly shriveled bodies sprawled at the far end of the flea market. Johnny got the impression that the man could not see the colonel or the sergeant. The policeman yanked out his alarm whistle and began blowing on it. The piercing tone of the thing must have carried for blocks.

Pamela had already vanished. The zombies that Johnny and Mel had been fighting also dashed away—right past the wide-eyed copper—as did the remaining creature that the colonel and Clegg were closing in on.

For a long moment, the policeman couldn't take his eyes off the defunct zombies sprawled on the cobblestones. Then he turned to Johnny, Mel, and Nina, glaring.

"I think you young people are going to have an awful lot of explaining to do."

CHAPTER 7

WEDNESDAY, JANUARY 29, 1936
GILBEYSHIRE, ROYAL KINGDOM

JOHNNY WAS PICNICKING with his parents on a rocky beach on Great Lake. They were all laughing and talking and having a fine old time. Without so much as a word, Mom and Pop began to walk up the shore. Johnny tried to follow, but he was caught in something like quicksand. He shouted for them to stop and help him. But they paid no attention. They continued to amble into the distance, growing smaller and smaller and smaller.

"Pop!" he panted. "Mom! Don't go!"

Someone grabbed him by his left shoulder and shook him. The lake scene dissolved away. When he opened his eyes, Nina was sitting next to him, still holding his shoulder and looking mildly worried. Johnny realized he was in the backward-facing seat of the Gorton's company town car, heading for Dame Honoria's estate. Through the back window he saw the colonel and his troopers galloping behind the vehicle.

Nina peered at him. "Were you having a bad dream?"

He rubbed his eyes with his knuckles. "Well, it wasn't bad until the end." He blinked out onto the rolling landscape of Gilbeyshire, green and fertile under a light overcast. "How long till we get there?"

Uncle Louie was sitting opposite Johnny, next to Mel. "Shouldn't be long now, kiddo."

It was only mid-morning, but Johnny was exhausted. They had spent the better part of the night in a locked room at Moorland Yard, the Royal Kingdom's national police headquarters. For several hours, it seemed they were under suspicion of killing two unidentified people, whose heads had been blown off in the Bixford Flea Market. Johnny was dying to tell the officials exactly what had happened, but he, Mel, and Nina had agreed that they should stay mum until someone came to help them. The whole business of the zombies was supposed to remain top secret.

The colonel and Clegg had stayed with them in jail all night, too, but they had been under strict orders from Mel to do nothing. The kids were in enough hot water as it was, without causing any further ruckus.

It was almost breakfast time when Rex Ward had finally shown up with an undersecretary from the Home Office, who ordered their release. According to Rex, the constable who had arrested them had been put on temporary leave of absence. He was told not to speak about the incident to a single soul. The authorities were indeed keeping the matter of bog zombies under wraps.

Uncle Louie, who had fallen asleep early the night before, wasn't even aware that the trio hadn't made it back to the hotel until the Home Office called his room at four a.m. He told Johnny he would have given anything to have been there when they were attacked. "Those bozos would have found out what a left hook and a right jab could do to their ugly mugs."

Johnny loved his uncle. But he didn't think even a big strong guy like Uncle Louie could take on five reanimated bog men with axes.

It sure was no coincidence that Pamela Worthington-Smythe had shown up with the zombies at precisely the same time that Johnny, Mel, and Nina were walking to their hotel. She had known exactly where they were. She was Percy Rathbone's number one helper—and girlfriend, too. And Johnny wouldn't be surprised if the pair had spies all up and down the country.

The last time Johnny had seen him, Percy had made it perfectly clear he despised the two Graphic siblings. Johnny couldn't figure out why—he hadn't even met Percy before the guy died on Okkatek Island, on the same trip where Johnny's parents had disappeared. But for some reason, Dame Honoria's son held a grudge against Mel and Johnny. And it was such an intense hatred that he wanted them dead.

If things had turned out differently last night, Percy might have gotten his wish. And poor Nina would have been a victim, too.

Everyone decided that it would be best to cut short the sightseeing and leave immediately for Wickenham, Dame Honoria's country house. Now that Pamela and the bog zombies knew Johnny and Mel were in Royalton, they might well try to ambush them again. It would be safer out of the metropolis.

Uncle Louie looked up from his copy of *The Morning Standard*. "Hey, look at this." He folded the newspaper back on itself, and then folded it again before handing it to Johnny. He jabbed at a little four-inch story in the middle of the page.

Johnny squinted at it. "It says that three foreign tourists were set upon in the Bixford Flea Market by ruffians. They defended themselves, and two of the five criminals died. The other three escaped."

Nina took a look at it, too. "Well, it's not inaccurate. It just doesn't tell the whole story. The whole story would read, 'Two creepy bog men get their heads blown off.'"

Johnny nodded. "That *would* make a better headline." But he knew if word of the bog zombies leaked out, there could be mass hysteria and panic. It was important sometimes to protect the public from the hard facts, he supposed.

Everyone in the back of the limousine was quiet for a moment. Out of nowhere came a ferocious growl.

A little embarrassed, Johnny shrugged. "Sorry, that was my stomach. Kinda hungry, I guess. Haven't eaten since before the show."

Nina sat bolt upright. "Look, look!" She pointed out the window. "Is that it, Mel?"

"Yes, it is," Mel answered. "The Gorton family home. I still remember it from when I was little."

Finally, Johnny thought, leaning over Nina to see. He caught his breath. Wow!

There stood Wickenham, crowning a verdant hill just a mile or so to the southeast. It was constructed of cream-colored stone, with a broad central section and two wings. Dame Honoria had once told Johnny that it had been built over two hundred years ago.

The sprawling old mansion had special meaning for Johnny. It was in a room upstairs where he had been born twelve-and-three-quarters years ago. It was sure a lot niftier place to get born than Zenith General Hospital.

A few minutes later, the limousine pulled up in front of the mansion's broad entry staircase. Dame Honoria was waiting for them, along with a dozen or so servants—all lined up, as if for military review. Maids and pages and butlers and cooks. Some of them were alive and some were ghosts.

Everyone piled out of the automobile and climbed the stairs up into the big country house. Johnny was even more impressed when he set foot in the grand foyer full of statuary and paintings. There were lots of battle scenes and old portraits. *How could you walk around here without stopping to look at the artwork all the time?*

"Now, before we have our lunch, I think we should gather in the library," Dame Honoria announced. "I want to hear everything that has happened." Leading them across the grand foyer, she glanced over her shoulder at Johnny, Mel, and Nina. "I understand you had quite an interesting stroll back from the theater last night."

Now *that* was an understatement, if ever Johnny had heard one.

The library was on the main floor corridor to the left of the foyer, and was just as impressive, in its own way. Books were shelved from floor to ceiling. There must have been ten thousand of them. And several folding banquet tables had been set up in the center of the room. They held a number of boxes filled with papers and books, which Dame Honoria explained had belonged to Percy. Every scrap was to be gone through, looking for clues. That was going to be a heckuva job. Johnny didn't envy Dame Honoria and Mel's task.

Everyone sat around an oval, mahogany coffee table near the fireplace. Dame Honoria asked all sorts of questions about the zombie attack, and the subsequent interrogation at the police station. Johnny was wondering how soon they would get something to eat when, Rex Ward arrived. He briefed everyone about the situation at the Home Office.

"The government's been working full speed, trying to control things up north and keeping the bad news from leaking out. Communications are still difficult, and transportation minimal. Because of the troubles and that blasted fog, there is still no way for Master Graphic and Miss Bain to travel in that direction. Honoria, I understand that you have explored other channels."

Dame Honoria nodded. "*Still* exploring, I'm afraid."

"In that case, I have another item of business to discuss," Rex said. "I've received a request from a friend in the Royal Marines. There is some need, apparently, for flying boat mechanics. Aircraft are being readied for missions up to the beaches of MacFreithshire. And I believe that Mr. Hofstedter is qualified to repair them. Is there any chance that Master Graphic and Miss Bain can undertake their efforts without him? I'm sure they'll be very well looked after by Colonel MacFarlane and his lads."

When he was told what the ghost had said, Uncle Louie reacted exactly as Johnny had expected.

"Well, that's very flattering," the big man said. "But I'm Johnny's uncle and Nina's guardian, and I'm not sure I ought to be running off right after they've been attacked."

But Johnny could tell his uncle was excited by the prospect. Since he didn't have etheric vision, Uncle Louie sometimes felt that he was useless when it came to battling miscreant spooks. This job sounded like a chance for him to really do some good.

"You know, Uncle Louie, it sounds like they need you," Johnny said. "Nina and I will be okay. I mean, with the colonel and half the brigade along, what could possibly happen to us?"

Mel nodded and gave her uncle an encouraging look. "They'll be just fine. Remember, Sir Colin said that their escort would also be a bodyguard."

Johnny figured the Home Office would hire someone who was pretty rough and tough. Like one of those muscular rugby players he'd seen in the newsreels. A guy like that could certainly handle a zombie or two.

"Well," Uncle Louie said hesitantly, "I feel like I should be there with you. But I think Rex is right. The colonel will take good care of you kids, better care than I can. So I'd be happy to help get those aeroboats in flying shape. But if I hear about any trouble, I'm coming back pronto."

Just then, Johnny's stomach rumbled again.

Dame Honoria eyed him and smiled. "I think the next item of business is lunch."

CHAPTER 8

JOHNNY AND NINA spent the afternoon wandering around Dame Honoria's estate and the surrounding countryside. One of the colonel's ghost troopers stood guard as Johnny took pictures for a photo essay on country life in Gilbeyshire. Wearing her etheric goggles, Nina was quite the center of attention when they visited the nearby village of Blackfield. A few of the merchants in the town wondered where they might buy a pair of the odd spectacles, as they would love to see their dead wife or grandfather. Even the ghosts were fascinated, especially those of a scientific bent.

Johnny enjoyed the visit to Blackfield, but had one troubling moment when they emerged from a teashop. Across the street in front of a grocery store, a little man was walking along. And to Johnny, he looked an awful lot like someone he had met back in Zenith a couple months ago.

Johnny had little doubt that it was Ozzie Eccleston, Dame Honoria's old ghost servant, now ensconced in a Rotonesian zombie body. At the end of last year it had been Ozzie who had delivered the etheric bomb ultimatum to the city of Zenith. In addition, he had sponged a couple of lunches off Johnny. He was a real bum, that guy.

Nina started to talk to Johnny, but he shushed her. "Look over there, Sparks. It's Ozzie Eccleston, probably come to spy on us."

A grin slowly spread across Nina's face. "So why don't we turn the tables and go do a little spying on him?"

They didn't have to go very far to do their surveillance, because Ozzie had nipped into the town's pub, The Laughing Fox. Johnny peeked through the open door for a few seconds, then slipped back out onto the sidewalk.

"He's already bellied up to the bar, and he's slurping on a pint of beer," Johnny whispered to Nina. "It looks like a couple people in there have picked up on his weird, musty smell. They were moving away from him. We'd better give Dame Honoria the bad news."

Back in the library at Wickenham half an hour later, they did just that.

Dame Honoria shot them a wily smile. "Thank you for this bit of intelligence. You needn't worry about Ozzie. I shall take it from here. I aim to have a little fun with my former employee."

MEL AND DAME HONORIA had already started going through Percy's archive of books and papers, all from the boxes that he had left in his chambers and in the attic. Assisting them was Percy's old tutor, Athelstan DeNimes, now a retired professor.

"Athelstan has offered to look into the matter of the bog zombies," Dame Honoria explained.

The professor nodded. "We need to understand how Percy has been able to reanimate such ancient corpses. Normally, unless they're properly cared for, these bog bodies quickly dry up and shrink when they're exposed to air. And the bones are very fragile, having been decalcified."

"What does that mean, 'decalcified'?" Nina asked.

"It means the calcium has leached out of them, leaving them

very porous. Percy has managed something remarkable, giving those ancient bodies enough strength and substance to function as warriors. My theory is that the ghost possession of these corpses somehow imbues them with vigor and power."

The old teacher was small and wiry, with white hair. He wore an old-fashioned gray suit and an overly large pair of horn-rimmed spectacles. The thick lenses magnified his watery blue eyes and made him look like some kind of strange tropical fish.

"Percy had quite a curious mind, you know," Professor De-Nimes told Johnny and Nina. "I recall his interest in the bog men years ago. He followed the news avidly whenever they dug one up. I think he liked to imagine what it might have been like to live in the ancient past."

Nina looked puzzled. "Why would anyone want to go back in time? They didn't have any of the modern conveniences back then. I sure wouldn't want to give up my ham radio set."

"Well, you know, quite a few scholars would time-travel, if they could," the professor said. Then he lowered his voice so Dame Honoria couldn't hear him. "Percy just never seemed quite that comfortable living in the present. I do wonder if I could have been a better mentor for him."

Johnny found the professor's insights into Percy very revealing. He wondered if the teachers back at Grover Falkland Junior High had given that much thought to Johnny's behavior, and to his decision to test out of school early. Maybe one of them felt like a failure for not persuading him to stay until he graduated at the usual age.

The phone on Dame Honoria's desk jangled loudly. She picked it up, said hello, and listened. Whoever it was did all the talking.

Meanwhile the professor continued his observations about her son. "The key to Percy's actions, I believe, lies in his overweening sense of righteousness."

"Overweening?" Johnny repeated.

"It means overbearing and arrogant, my young friend. *His* truths are greater than any others. *His* causes are the worthiest of all. He is justified in doing *anything* to achieve the ends he desires."

"Was he like that when he was a kid?"

"Oh, yes. Absolutely. He was prickly and difficult to teach. He had few real friends. You had the feeling that he loved humanity, but couldn't stand people. As you know, his father died at a young age. His mother was off most of the time, fighting for her cause."

"The vote for women."

"Got it in one."

"I can't believe women couldn't vote when Dame Honoria was younger," Nina piped up. "In just nine years, I'll be able to vote, and no one better try to stop me!"

At that moment Dame Honoria said goodbye to her caller, and looked up at everyone, wearing a huge smile.

"You seem unusually happy, Honoria," the professor said.

She beamed at him. "Very perceptive, Athelstan. I have a little surprise for everyone. Tomorrow we're going on a picnic. And then we're visiting an old friend of mine."

A picnic? Johnny thought. It was hardly the time of year to be eating outdoors. And weren't there more important matters to attend to—like fighting zombies?

But Dame Honoria was their hostess. She called the shots.

CHAPTER 9

THURSDAY, JANUARY 30, 1936
GILBEYSHIRE

THEY WERE ON THE ROAD for an hour and a half the next morning before the chauffeur finally turned the car up a narrow country lane that curved through an orchard of apple trees. They ended up by the grassy banks of a burbling stream, beneath some leafless willows. The air was crisp, but everyone had on warm clothes and didn't mind plopping down on heavy woolen blankets by the water.

Bao and Evvie, who had been riding up front with the chauffeur, joined them—though, of course, unable to eat anything.

Johnny was impressed by the picnic that Dame Honoria's cook had laid out for them. The best restaurant in Zenith would have a hard time topping it. First, there was potato and leek soup, which had been kept warm in a big vacuum flask. Then came what Johnny thought was a piece of pie—but inside the crust was a mixture of pork, carrots, celery, and onions, all held together by some kind of jelly. Bread and cheese. Some grapes and fresh slices of apple. Then came the sweets: brownies, éclairs, and a gingerbread cake with a dollop of lemon curd on top of it. Another vacuum flask contained hot cocoa, which Johnny and Nina drank. Mel, Uncle Louie, and Dame Honoria opted for hot tea.

Half an hour later, stuffed to the gills, Johnny asked if there was time to amble downstream and talk to the man who was fishing there. Dame Honoria said that was fine, just don't take too long. The man, in tweed jacket and waders, turned out to be a brigadier general who was on leave from the Royal Army after being wounded in an action in one of the desert realms. He was quite happy to let Johnny take some photos of his fly-fishing technique.

"It's Brigadier John Stafferton, spelled S-t-a-f-f-e-r-t-o-n," the lanky man with hawkish features said when Johnny asked for his name. "As I explained, currently on leave, recovering from wounds. Though I may be reactivated soon."

Johnny wasn't sure what to say. "Is that good or bad?"

"Oh, good. *Very good.* Life's been rather boring these past months, without a brigade of my own."

"Where's your assignment?"

"Sorry. Can't say, young man. Top secret, don't you know. And by the by, who is the officer standing behind you? I should enjoy an introduction."

Johnny hadn't realized that Colonel MacFarlane had walked up behind him. Obviously the brigadier had etheric vision. Johnny introduced the two and they hit it off immediately. The brigadier, it turned out, had made a study of the First Border War and was particularly interested in the Battle of Digsby's Run, where the colonel had died. He invited Johnny and the dead cavalryman back to visit anytime.

After the picnic, they drove another half hour, ending up at a grand country estate. The place even had uniformed guards stationed here and there. After telling the others to stay in the limousine, Dame Honoria got out and made immediately for the sprawling pile of limestone that was clearly the estate's main house. A trim, middle-aged man in a crisp dark suit came down the front steps, striding straight for Dame Honoria. They talked for a moment, then came over to the long, black automobile.

"All right then," Dame Honoria said. "Come along this way."

Johnny was surprised that they didn't go into the big house, but instead proceeded through some stables and past a large barn. Whoever lived here had a lot of horses and a lot of laborers, all looking quite busy.

Finally, they came to an old greenhouse, with many of its windows purposely soaped over to diffuse the sunlight. The man in the dark suit knocked at the door, and a muffled "Yes, come in" emerged from inside. Their guide opened the door and gestured for them to enter. They all filed in, followed by the colonel, Bao, and Evvie.

Johnny was dying of curiosity. Who was it they were dropping in on? Dame Honoria had been perfectly mum.

Inside was a place of dazzling beauty, packed every which way with tables full of gorgeous orchids. Hundreds and hundreds of them in all the colors of the rainbow. Johnny had never seen anything like it, even at the Zenith Botanical Garden. It was warm and humid, and smelled of damp, rich earth.

There was a small, slender gardener working at one of the tables, his back turned to the new arrivals. Except for a fringe of brownish hair, he was bald, and his ears stuck out a bit. He had on a blue, knee-length workman's coat. Putting down the water-misting bottle he had been using on an orchid, he turned around. "Yes, Oates?"

Almost instantly, Johnny knew where he had seen that face.

On every royal banknote that he had in his wallet.

On every coin that jingled in his pocket.

It was King Robert!

"Your Majesty," the man in the dark suit said, with a slight bow. "Dame Honoria Gorton Rathbone and her friends."

"Your Majesty," Dame Honoria echoed, making a small, arthritic curtsy.

"Hello, Honoria," the king said. "So good to see you."

"And you, as well, Your Majesty," Dame Honoria replied. "Let me introduce my companions. First, Miss Melanie Graphic."

Mel made her own curtsy. Not a very smooth one, Johnny thought. But Nina did hers like an old pro. And Uncle Louie bowed deeply from the waist, having removed his hat.

So when Dame Honoria said, "And this is John Joshua Graphic, my godson," Johnny knew just what to do. He put his right hand on his stomach, his left hand behind his back, and bowed.

The king smiled at them all and said, "Hello. Pleased to meet you. I have read all about your adventures."

He then invited them over to a glass-topped table surrounded by a few metal lawn chairs. He gestured that everyone should be seated.

"Tea and crumpets will arrive shortly," he said, taking off the gardening gloves he was wearing. "Now I understand that you have some transportation problems."

"Regrettably, the fog up north has brought traffic to a virtual standstill," Dame Honoria said. "My friends in the Home Office and the Special Ghost Service asked me to speak to you on their behalf. They desperately need to get troops and agents on the hunt for all these poor, kidnapped children. As I discussed with your aide the other day—"

The king put up his hand. "Say no more, Honoria. I've already authorized the use of Old Sal for these operations."

Johnny figured that Old Sal must be some kind of train, because it sure didn't sound like a flying boat. But he wondered how it could get through, when other trains couldn't.

"And since Johnny and Nina are here to gather intelligence in the affected counties," Dame Honoria continued, "we would request that they be allowed to ride on Old Sal, as well. After all, they have proven themselves extremely capable in dealing with my errant son Percival, whom we believe is behind the troubles."

"Rest assured, Honoria, I know all about their heroism out in Rotonesia and in Zenith," the king said. "They saved that great city from utter destruction, did they not?"

Johnny was shocked. "But no one's supposed to know about that."

Dame Honoria looked slightly appalled at his outburst. But the king merely chuckled.

"We kings have ways of finding things out, Johnny," the monarch said. "Even very secret things. It's part of our job."

Two servants appeared with pots of tea and plates of toasted crumpets with strawberry preserves. They set down the refreshments and took their leave.

As they all sipped their tea, it came out that the king and Dame Honoria had known each other since they were children. The king's younger sister had gone to school with Dame Honoria and had been a fellow suffragist back in the teens.

"You know, Honoria, I remember being so jealous of your etheric vision when we were younger," the king recalled. "And I still am. I have Oates here, who can see and hear specters. I call him my 'ghost eyes.' But I believe I'd almost trade my crown for a chance to see real ghosts."

Johnny had an idea. He glanced at Mel, who nodded. They both turned to Nina, who looked giddy with excitement.

"But you can, Your Majesty!" Nina exclaimed. She pulled open the top of her shoulder bag and extracted the etheric goggles, flipping a little switch on the battery pack. "Now these won't fit you, Your Majesty, but just hold them up to your eyes."

Looking skeptical, the king took the peculiar eyewear and did as instructed. A grin began to spread across his face.

"Good heavens!" he declared. "Who is this fine looking military man?"

"Colonel Horace MacFarlane, Your Majesty," said Dame Honoria. "He and his men of the First Zenith Cavalry Brigade were absolutely vital in the effort to defeat Percival last year."

The colonel snapped to attention and made a crisp salute.

The king nodded at him. He began to peer around his orchid house. "My word. That must be Sir Winston. He was my mother's uncle. I'm told he loves to haunt the castle."

Johnny saw a ghost of middle age at the end of the orchid house, waving at the king. He had on hunting clothes and appeared to have been killed by a shotgun blast—hopefully accidental.

Then the king's gaze fixed on Bao. "And this pretty girl?"

"The young lady is Bao," Dame Honoria said. "We found each other during my captivity on Old Number One. She has been in my service ever since."

Bao made a curtsy and started giggling.

"And the young man next to her?" the king asked.

"The gentleman is the late Lord Hurley of Evansham," Dame Honoria said. "He and Bao are great, good friends."

"I can see the family resemblance, Lord Hurley," the king said. "I'm acquainted with your brother, the current Lord Hurley. And please do accept my sympathy with regard to the abduction of your nephew from St. Egbert's School. Along with the rest of the kingdom, I'm praying for his safe, expeditious return."

Evvie's face turned into a mask of shock.

"I have a nephew?" he said with genuine surprise. "And he's been kidnapped? This is terrible. *Terrible.*"

CHAPTER 10

BASIL HASTINGS NEVER THOUGHT in a million years that he would ever feel the least bit nostalgic for St. Egbert's School. Those lumpy, thin mattresses. Those cold-water showers. Those miserly meals of tough, stringy beef and overcooked peas.

Now it all sounded like a bit of heaven.

It had been nine days since the creatures had taken them captive on that horrible night of fire and destruction. All during that time, the boys of St. Egbert's had slogged slowly northward. Up forest paths and narrow country lanes, always at night. Sometimes in chill drizzles. Sometimes through that miserable, thick fog that popped up out of nowhere. More boys and girls joined them along the way. Some of them were from schools like St. Egbert's. Others were the children of locals—farmers' and shopkeepers' sons and daughters.

A couple of times they were lucky enough to spend the night in deserted buildings—an abandoned school and a vacant granary. But most of the time, they were forced to sleep on the ground.

Those who needed them were allowed to pilfer coats and blankets along the way, for warmth. Basil thanked his lucky stars that he had on his school clothes and overcoat. Some of the St. Egbert's boys were still in their pajamas and robes. Food was whatever they could scavenge. Unfortunately, they had to go to the bathroom out in the bushes. Basil longed for a lovely, porcelain toilet.

Communications from the creatures never amounted to much. They ordered the children around in their low, harsh voices, which sounded like tubas gargling ball bearings.

"Go!"

"Stop!"

"This way."

"That way."

And most ominously, "Escape means death."

At first, of course, the kids whined and jabbered and cried.

But as Basil suspected, the creatures—all dirty and leathery, and smelling of fish and stinky cheese—didn't take kindly to protesters and chin-waggers. And more than a few fuzzy young cheeks were slapped hard. *Very hard.* He was glad he had kept his mouth shut. As his old pater used to say, "Basil, no one likes a complainer."

Late one night, Basil was lying on a wet spot of grass off a narrow shepherd's path, near what he thought might be the village of Nashton. He had curled up as tightly as he could, trying to warm himself. Tucking up against another boy for warmth—let alone a girl—was, of course, out of the question. Things were not *that* desperate. As he struggled to fall asleep, he could just barely make out the whispered conversation between Goldsworthy, Carson, and Leith.

"There are a dozen of them," Goldsworthy was saying, "and over forty of us. If we wait for just the right moment, a bunch of us ought to be able to get away. They can't catch us all."

"But they said they'd kill any escapees they caught." Carson's voice was quite sensibly quaking with fear.

"Listen, Carson, that's just a bluff. If they wanted to kill us, they would have done it back at the school. Whatever their reason, they need us alive. I don't think these palookas will be knocking us off without a very, very good reason. You can bet on that, pal."

Basil smiled in the dark. He knew that Goldsworthy's slang came from watching way too many crime movies. For some reason, Goldsworthy fancied a future career as a gangster chief. To Basil, it seemed like a peculiar dream for the son of a banker. Or perhaps not.

There was a long silence, then Leith spoke up.

"The problem, Goldsworthy, is how do we get forty frightened kids to do what they need to do when they need to do it?"

"It would be like herding cats," Carson put in.

Basil couldn't help himself, and a chuckle escaped from his mouth.

"Hastings, are you awake?" Goldsworthy whispered.

"No," Basil replied, smiling in the dark.

"Be that way, then, you witless prat," Goldsworthy hissed.

There was another pause in the plotting. Leith again broke the silence.

"I think just the three of us should give it a go. Slip out while the slipping is good. They won't know what happened until the morning. We might even be able to bring back help."

"I don't know." Carson could not control that quaver in his voice. "We haven't thought it through very well."

Goldsworthy snorted. "Why do we have to? We just sneak away. How can they possibly track us in the dark?"

Basil didn't know if this lot was being brave or brainless. Possibly both at the same time.

"That's two to one, Carson," said Leith. "Stay if you want. But Goldsworthy and I are making a break."

Basil could hear Carson's heavy breathing, almost as if he were hyperventilating. It didn't sound as if he enjoyed making his decision. After a moment, he squeaked, "All right, I'll go."

"Good man, Carson," said Leith, sounding full of bluster.

"Knew you'd do the right thing," Goldsworthy said. "Now after the next creature comes and goes, we all crawl off together. When it seems we're safely out, we divide up. Harder for them to catch us, then."

Except for the light of the creatures' torches and oil lamps some distance away, the woods were perfectly dark. Basil, though he didn't like Goldsworthy or Leith, was starting to feel fearful for them. This wasn't some fictional boys' adventure story. They could get hurt or killed. Better by far, Basil thought, to hang tight and wait for the inevitable rescue.

Exhausted right down to his bones, he had nearly drifted off into a fitful slumber when he heard the crinkling and crunching of grass and twigs and gravel, as the three boys began to crawl away. He genuinely hoped they would make it.

Transfixed, he held his breath for what seemed a long time. But it was likely less than a minute. Nothing happened. As exciting as the great escape may have been, now it was time to sleep.

BASIL'S MORNING WAKE-UP CALL came in the form of a kick to his right leg by one of the creatures. He stumbled to his feet and started to shout some angry words. But the leathery face that glared down at him quickly shut him up. This was the one that had grabbed him at St. Egbert's, and Basil knew not to give it any lip.

The creature shoved Basil into a line of captives that was forming. "Time to go."

It seemed as if the villains had a hard time talking. That might explain their anti-social qualities, Basil supposed. Some other kids laughed when he suggested they might be bog warriors come back to life. Incredible, perhaps, but it was the best theory he had.

One of those dense fogs had come in, so he could only see a few of the other boys and girls. Wherever it was they were going, these ground clouds would slow them down. That had to be a good thing.

Suddenly Basil remembered what had happened in the night. The three boys had escaped. Surely by now their captors would know that they were missing.

Prodded forward, the gaggle of bedraggled children and teenagers began to move.

That's when Basil observed something odd up ahead. He picked up his pace, and two hulking figures became clearer in the fog. They were carrying squirming bodies over their shoulders.

Basil trotted up ahead of a half-dozen other captives and was shaken by what he saw.

One of the creatures was hauling Carson, distinguishable by his limp, blond hair and big ears. The other monster had Leith, whose blue-and-white school scarf was still tied jauntily around his neck. They had gags in their mouths and were bound hand and foot.

But where was Goldsworthy?

Basil scooted forward again, provoking some girls to snap angrily at him for pushing. He ignored them and kept going, until he was first in line, behind the creature that seemed to be the chief of the kidnappers. They were still on the shepherd's path, entering out onto a meadow.

Goldsworthy was nowhere to be seen. Neither walking nor being carried.

Had he made it?
Had he escaped?
Was he bringing help?
Or had he met some other, darker fate?

CHAPTER 11

SATURDAY, FEBRUARY 1, 1936

EN ROUTE TO HIGGSMARKET, ROYAL KINGDOM

THE JOURNEY TO HIGGSMARKET was a slow, ninety-mile trek north through thick fog. The town car couldn't have been going more than fifteen or twenty miles an hour. But the interminable drive gave Johnny and Nina plenty of time to hear what Rex Ward had to tell them about current intelligence from MacFreithshire.

The county was still cut off, with roving gangs of zombies terrorizing residents who had stayed. It was hard for the army and police to stop the scoundrels, because they appeared and vanished with unseemly ease. The patchy fog—which came and went without warning—also made things difficult for the good guys. But somewhere those zombies had to have a base. And when it was found, the army would act decisively.

As excited as Johnny felt, it was strange not having his sister *or* Uncle Louie with him.

Uncle Louie was on his way to the Rowestoft aeroboat port, to take up duty repairing Como Eagles. Right up until he left, he had expressed doubt about leaving Johnny and Nina, even for just a few weeks. But Johnny could tell that this was what Uncle Louie really wanted. He had been raising kids for a long time and deserved an adventure on his own.

Mel, of course, stayed at Wickenham with Dame Honoria and Professor DeNimes, studying the piles and piles of papers and books that Percy had left. When Johnny heard what Dame Honoria had planned for Ozzie—the sneaky zombie spy who was still lurking around the neighborhood—he had a good laugh. Hopefully, her scheme would work.

On the drive to Higgsmarket, Nina wore her etheric goggles. She kept looking through the car's rear window, apparently to make sure that the colonel and his boys were still galloping along behind. And she intently lip-read everything that Rex said, asking him to repeat himself a few times. At one point she asked why he had on a Barovian uniform, since he wasn't a Barovian. And what about the target over his heart? Johnny had wondered the same thing.

"My stock in trade," the ghost answered, "was spy craft. My superior sent me on a secret mission to Barovia late in the war, to find out about certain troop movements. I speak perfect Barovian, and I wore this enemy uniform, so I wouldn't be detected. But someone betrayed me. They captured me, tortured me, and summarily put me before a firing squad. Shot to death. I think you'll find five bullet holes in my chest. And, of course, I'm doomed to wear these blasted enemy rags through all of eternity. What I'd give to have died in a nice tuxedo or even a tweed hunting jacket."

"So what will be happening when we get to Higgsmarket?" Johnny asked, eager to get off the topic of gentlemen's attire.

"We'll meet up with your official guide. Goes by the name of Marko. He comes highly recommended, I'm told. He'll want to brief you on his strategy for guiding you through hostile country. Remember, you're under instructions to only observe and report."

Johnny was anxious and apprehensive about working with this new guy. He and Nina would have to depend on him to keep them safe during the mission. He sure hoped that Marko knew his stuff.

"You can enjoy a little sight-seeing in Higgsmarket and get a good night's sleep," Rex continued. "Then tomorrow morning we'll head down to the rail yard to board Old Sal."

"What's Sal like?" Johnny asked.

Rex looked at him with a raised eyebrow. "Best that you wait and see."

BACK IN ROYALTON, people had seemed oblivious to the crisis in the north. But in Higgsmarket, Johnny sensed an air of nervousness. People rushed up and down the sidewalks. Johnny didn't see very many smiles, just grim and wary looks. He caught snatches of conversations as he and Nina walked along.

"… have enough water and food for a week…"

"… sending the young 'uns to Gran's in the south…"

"… don't think they're telling us everything…"

When they walked by a grocery store, Johnny was shocked to see that most of the shelves had been stripped nearly bare. This is what people did when they were facing natural disasters and other emergencies—stock up on food and additional supplies. And there seemed to be a lot of soldiers and police officers about.

Johnny took a few pictures of the main shopping street and caught a glowering look from a policewoman directing traffic at a busy intersection. No, things definitely did not seem normal in Higgsmarket.

In the teashop where Johnny and Nina had lunch—delicious little sandwiches of ham and deviled eggs—Johnny asked the waitress why everyone seemed so jumpy. He was anxious to hear what the locals knew.

"Well, m'dear," the rosy-cheeked woman said, "you'd be jumpy too, with that business in MacFreithshire being so close. Lots of people think that whatever is happening up there might be more than gangsters run amok."

"What do you mean?" Johnny asked.

"My sister Agnes lives near Chippington, and her letter said that those that've seen the hooligans say they don't look human. Brown as mahogany, they are. Odd of figure. Terrible strong."

The waitress patted Nina's hand. "Not that there's anything wrong with dark skin, m'dear. But their skin isn't soft and pretty like yours. It's leathery and unnatural. And what kind of monsters take children, yet ask for no ransom. There's more here than meets the eye, if you ask old Stella."

"I wish we could tell her what we know," Nina whispered just before the dessert tray arrived, loaded with small pieces of cake.

"I wish we could too, Sparks," Johnny said. "But telling her about Percy and the zombies would only make things worse."

As Nina wrote down some notes for their first story in her narrow reporter's tablet, Johnny placed his camera bag down on the floor next to his stool. He told her some of the things that she might want to jot down, and she shared her thoughts.

The two friends were sitting at the counter with their back to the door. Johnny sipped on his cup of tea and nibbled on his chocolate cake, thinking about what a huge scoop their articles and photos would be—once publication was allowed. He wouldn't be at all surprised if their stories won some big awards. Though he didn't brag about it, Johnny was awfully proud of winning the *Clarion*'s Newshawk award at the end of last year. He could make a habit of something like that.

He was daydreaming about future accolades, with a goofy grin on his face, when the rosy-cheeked waitress came out of the kitchen. Her jovial face morphed into a mask of indignation.

"You there!" she barked, looking right between Nina and Johnny. "Out! Or I'll have the police on you!"

Johnny twisted violently around, nearly falling off his stool.

There, facing him in a half-crouch, was a boy about his own age, with wild, shaggy blond hair and a grimy face.

The two of them briefly made eye contact—both equally startled.

The boy took a few steps backward, then turned and bolted out the teashop door.

With Johnny's camera bag in his left hand!

CHAPTER 12

JOHNNY HEARD NINA SHOUT HIS NAME as he scrambled out of the teashop onto the crowded sidewalk. He almost lost sight of the blond-haired boy. But he could tell that the camera thief had darted to the right. Pedestrians howled their disapproval as the bandit bulled his way through the crowd.

"You there, stop!" someone shouted.

"Delinquent!" a woman screeched.

"Blasted ruffian!" cried a well-dressed businessman.

As Johnny plowed after the robber, he collected a few scolding words of his own, even as he repeated, "Sorry… Sorry… Sorry."

It wasn't easy getting through the crowd. But when he arrived at the first intersection, about a hundred yards from the teashop, Johnny could see that up ahead, no one was being shoved or budged. No one was shouting at a rude boy. The thief must have gone either right or left.

Johnny peered to the left across the main street, but saw no one running off that way. Then he swiveled to the right and caught sight of the blond-haired boy vanishing around a curve in the road. He set off after him, knees high, feet pounding the decrepit sidewalk. As he blasted around the curve, he saw his quarry receding in the distance.

This kid is a lot faster than me, Johnny thought as he dashed along. *But I gotta catch him or I'll lose my camera.*

Just then, he heard the clatter of hooves on the cobblestones, then a few shouted words: "Master Johnny, climb on board!"

It was the colonel and Buck!

Johnny, completely out of breath, nodded and took the colonel's hand. The old ghost soldier hauled him up into the saddle and told him to hang on.

And off they galloped, just in time to see the blond-haired boy cut down an alley. A few seconds later they arrived at the same spot, which was the entrance to an arcade. The colonel headed Buck into the arched passageway.

Small shops lined the little arcade. A cobbler, a fishmonger, a tailor, a bookseller, a toy shop. And here and there, ghosts mooned about, as ghosts often did. A soldier from the continental wars of the early 1800s. A lady from several centuries ago, in a spectacular dress with fine embroidery. Oddly, they seemed unsurprised to see Johnny and the colonel. They said nothing and did nothing. They just stared.

A young boy and a woman—neither of them ghosts—came out of the toy shop, the lad proudly hugging a colorful, pressed-metal roadster. They both gasped. Johnny presumed they couldn't see the colonel, and were taken aback encountering an ordinary kid in hiking clothes, hovering up in midair.

The woman stopped and gave Johnny a disapproving look. "What in the world are you doing up there, young man? You could get hurt!"

Johnny briefly explained why he was levitating and what he was doing. He asked if they'd seen a blond-haired boy running through.

As the woman shook her head, her son tugged at her sleeve.

She looked down at him. "Yes, Oswald?"

"I saw him," the tyke said, a bit shyly. "He had a green bag and he went that way." The boy pointed to the far end of the little shopping street.

Johnny thanked them. The colonel flicked the reins and nudged Buck's flanks with his heels. They began trotting away.

"You'll need to dismount, boy, or you'll bump your head," the woman shouted after them. "There's a low, narrow passageway that leads out into the pottery yards."

"Thanks, ma'am," Johnny bellowed back. "I'll do that."

They emerged from out of the tunnel into a broad courtyard. There were brick factory buildings on three sides, although they seemed to be abandoned. Many of the windows had been broken. A big, weatherworn sign on one of the structures said "Higgsmarket Potteries, Ltd." But it had come partly loose and was tilting down. Johnny didn't see a single person.

"I'm fearful that your young thief could have gone to ground anywhere out here," the colonel said.

Johnny wanted to scream in frustration. He really liked that Ritterflex camera. Now it was gone. And he didn't know if he could find another camera like it in Higgsmarket.

"I'm sorry, Master Johnny. If we had the whole brigade here, we might have a chance of finding him. But this is akin to hunting for a needle…"

"… in a haystack," Johnny groaned, completing the simile.

He felt terrible!

The camera was gone. Probably for good.

As he trudged back to the teashop to get Nina, he thought about what he should do. He had to notify the police, because that camera was worth at least seventy-five dollars. Then he figured he ought to go around to as many pawn shops as he could. The kid would probably try to sell the Ritterflex at one of them. And what would happen to the film already exposed? What a mess.

THE NEXT MORNING Johnny again faced a mystery that had baffled him since they had arrived in the Royal Kingdom. There it was, sitting in a little rack in the middle of the hotel breakfast table. Toast. But it was cold. What was the point of that? Didn't it make more sense to put butter and jam on nice *hot* toast? Who wouldn't prefer that? He scraped some butter onto the cold toast and began to munch despondently.

The Ritterflex was gone, stolen. And this stupid town didn't have a decent camera store. Even the pawnshops Johnny had visited yesterday afternoon didn't have anything good. He would have to buy a crappy folding camera at a chemist's. Now he was worried that the chief wouldn't be happy with the quality of his pictures.

Nina arrived at the table and began to butter her own cold toast. She tried to lift his spirits, telling him he was such a good photographer that he could probably cover the whole story with an ordinary box camera.

But Johnny didn't feel like being comforted. "I've never had a camera stolen before. And wouldn't you know, it has to happen just before we leave on one of the biggest assignments ever."

"And that would be this morning."

Rex Ward, the secret ghost agent, had come down through the ceiling and landed right next to Johnny—who looked at him, prompting Nina to do the same. Even without her etheric goggles, she was well trained in the craft of looking at dead people she couldn't see.

"You mean we're leaving soon?" Johnny asked.

Rex nodded, while gazing enviously at the overloaded breakfast plates.

"Oh, to be able to eat and smell some fried eggs and kippers," he sighed. He blinked back at Johnny. "Sal leaves at eleven this morning. The SGS officer I've been in contact with has made the arrangements for you."

"What happens when we get to Chippington?" Nina asked. She had put on her etheric goggles, which drew perplexed stares from a few other breakfasters in the dining room. Johnny had to admit the glasses made her look plenty weird.

"Simple enough," Rex said. "You'll head off with your escort and several ghost couriers, to bring back your reports. And you will try earnestly to not get killed or captured."

Johnny wondered if Rex was just trying to be funny, and waited for him to smile or wink or something. Wasn't that the escort's job? To keep them safe?

"And speaking of your escort," Rex said, "here he is." The ghost made a head nod toward the dining room entrance.

Johnny turned and looked quizzically at the approaching black-haired teenager, who swaggered into the room as if he owned the place. He was wearing a tan trench coat that was, at the moment, unbelted, and a dark, wool suit that looked fashionably up to date. Johnny caught the odor of his scented hair oil. A bit of a dandy, apparently.

Johnny frowned. Was *this* the guy they had hired to guide him and Nina and protect them from zombies? This character didn't even vaguely resemble the rough, tough rugby player Johnny had hoped for.

Behind the kid came a red-haired girl in a well-tailored, double-breasted, green plaid suit. Johnny noticed her eyes—a shade of violet that he had never seen before. Two ghosts—a dark-skinned boy and a little girl—floated above them.

"Johnny, Nina," said Rex, "I'd like you to meet Marko Herne.

Mr. Herne thought it best that you have more than one escort. So you'll also be accompanied by his associates. This is Iris Budd, the late Raj Gupta, and Iris's late sister, Petunia."

Marko didn't seem much happier to see Johnny, than Johnny was to see Marko. Johnny got a distinct impression of coldness and disregard from this kid, and he had no idea why.

The curt, quick handshake that they exchanged confirmed it.

Marko was actually glaring at Johnny, as he nudged a thick strand of black hair off his forehead. "I have something for you."

He swung his left arm around to the front.

"Holy maroley!" Johnny blurted, amazed. "You got my camera bag! Is the Ritterflex in there?"

"Yeah, and you're lucky I found the bloody thing." Marko didn't exactly look happy about it. "Now what I want to know is how stupid can you be, letting a street rat grab it so easy?"

CHAPTER 13

SUNDAY, FEBRUARY 2, 1936

WICKENHAM, GILBEYSHIRE

EXCEPT WHEN GRANDMOTHER or Mel sent her off on an errand—usually to refresh the contents of the teapot—Bao had spent most of her first few days at Wickenham haunting the great library.

Grandmother sat at a huge desk and went through stacks of papers one by one, scribbling notes down as she progressed. She riffled through books and boxes. Professor DeNimes and Mel did the same, but at much smaller desks. Bao wished that she could read well enough and was smart enough to do the same thing—to help her friends. But she was having a hard enough time just reading *Ellie Owl and the Midnight Hoot*.

Despite being warned by Grandmother to not bother anyone, Bao's curiosity got the best of her. When Grandmother left the library late one afternoon, Bao zipped over to Mel and asked what exactly it was she was looking for.

Mel put down the papers she held in her hands. "Well, Bao, you know that Percy turned himself into a zombie."

Bao, floating several inches above the floor in front of Mel, nodded earnestly, remembering with a shudder that creepy man.

"We're trying to figure out how. And then we want to stop it from happening ever again. I'm looking at some articles that Percy clipped out when he was a teenager. They're mostly about cricket stars and test matches and whatnot. There are even a few about baseball. Nothing to do with ghosts and bombs and zombies that I can see. But everything has to be checked out."

Bao listened intently. The little ghost girl agreed with Nina. Zombies were *gross*. She hoped that Grandmother, the professor, and Mel could figure out how to do away with them.

But boxes and boxes of Percy's papers covered several tables that had been set up in the library. Bao thought that it would take a very long time to get through all of them.

When she wasn't helping Grandmother and the others, Bao spent her time with Evvie, the late Lord Hurley of Evansham. The two ghosts had met when they were about to go into the etheric bomb that Percy had built. Bao was a little girl from an ancient mountain tribe and Evvie was a teenaged nobleman of the Royal Kingdom. They hit it off splendidly, becoming the best of friends, despite their many differences.

The pair often went exploring around Wickenham. Through the attics. Down into the basement. Out in the barns and stables. Around the gardens and the great maze. Over to the village of Blackfield, where they helped ghosts from the estate spy on Ozzie Eccleston, one of Percy's gang.

Bao didn't like to be forward and ask about Evvie's family. But one afternoon, when they were sitting on the ornate wrought iron fence by Wickenham's little lake, she couldn't help herself.

"Why didn't you go to see your family when we were in Royalton?" she said, swinging her legs beneath her. "Didn't you want to see your brother and everyone?"

"Well, old girl," Evvie said, "the thought did occur to me. But the fact is that I'm dashed embarrassed about being a ghost. Our father died in '09. And what did I go and do as soon as I became Lord Hurley? I took that blasted expedition up the Roobuco River and promptly got myself drowned. At the tender age of sixteen. I can only imagine how angry my mother and brother were at me, after warning me against going."

"But that was a long time ago, Evvie," said Bao. "You should talk to your brother again. He'd want to know that you're all right, even if you're dead."

"I suppose so," Evvie sighed. "But I feel that with my nephew being kidnapped, his fate unknown, it would be deuced awkward for me to show up on their doorstep. And I don't even know the poor lad's name. No, no. They have bigger fish to fry than having a reunion with a dusty old wraith."

Later that afternoon, Bao and Evvie were hiding up in a shadowy corner of The Laughing Fox pub. They knew that Dame Honoria's scheme to take care of Ozzie Eccleston was about to unfold.

Down below, local men were playing darts and drinking beer, oblivious of the ghosts up above them. Some women sat at a side table, jabbering loudly at each other. A clump of men were standing around talking about the weird business up in MacFreithshire and what it might mean for the Royal Kingdom. Cigarette and pipe smoke filled the air.

And at the bar, all by himself, sat Ozzie, sucking on a tall ale and voraciously consuming a plate of sausages and boiled potatoes. When he had just been a ghost, he hadn't been able to eat or drink anything. As a zombie, he seemed to spend most of his time doing just that. Grandmother said it was a wonder that he hadn't gained a hundred pounds.

A few moments after Bao and Evvie arrived, another man sauntered up to the bar and took the stool right next to Ozzie. The zombie looked to his right and nodded. Obviously he didn't recognize the fellow, who happened to be one of Grandmother's gardeners. Bao knew him as Phillip.

"Evening," Phillip said, after he ordered a beer for himself. "Don't believe I've seen you at The Fox before."

Ozzie shrugged. "Then you haven't been here lately. I practically live in the place."

"Don't look like you're from around here."

"From Rotonesia, actually. On the grand tour of the Royal Kingdom. History buff, don't you know."

"Well then, welcome to *our* little piece of history. It looks to me like you're just about out of our local brew there. Can I buy you another?"

Ozzie's little Rotonesian face lit up. "Good chap! Kind of you. Yes, please."

And that was the first of about seven large mugs of beer that Phillip bought for the zombie—who about two hours later was face down on the bar, muttering to himself.

Phillip nodded at a solitary man who was sitting in a corner. The fellow trotted over. Together they hoisted Ozzie to his feet and trundled him out of the pub. Their noses were wrinkled up, probably from being so close to that dank, musty smell the zombie gave off. Bao and Evvie zoomed outside to watch them stuff Ozzie into an automobile. From there it was a quick trip back to Wickenham.

Grandmother and Mel were waiting out in the garage with several more workers from the estate, standing around a large wooden crate, the end of which was open. Stenciled on all sides were the words: FRAGILE. KEEP UPRIGHT. Inside the crate were blankets, copious quantities of tinned meat, water, a small chemical toilet, flashlights, and other supplies. There were several air holes drilled in the sides, as well.

As Phillip and the other man extracted a limp, drunken Ozzie from the auto, Grandmother said, "It's not my wish to harm him, but to teach him a lesson. It was his choice to be trapped in a dead body. Now he will have ample time to ponder his misdeeds."

Bao knew that once Ozzie was put in his box, the box was to be express-shipped all the way back to Old Number One, the island that Grandmother's father had owned. That's where Percy had made the second etheric bomb. And that's where Ozzie and the Steppe Warriors had held Grandmother captive after they abducted her.

The shippers were instructed to ignore any urgent pleas from inside the box. Once the crate arrived on the island, it was to be opened and Ozzie released to his exile. Since the island was uninhabited, there would be no pubs or cafes or grocery stores. So, no more sausages and beer for him.

As soon as the last nail was hammered in, Bao shouted gleefully, "It's just what you deserve, you mean, mean man!"

"Don' think you've won," came a slurred, muffled voice from inside the crate. "Percy Rathbone'll have the last word. And then all of you can go hang!"

CHAPTER 14

JOHNNY WAS FURIOUS!

He had never met anyone—living or dead—who was as rude as this kid Marko.

The scene at breakfast kept replaying over and over in his head, as he walked to the Higgsmarket rail yards later that morning.

When Marko had called him stupid for letting his camera get stolen, Johnny felt as if he'd actually been slapped in the face. Even Nina looked angry. Johnny had started to defend himself, but Marko kept talking, his voice harsh and accusing.

"If I'm going to keep you alive in zombie country," Marko had said, jabbing a finger at Johnny's chest, "I need to know that you're not a chowderhead. You've gotta do what I say, when I say it. I'm in charge, got it?"

People around the dining room were staring at them. One waitress looked as though she might intervene.

"This isn't any picnic, mate," Marko continued, now lowering his voice. "And I'm not putting Iris and myself at risk because of some camera-toting cowboy from the Plains Republic. Got it, mate?"

By the time Johnny finally had a chance to respond, his blood was boiling.

"Now you let *me* make a few things clear. I've traveled across the Greater Ocean and seen things you couldn't even imagine, *mate*. I nearly died a half-dozen times, *mate*. I saw the etheric bomb explode, *mate*."

He gave Marko the coldest stare he could muster. "So just because I had my camera stolen, it doesn't mean I don't know what I'm doing. Got that, *mate?*"

Rex had tried to smooth things over. "Now, now, lads, we don't want to start off this partnership under a dark cloud, do we? Let's just chalk it all up to this dashed fog. It's got everybody on edge. Even us ghosts."

So Marko had grumbled that he was sorry for being so blunt. Johnny had accepted the apology, but he didn't believe Marko meant a word of it. Johnny didn't know how he could spend a day with this arrogant jerk, let alone a week. But if he was going to carry out his spying assignment, he had to put up with the guy.

Now they were all heading to the rail yards, where the king's train awaited them. Johnny and Nina strode directly behind Rex Ward, with Marko and his pals up ahead. Farther back, the colonel led a half-dozen members of the First Zenith Cavalry Brigade, including Sergeant Clegg. They turned onto a side street filled mostly with tradesmen's shops—plumbers and electricians and builders. Local ghosts stared at them rudely, as many ghosts do.

Both Johnny and Nina had on their backpacks. And Johnny was clutching his camera bag with a fierce grip. He would never so much as leave it on the floor again. *Never. Ever.*

Along the way, he sidled up to Rex and, in a low voice, asked him a question. "What's the story with these two kids?" He pointed at Marko and Iris, walking ahead of them.

"Don't be fooled by their age and appearance. Marko is tough and street-smart and knows his way out of a tight spot. He comes highly recommended by the Higgsmarket constabulary. And Iris knows MacFreithshire like the back of her hand."

"But they can't be much older than I am," Johnny protested.

"According to Marko's application for security clearance, he's sixteen."

Johnny snorted. If that kid was sixteen, then Johnny was four-teen. And that wouldn't be the case for over a year.

They came into the square that faced the front of the Higgsmarket rail station, a great layer cake of red and tan brick, and many tall, arched windows. Taxicabs were peeling in and out on the street in front of it, dropping passengers off and picking them up.

Following Rex, they marched through the crowded, noisy station, then outside. The travelers made their way across the tracks and around the near end of a huge steel shed.

What Johnny saw then absolutely took his breath away. A streamlined railroad locomotive built of stainless steel. It looked like a giant bullet on wheels, with functional adornments here and there. Behind the mirror-polished engine were eight rail cars.

"Wow!" he exclaimed. "This is Old Sal?

"That she is," Rex answered proudly. "The Super Automated Locomotive. Old Sal."

Johnny had never seen anything like it. "I bet she can fly like a rocket."

Rex nodded. "I'm told she can do one hundred and fifty miles per hour, on a straightaway of the proper track."

Both Johnny and Marko whistled at the impressive speed.

"It's the king's personal train," Rex continued. "Because of that, it has a unique system to prevent derailment. A special sensor alerts the engineer if there are obstacles ahead. Say, a fallen tree."

"We'll be up to Chippington in no time at all on this little buggy," Marko enthused.

"Afraid not," Rex said. "We won't be traveling on mainline track, which Sal requires for full speed. And if there's fog, we'll have to slow down."

"Is she steam-powered or diesel?" Nina peered at him through her goggles.

Rex offered a teasing little smile. "Actually, neither."

"What do you mean?"

"Sal is electric. She runs on batteries and you'll notice she makes hardly any noise."

Johnny was astounded. "But that's impossible. You can't power a train like this on electric batteries."

"He's right," Marko put in. "It can't be done."

"Normally, I'd agree," Rex said. "But Sal was built for the king by some of the best ghost scientists in the world. No one has revealed exactly how she works, but rumors are that ghosts in the circuits somehow make for an exponential increase in electric efficiency."

Johnny grinned at Nina. "It's going to be fun traveling on this baby, isn't it, Sparks?"

But Johnny and his group were not the only passengers that Old Sal was carrying north that morning. There were a number of living soldiers aboard. And wraiths of the Special Ghost Service floated and darted all over the place. Rex explained that they were all tasked with hunting for and rescuing the missing children.

To Johnny's dismay, his group ended up in the very last carriage, which was some kind of baggage car full of supplies. Rex apologized, but explained that it was the only place there was any room for them. So Johnny and Nina crowded into the car together with Marko and Iris. Raj, Petunia, and Rex found perches on top of some crates. The colonel and his lads were to ride escort outside.

Everyone settled down on the hard benches in back, waiting for the departing whistle. The silence was awkward. Johnny decided to do a little fence mending. He turned to Marko. "I was wondering, how'd you find my Ritterflex?"

Marko didn't even look at Johnny. "Heard about the theft down at the police station. Knew you were the shutterbug from Zenith. Knew you'd need it. Seen your stuff even, once or twice. Pretty good. Like that shot of the nice-looking bird in the mustache."

Johnny moaned. His picture of Mel on the Night Goose, wearing the fake mustache, would never stop haunting him. When they wrote Johnny's obituary, hopefully when he was a hundred, they'd call him the photographer who shot the mustachioed girl.

"Your sis, right? Tell her if she's ever in Higgsmarket to look up Marko Herne. He'll show her a fine old time." Then Marko made a weird clicking noise out of the side of his mouth and offered a sharkish grin.

Johnny almost laughed out loud, imagining what Mel would make of this impudent character. What would the two of them even have to talk about?

"So I heard what the thief looked like and knew right off who it was. Weasel Pitt, the pest. Put out word among my ghost mates. Where's that rotten little blighter at? Found him last night, made him an offer he couldn't refuse. A nice, big knuckle sandwich."

Iris laughed. "Marko here's on a first-name basis with nearly every underage lowlife in the county."

As much as Johnny didn't like Marko, the guy had done him a huge favor. Without his Ritterflex, Johnny couldn't get the high-quality shots that might run someday in the *Zenith Clarion*.

But somehow, Johnny had to make one thing clear to the guy. Johnny and Nina were here to do a job—get their stories and photos, and find out anything they could about Percy and the zombies. Marko's job was to protect them while they did it. He was their guide and their escort. But he *wasn't* their boss.

Finally, under a dismal gray sky, a whistle sounded and the train lurched forward. As it picked up speed, Johnny looked over at Nina, who was sitting next to Iris Budd.

Iris seemed the polar opposite of Marko. While he was humorless and moody, she bubbled with enthusiasm for the mission. She was examining the etheric goggles with a look of amazement.

"Would I love to have a pair of these, Nina. Simply amazing that Johnny's sister came up with them. She must be some kind of genius."

Nina nodded proudly. "That she is."

"Any idea how much they cost?"

Nina shrugged. "Not a clue. I mean, these are the first pair anywhere. But when I see Mel again, I'll ask."

"You know, our mum can touch Pet and hold her—thanks to me—but she has no way of seeing the girl. I'm the only one in the family who can. But if Mum could actually look at Pet whenever she wanted to… Well, that would just be brilliant."

Before long, the scenery outside the window became obscured by fog. But the train kept advancing at the same speed. After about an hour, Rex excused himself. He said he needed to talk to someone up front.

A short time later the ghost returned. "It's a right old peasouper out there." He shivered as if he could actually feel the chill. "One of the worst I've seen. Somehow it's given me a headache. Haven't had one since I was alive. In any event, we should be in

Chippington within—"

Before he could finish his sentence, a horrific, deafening scream of tortured steel came blasting at them from the front of the train.

Johnny felt the whole world lurch violently sideways.

Was it an earthquake?

But before he could think another thought, he was thrown into a pile of stacked boxes, as if tossed by a giant's hand.

Stunned, he became aware that the floor of the car was rapidly tipping up toward the sky.

Boxes began to tumble over on top of him. He raised his arms to cover his head, trying to protect it from the onslaught. He was being battered and bruised from all sides. Confused, he struggled to figure out what was happening.

Then the lights inside the car winked out, and everything went black.

CHAPTER 15

THERE WAS SILENCE in the railroad carriage. In the distance, metal continued to grind and wood to crack.

It took Johnny half a moment to clear his head. He had to make sense of where he was, of what had happened.

One thing was clear—the car was tipped on its side.

He seemed to be okay.

But what about the others?

"Is anyone hurt?" he bellowed into the darkness, his heart racing.

Out of the corner of his eye, he saw some movement. A small shape of luminous green floated along up above the scattered boxes. It was the girl ghost, Petunia Budd.

She began to call out, in that papery sort of ghost voice, sounding very scared.

"Iris! Iris!"

A germ of fear formed in the pit of Johnny's stomach, like the first hint of nausea. The train had wrecked, probably derailed. And what had happened to Nina? Why wasn't she saying anything? If only Johnny could see better. But the dense fog outside offered little illumination.

Johnny pushed several boxes aside as he stood. "Sparks! Sparks!"

There was some thudding and clunking as more boxes were manhandled.

A shaky voice came out of the darkness. "I'm okay, Johnny."

"Are the rest of you guys all right?" Johnny hollered.

"Yeah, I guess so," came Marko's voice.

The boy ghost Raj floated into view. "Me, too. But then I'm already dead."

"Rex?" Johnny yelled. "Where are you?"

"Over here." The ghost agent emerged from the darkness at the front of the carriage. "Well, this certainly throws a spanner into the works."

Johnny groaned. "So much for a train that can't be derailed."

"The enemy must have figured out a way to outsmart the sensor wheel," Rex said.

Petunia was still darting around nervously up above them. "Iris! Iris!" she panted. "I can't find my sister!"

"Okay, everyone," Johnny said. "Let's help Petunia find Iris."

Johnny was worried. Iris hadn't made a peep since the wreck. She could be seriously hurt, lying unconscious beneath the boxes that had been strewn around. This could be bad.

Nina had on her etheric goggles now and took charge. "She's here somewhere. Raj and Petunia, can you fly slowly around where she was sitting? Maybe we'll spot her."

Under the very pale green glow of Petunia and Raj, everyone began to pick up boxes—some of them surprisingly heavy—and move them to the side. They found Iris a moment later, crumpled beneath boxes of pork loaf—rations for soldiers up north.

Rex and Marko hefted the boxes off her, and Petunia zoomed down to hug her sister. That's when the battered girl slowly came to, with a fluttering of her eyelids. Johnny could tell that she would have one terrific shiner. Too bad for a girl with such amazing violet eyes.

"Iris, are you all right?" Marko sounded anxious. "Are you hurt?"

Slowly rising to a sitting position, she shook her head, nodded, then shook her head again. "Dunno. Maybe."

"Let's get her up," Johnny said.

"Right," Marko agreed.

The two boys tried to haul Iris to her feet. That was when they discovered something was wrong. *Very* wrong.

The girl screamed in agony as they tugged on her arms.

Johnny had never heard a person make such a terrible noise. "Ease her back down! Now!"

Johnny didn't know what to do. He looked at Marko, but Marko seemed just as baffled.

Nina elbowed her way onto the scene, goggles pushed up on her forehead.

"Let me check her out. I earned a first-aid badge from the Woodland Guides. Johnny, get out your flashlight."

My flashlight! Johnny thought. *Of course!* Both he and Nina carried one in their backpacks. But he'd been too stunned by the crack-up to even remember it until now.

While Johnny pointed his flashlight at Iris, Nina squatted down by the injured girl. "Now, this may hurt a little bit, Iris, but be tough." Nina prodded gently at the right arm—shoulder, upper arm, and forearm. Iris didn't make a peep. But when Nina started to feel the left forearm, Iris screamed again, though not so horribly.

"Nuts!" Nina muttered. "She's got a broken radius bone, I bet. Let me feel it again, Iris. I'll try to go easy."

Iris nodded. She bravely allowed Nina to probe her forearm again, though she did whimper a bit at the pain.

"I think it's a partial break," Nina announced. "Bad, but not real bad."

Petunia was floating right above Iris and Nina. "You be careful with her," she snapped. "She's my little sister!"

But Nina, not seeing the ghost, let alone her moving lips, never heard her scolding.

From outside came the sounds of men hollering and shouting, of gunfire and clashing blades.

Johnny put up his hand. "Everyone, quiet. Listen."

They all went silent. Something was happening out there in the fog. And it didn't sound like a tea party.

There was more shouting and shooting. And the noise seemed to be getting closer.

Just then, Colonel MacFarlane, still mounted on Buck, flew into the railroad car, stopping right in front of Johnny.

"Am I glad to see you, Colonel! What the heckfire is going on?"

"The scoundrels threw something on the track from the embankment a short way ahead of Sal," the colonel answered. "Something big enough to derail the train."

So there had been no time for Sal's anti-derailment warning system to work, thought Johnny. No wonder they were in this pickle.

"As soon as the SGS forces and soldiers started coming out of the passenger cars, they were ambushed," the colonel continued. "There's a devil of a fight going on. I fear it may spread back here. We have to get you out of this car and into the woods. Now!"

Over a desperate few minutes, the colonel and Buck hauled Nina, Marko, and Johnny up out of the car and flew them into a dense thicket of trees nearby. Then, with Petunia hovering overhead, the colonel gently lifted Iris out. She cradled her arm as best she could.

From the safety of the woods, Johnny heard more shouting and shooting. But there was also another noise—a guttural bellowing from things that sounded not quite human. He had no idea what exactly was happening out there in the fog. But it didn't take much imagination to understand that they were in terrible jeopardy.

They all kneeled in the dirt amidst the twigs and branches, with the colonel and his men arrayed around them. Private Boo, normally the most good-natured of ghosts, seemed almost as if he were in pain, rubbing his temples and grimacing. And the stalwart Corporal Marchiano hugged himself as if he were freezing cold. Johnny wanted to ask what was wrong, but there were far more pressing matters at hand.

Marko actually looked at a loss. It was pretty clear that this mess was a lot more than he had bargained for.

"Ask the colonel if he has any ideas," he whispered to Johnny.

Johnny caught the colonel's eye. The ghost officer and the other troopers had dismounted, so they wouldn't be as visible. "Colonel, what do we do?"

The colonel was about to answer when a terrible scream—much closer than before—cut through the fog.

"You and the others sit tight here," the colonel said. "Sergeant Clegg and Private Boo will stay. I aim to sortie up the tracks with the rest of the lads. See if we can help those SGS and army boys up front. They sound like they're in trouble. We'll find you later. We could use your help, Captain Ward."

Rex nodded, pulling his army revolver out of its holster. "Quite right. I think it's time we got into the action. May I ride with you, Colonel?"

With a wave to Johnny and the others, the colonel, Rex, and the four troopers set off through the brush and fog.

Even in a tight spot like this, Johnny's photo instincts took charge. He grabbed his camera and began to creep forward to the edge of the vegetation. But before he could get more than a few feet, he felt a hand on his shoulder, sharply tugging him back.

It was Marko. And he seemed to have regained his bossy attitude.

"What do you think you're doing, you fool? Those goons out there will see you. You'll get us all killed."

Johnny yanked away from him. "Can't you get this through your thick skull—I'm a news photographer! I've done this before and I know what I'm doing!"

That's what happens when you get stuck working with an amateur, Johnny thought as he snuck forward. *Marko may know his street thugs and pickpockets, but he doesn't know much about a news lensman's job.*

When he reached the edge of the railroad bed, Johnny saw a trio of hulking figures—zombies for sure. They had axes and bludgeons in hand, and were surveying the ruined railroad carriages. They were standing with their backs to Johnny, making the scene a perfect shot.

Johnny looked down into the camera's viewfinder, focused the lens, and snapped the shutter. The flashbulb flared.

And before its light faded away, the three hulking figures had turned and were charging straight at him.

CHAPTER 16

JOHNNY TORE BACK INTO THE WOODS.

"Sergeant Clegg! Help! Three zombies! Coming at us!"

The beanpole ghost soldier leapt onto his horse. "Private Boo and I will decoy them away. You and the rest head into the woods, out of sight."

Marko glared at Johnny. "Told you not to do that." He grabbed Iris by her right hand and, in a crouch, began to lead her back into the brush. Petunia floated close behind.

"Don't go too far," the sergeant warned. "We'll find you later."

And at that, Clegg and Boo burst out through the undergrowth into the open, whooping and hollering.

Then came a rapid clanging of blades. Johnny could hear the receding hoofbeats, the clunking of hobnail boots, and finally one blast from the sergeant's shotgun.

"What happened?" Nina asked.

"Clegg and Boo must have lured those zombies away," Johnny told her. "But there might be more. We gotta hide farther back in the trees."

Nina grabbed her backpack and swung it onto her shoulders. "The trick will be keeping together out there in this fog. You can barely see your hand in front of your face."

"Then we'd better catch up with Marko and the Budd sisters, or we might lose them."

As Johnny turned to go, he felt a tugging at his elbow. It was the ghost boy, Raj Gupta.

"Let me bring up the rear. I can warn the rest of you if someone's coming. I'll be okay. I think whoever is after us is looking for living kids, not a dead boy like me."

They set off at a right angle to the derailed train, going single file, brushing aside branches and twigs. They soon caught up with Marko, Iris, and Petunia. From then on, Johnny tried to make sure that he could always see Iris up ahead and Nina behind. To lose sight of one of them could be big trouble.

But that's exactly what happened.

Just after carefully climbing over a fallen tree trunk, Johnny looked up and saw the faintest shadow of Iris vanish before his eyes—as if by magic—right into the dense fog.

"Iris," he whisper-shouted. "Slow down! I can't see you!"

Then he quickly turned around, looking for Nina. He couldn't see her either!

Panic rose up in his throat like some bitter acid.

He seemed to be all by himself in the dark, dismal woods, immersed in a gray soup. In a strange country. Surrounded by rampaging zombies.

Okay, he thought, *calm down. Take a deep breath.*

The best thing he could do was keep moving forward. That's the only way he'd find Marko and Iris. And if he went back to look for Nina, she might pass him in the fog.

He darted forward only a few dozen steps when he heard a familiar and very welcome voice behind him.

"Don't go so fast. You'll break a leg."

It was Nina, emerging from the murk. When she saw his face,

she looked concerned.

"What's the matter, Johnny?"

"I lost sight of Iris. I'm trying to find her. Why in heckfire hasn't Marko stopped? We must be far enough from the train to be safe."

Raj zoomed up to them. "Let me go up ahead and find the others." He darted away, vanishing into the fog.

Johnny and Nina tramped onward. A couple of minutes later, they stumbled upon Marko, Iris, and Petunia—with Raj floating above them, looking this way and that.

The sisters stood side by side, Iris clutching her broken arm next to her chest. Petunia was patting her hand, repeating, "Poor baby, poor baby."

"Oh, don't fuss over me, Pet," Iris said. "A little broken arm's nothing to worry about."

Johnny went up to Marko, scowling. "I thought you were supposed to be looking out for Nina and me. You're going too fast. You've gotta make sure that we can all see each other when we're moving through this fog."

Marko's face flushed with anger. "I set the pace, mate, and you follow. If you're not fast enough, then I guess I'll have to slow down. I just didn't think you were that sluggish."

Now Johnny was really mad. He'd always thought that, for a runty kid, he could move pretty quickly. And this guy was calling him sluggish.

"Listen, Marko. I was the third fastest kid in my phys ed class back at Grover Falkland Junior High. And the football coach said that if I could put on a few more inches and pounds that he'd like me to go out for junior varsity and—"

"Stop it, you two!"

Both Johnny and Marko were startled by the interruption. They swiveled to blink at an angry-looking Nina.

"We're running for our lives, and you two are arguing about who's fast and who's slow. Save it for later. You should be worrying about Iris."

Johnny took a deep breath and nodded. Nina was right. "Sparks, do you think you can splint Iris's arm until we get to a doctor or nurse?"

"If I can find two or three solid sticks and tear a few pieces of cloth from someone's clothes."

"Then what?" Marko still sounded hostile.

"We wait for Clegg and Boo to find us," Johnny snapped.

"And if they don't?"

For that question, Johnny could only think of one answer.

"Then we go on without them."

TWO HOURS LATER, they were still waiting. Johnny strained his eyes, trying to catch a glimpse of the sergeant or the private emerging from the fog. But the two ghost troopers never appeared. Johnny decided that if he and Nina were going to continue on their mission, they'd have to do it without the colonel, the troopers, and Rex.

And that meant they had to rely solely on Marko to guide them and keep them safe. But Johnny needed to make it clear that he wouldn't follow the guy's orders blindly. This was still all about getting Johnny and Nina behind enemy lines. And finding out what Percy Rathbone was up to.

"I say we plow on to Chippington-in-the-Vale," Johnny announced. "We'll go on just as we've planned."

Marko fixed a narrow-lidded stare at him. "The SGS hired me and Iris to take you around MacFreithshire. It's pretty clear, though, that this'll be harder and more dangerous than we ever thought. I've decided that we give up on this attempt and back-track to Higgsmarket as best we can."

Was Marko serious? Did he really think Johnny would give up just because of one little zombie attack? Johnny had been through lots worse. Anyway, Higgsmarket had to be dozens of miles back.

Johnny thought it would almost be a relief to be rid of Marko. "You do what you want. Nina and I took on this job and we intend to finish it. Got that? Now which way is Chippington?"

Marko shrugged. "How would I know? I can't see anything in this bloody fog."

Nina grabbed her pack up from the ground. "Anyone in my Woodland Guide troop back in Zenith would know just what to do." She pulled a compass from one of the pack's many pockets, held it in her hand, and squinted down at it.

"I understand that Chippington is northwest of Higgsmarket. That way, I think." She pointed straight ahead.

Marko whispered a few words to Iris and Raj, then turned back to Johnny. "Well, I guess I don't get paid unless I bring you back alive. So, we'll stick with you for now. Lead on, Miss Bain."

WITH NINA NOW AT THE FRONT of the line—regularly checking her compass and looking at the map that Iris had brought—they tramped through the foggy woods. This time, they took care to stay close to each other. But for a change, the dismal ground clouds lifted slightly, and they could clearly see a two-lane paved road that curved through the forest of oaks and elms. They took only a moment to get there.

Iris, still holding her splinted arm close to her, looked around and smiled. "This here's Kilborn Road. The main road into Chippington from the south. We just follow along a few miles, and we can walk right into town. I spent time here when I was younger."

"I died in Chippington," Petunia put in. "Typhoid fever."

Iris put her good right arm around Petunia's narrow little shoulders and pulled her close.

It always made Johnny feel bad, hearing how a kid ghost had died. But what could anyone do? Death was a part of life.

Just at that instant, he heard the rumble of a truck up ahead, coming their way. They couldn't be seen by the army or the police! If they were, that would be the end of their zombie adventure. The cops or the soldiers were sure to take them back to some safe place, far away from any bog zombie action.

"Everyone!" Johnny shouted. "Off the road. Now!"

Not fifteen seconds later, three big trucks—they called them lorries here—came rolling by, heading south. They were painted the olive drab of army vehicles everywhere and were open in back. Johnny figured there would be soldiers in them, or policemen. And there were, in a manner of speaking.

All three trucks were packed with uniformed men, also in olive drab, who had been bandaged up and patched together. Most were seated on benches, but a few lay on stretchers, being tended to by medics. They looked as if they had been in a real fight, and had taken the worst of it.

If the zombies could do this to trained soldiers, what could they do to four kids with no weapons at all?

CHAPTER 17

LATE IN THE AFTERNOON, Johnny and his companions—exhausted, dirty, and sweaty—tramped into Chippington-in-the-Vale. They were shocked to see what looked like a prosperous village so empty and abandoned. Johnny noticed a couple of faces watching them through windows, and someone running across a street up ahead. But that was all. Hardly anyone seemed to be around. Even the ghosts acted wary of the newcomers.

With ghosts on his mind, Johnny kept looking back down the road, hoping to catch sight of the colonel or Sergeant Clegg or anyone from the First Zenith Brigade. But no one appeared through the fog.

One wraith, however, did approach them. She was a horse-woman, wearing high leather boots, a black jacket over a white blouse, tan jodhpurs, and a badly dented helmet. In her right hand, she carried a short whip, which she kept cracking against her left hand. And oddly, following right behind her, practically like a pet dog, was the ghost of a fox.

"Oh, look at the pretty fox," Petunia said. "Does he belong to you?"

"He belongs to no one," the dead rider answered. "Let's just say we've become fast friends. Ever since I was thrown from my horse and landed on top of him. Ended things for both of us."

Petunia reached down to stroke the fox, who quickly darted away, behind the woman's legs—considerably shyer than his mistress.

"Name's Lady Cordelia Graves-Burgoyne, by the way. Listen, chaps. If you've come to do some shopping in old Chippie, I'm afraid you've picked the worst possible time. We've had an infestation of rude tourists from the north. Never seen anything like them before. Nothing but a bunch of thugs and criminals. Ransacked the town and set fire to St. Egbert's School."

Nina peered at Lady Cordelia through her etheric goggles. "Didn't the townspeople do anything to fight them off?"

"They came and went so quickly, we hardly had time to react. I took after a few of them. Tried to administer a good whipping, but my riding crop just went right through them. Moments like that are when I utterly detest being a ghost."

"If you really want to wallop them, I could help you," Johnny said. "All you have to do is agree to work for me."

"Work for you?" She laughed, as if the notion were ridiculous. "My dear boy, I am a Graves-Burgoyne. No Graves-Burgoyne has ever worked a day in his or her life!"

"Well, maybe you can consider it something other than work, Lady Cordelia. I won't be paying you, after all. Maybe you can volunteer to help."

"Well, that's more my cup of tea. Always felt that the nobility was obligated to help the common folk whenever possible. *Noblesse oblige*, don't you know."

Johnny heard a low rumble coming from Marko. He could sympathize—this woman didn't seem to have a clue how insulting she sounded. But she could serve a purpose, now that she had agreed to be useful. Of course, she would be vulnerable to injuries from zombies, as well. That was the arrangement when a ghost interacted with the real world—they could inflict pain, but also receive it.

"All right, then," Johnny said. "We have a deal. So I'm empowering you to go after any of those foreign tourists and give them a good thrashing with your whip. Whenever and wherever they appear."

The ghost grinned. "Now *that* sounds like a ripping good time. Though I must admit, I'm feeling a bit of a twinge in my elbow. Still, I should be able to crack the old whip a few times."

"One more thing," Johnny said. "Do you know of any good lodgings around here?"

"Try the Dusk Rose Hotel, up on the hill. You can't miss it— it's just across from the infirmary."

With that, the ghost snapped a cheery "Tally ho!" and marched off with an air of militant determination. The fox trotted behind.

"I think I'm rooting for the zombies in that fight," Marko snorted under his breath. "Upper crust like her always get under my skin."

JOHNNY FELT INCREDIBLY LUCKY that a doctor was on duty at the infirmary—a kind of dinky hospital. The doc wanted to know why a bunch of children were on their own in the midst of this emergency. She said that if her phone hadn't been knocked out, she would have reported them to the authorities. Nonetheless, the wiry, middle-aged woman made sure the bone was properly aligned, then put a plaster cast on Iris's arm and fitted her with a sling. She also checked out the girl's black eye and said it would feel better in a few days.

As they left the doctor stood eyeing them, her hands on her hips, still very much the disapproving adult. "Be it on your heads, then, if you come to a bad end on your ridiculous adventure. Don't say I didn't warn you."

"I get what you're saying, doc," Johnny replied. "It's dangerous. But we have to keep going. It's important we finish our mission. There's a lot here going on that you probably don't know about, but we—

Johnny felt a tugging on his sleeve. He turned and saw Petunia blinking up at him.

"Would you please tell the doctor that I'm sick, too," she said. "My whole body is sore and I have a headache."

Johnny patted her on the shoulder. "I'm sorry, Petunia, but I don't think the doctor can treat a ghost."

But it was pretty weird, he thought, that so many ghosts were complaining of pain. Sure, wound a ghost and it hurts him or her for a while. But mostly, ghosts were not supposed to feel ill. So what was up?

When they walked into the Dusk Rose Hotel a few minutes later, they found an innkeeper who was only too glad to see paying guests. He hadn't had any for several days and offered them four rooms for the price of two. He even threw in a free supper of mutton stew, to boot. Like the doctor, he was quite surprised to see a troop of kids out on their own. He thought they had all been evacuated after the attack on St. Egbert's. But unlike the physician, he seemed to have no parental tendencies. To him, they were simply paying customers.

Johnny was especially relieved to have a comfortable bed and room all to himself. He wouldn't have to share with Marko. He could at least count on a good night's sleep.

After settling in, Johnny tried to make a long distance call from the telephone at the front desk. He wanted to contact Dame Honoria to tell her that he and Nina were okay. But the hotel phone was out of service, too.

At the long table in the dining room that evening, the four living kids gobbled up their mutton stew in silence. It was tasteless and chewy, Johnny thought, but probably nutritious and undoubtedly filling. They might not have another hot meal like it for days to come. Marko practically wolfed down his chow, then excused himself. He said he wanted to go to the pub down the street and see if anyone there had recent news about zombie attacks in the area.

"When we were at the infirmary," Johnny said, catching Iris's eye, "Petunia said that she wasn't feeling good. She wanted the doctor to look at her."

Iris gave him a sad smile. "She knows she's dead and she knows she's a ghost, but she still is just a little girl, too. She misses being the center of attention. Our mum doesn't have etheric vision, so I let her know when Pet needs a little loving. And then I put Pet right in front of Mum, and Mum gives her a long, tight hug."

"But does Petunia ever feel sick?" Johnny wondered.

"No. That's what's odd about this. Because she never complains about feeling ill."

Iris's words made Johnny curious. He turned to Raj, who was sitting at the end of the table, looking on enviously as the youngsters filled their stomachs. "How are you feeling, Raj?"

"I have a bit of a headache," the ghost said, rolling his shoulders.

"Ever have one before, since you've been a ghost?"

Raj shook his head. "Nope."

"It is a little peculiar," Johnny said, remembering that Private Boo was also feeling unwell. What was going on?

There was something else on Johnny's mind. "Iris, I'm curious. How did you and Marko get involved in this kind of work?"

Iris set her spoon down in the mutton stew and daubed at her mouth with the blue linen napkin.

"Marko lost his mum young. He lives with his bachelor uncle, who's a copper. And he's always wanted to be a copper himself, when he grows up. Well, being streetwise and knowing his way around Higgsmarket, he started to pick up bits of information about this and that. He became an informant on crimes committed by kids. He even saved an old lady's life once, when her nephew was mistreating her. Now Marko's practically on the force."

"But why is he so, well, *abrupt?*" Nina asked. "He doesn't seem to know the common courtesies."

Iris shrugged. "He's just acting the way he's seen his uncle act, the way he's seen other coppers act. He doesn't really care about the social graces, that's for sure."

"So how'd you get involved with him?" Johnny had been wondering whether their relationship was strictly about business.

"My dad never had the knack of making much money. So being one of the few people around Higgsmarket who can see ghosts, I'm appreticed to an etherist in town. She's teaching me what she knows, and I can bring home some coin that way. And in a few years, I'll have myself a good trade."

"You're not in school?" Nina asked.

"Not anymore. But that's where I met Marko, before he went on the streets as an informant. I sometimes go spying with him, when he needs a girl to check things out. For this assignment he wanted another set of eyes that could see ghosts, so he asked me to come along."

She pointed to the plaster cast on her left arm. "Don't know how much use I'll be, though." Then she looked at Johnny and kind of fluttered her eyelashes. "Marko told me a little about you, Johnny. I understand you're quite the hero."

A big, goofy grin broke out on Johnny's face. He was about to describe his dauntless deeds of the past few months when he saw Nina glaring at him.

"Well," he stammered, "I didn't do it alone."

Before he could explain, Marko tramped into the dining room and came over to the table.

"Find out anything?" Johnny asked.

Marko sat down. "I overheard two men at the pub. Tomorrow the police are planning a sweep of the town for kids. To haul them south to safety. You know what that means?"

"That means there better be no slugabeds in this outfit tomorrow morning," Johnny said grimly. "We gotta get outta here as early as we can."

CHAPTER 18

AFTER A HURRIED BREAKFAST of porridge and tea at the inn, Johnny and the rest headed north out of Chippington, in the direction of St. Egbert's School. It was well before dawn, so they managed to dodge any officials that might have wanted to drag them off to safety.

"I know right where St. Egbert's is," Raj had said, flying ahead. "When I was alive, I went along with my dad to deliver eggs to the school."

Petunia said she felt better this morning, although "my left knee hurts a bit." Johnny still was puzzled by the sudden appearance of aches and pains in his ghostly friends. It might indicate something important. But he had no idea what.

It took a brisk thirty-minute walk to arrive at the burnt and shattered remains of St. Egbert's. Johnny was appalled by what he saw. A library and medieval chapel destroyed. Books and clothing scattered about, soggy and ruined. Charred hulks of dormitories and classroom buildings. St. Egbert's had practically been wiped off the face of the earth.

"How could anyone burn books?" asked an outraged Nina.

Sparks was a real bookworm. Johnny figured that to her, destroying a novel or volume of history was almost as bad as committing murder.

They were walking across the grounds when someone popped out of an old shack at the near end of the soccer pitch. In a flash, a stubby, powerful man of about fifty rushed at them, an old, two-handed battle sword held at the ready.

Realizing there was no threat, he regarded his unexpected young visitors with a look of bemusement. He let the tip of the heavy weapon rest on the ground before him.

"What in the world are you young people doing in a place like this? Don't you know what happened here two weeks ago? Boys your age were taken by zombies! For all I know, they might have been made into meat pies by now."

The man had a wild mop of brown hair, a prominent red nose, and a lazy left eye. His well-worn green coat looked as if he had been rolling around in the dirt.

Johnny, who found it a little hard to look at the guy, what with his eyes going in different directions, stepped up and made introductions. He even introduced Raj and Petunia, although he wasn't certain the man could see them.

"We're here to do some fact-finding about the attacks," Johnny explained.

"Yeah," Marko said. "Johnny here is a news photographer who's been sent to report on the troubles in MacFreithshire. And Nina is helping him write the stories. Iris and I have been hired to guide them around and keep them safe."

"Were you here when the attacks happened?" Iris asked.

"That I was," the man answered. "Name's Angus Snodgrass.

I've been the groundskeeper here for two decades and I've never seen anything like what happened that night. Dozens of boys taken. None of them heard from since." He shook his head in disbelief.

"Any tips on how to fight zombies?" Marko asked. "If we run into some of these blokes, I want to be prepared."

"Well," Johnny interjected, "I can tell you that they're big and strong and fast. And the best plan is to keep out of their reach. Whack 'em and hit 'em with everything you've got. That's what we did that night in Royalton."

Angus fixed Johnny with a quizzical expression. "You fought 'em?"

"We did," said Nina. "But it was a bobby who saved our bacon."

Angus looked at Johnny and Nina with a certain admiration. "Then I guess you've had as much experience with the creatures as I have. I agree with you about staying out of their grip. That's why I'd advise you to turn tail and head back where you came from. Don't press your luck."

Johnny shook his head vigorously. "But the whole point is to get pictures of them. And write stories, too." He thought it best not to say anything about their spying mission—he didn't know who might be in cahoots with Percy.

"And I can't talk you out of it?" Angus asked.

Johnny shook his head again. He didn't blame adults for trying to take care of kids. That was often their job. But he kind of wished they would stop trying to take care of *him*. Hadn't he proven himself quite capable in that department?

"And you've no weapons?"

"Nope," Johnny said.

"Well, you won't last long without some. Come along and we'll see what we can find for you."

They all followed Angus into the shack, which was clearly his home. There was a cot and a dresser, with a table and chairs and a stove. There was also a heavy wooden cabinet, held shut by two big padlocks. Angus unlocked them and revealed his collection of weapons. Several swords and axes. Two shotguns. A hunting rifle. Two army revolvers.

Marko seemed *very* impressed as he studied the groundskeeper's arsenal. "Guess I'll take a pistol there."

"'Fraid not, laddie," Angus replied. "No one shoots Angus Snodgrass's guns but Angus Snodgrass."

Marko looked offended. "I'll have you know I'm perfectly competent to handle a firearm. I'm practically a copper myself. I won't do anything stupid with it."

"That's as may be, but these weapons are my responsibility, and I won't be putting them into the hands of young people I don't know. Besides, a pistol like that won't do you much good. I shot one of the monsters with my revolver, but it seemed just to tickle him a bit and make him even madder."

"But what about a shotgun?" Johnny asked, thinking back to the attack in Royalton, when Sergeant Clegg had dispatched a couple of zombies with his sawed-off shotgun.

"Aye, a shotgun might do the job," Angus said. "It'd give them a good thumping. The only thing is, a shotgun has a bit of a kick. Unless you're used to firing one, you could end up getting knocked on your bum. And then you'd be in a tight situation, should you have missed."

Johnny was actually relieved. He didn't like guns. Not one bit. It was just too easy for accidents to happen—especially when guns were in the hands of inexperienced shooters. Uncle Louie had carefully taught Nina how to use a rifle, but their hunting trips still made Johnny nervous.

"What we need more than weapons," Marko said, "is some information on these zombies. Where did they come from?"

"I'm pretty certain I know," Angus said. "From Blackcombe Bog."

"What makes you think that?" Nina asked.

"I've been in these parts since I was a pup. The legends about the bog men have been passed down from generation to generation. We all grew up hearing stories about the Eldurians."

"Who are the Eldurians?" Johnny had never even heard the name before.

"A warlike tribe that lived in this part of the country a couple thousand years ago, back when the Imperium sought to conquer every inch of the land. The Eldurians were the only tribe able to beat back the invaders. They were terrific, fierce fighters. After battles, the Eldurians honored their dead warriors by placing their bodies in the bog."

Iris raised her good arm, like a student in class. "Didn't they find a bog man just a few years ago? Someone went to the bog to cut peat for their stove, and ended up uncovering a bog body."

"Aye, and they gave the bog man to a museum for studying. But now I'm told by people up by Blackcombe that the whole bog's been disturbed. Dug up, torn up, whatever." Angus crossed his arms and shook his head in disapproval.

"Then we need to go up there to check things out," Johnny said.

"Now wait a minute," Marko objected. "I agreed to escort you around Chippington and the surrounding area. But the bogs are off limits. It's dangerous to even walk near them. I can't keep you safe in a place like that."

"But we can't gather information if we have to stick to the safe areas." Johnny continued to be frustrated with Marko. He felt like he had been assigned a babysitter on this trip instead of an escort.

"May I remind you," Marko said, "about how yesterday someone took a flash photograph that brought zombies after us? That led to us being separated from our ghost escorts? Maybe that person should be a little more concerned about safety and security."

Johnny blinked at Marko, stung. He knew he had been stupid to use the flash. But he was too embarrassed to admit it. And besides, what could he do about it now?

Nina cleared her throat. "If we're smart about it, we should be able to stay out of sight. The fog will give us good cover, and I can use my compass to navigate. But it won't work unless we all stay calm." She cast a pointed look in Marko's direction.

Marko let out an exaggerated sigh. "Well, at least if I die young I'll make a good-looking corpse."

"That you will, Marko," Iris said with a laugh. "That you will."

Angus told them to help themselves to supplies in his hut. Johnny took heavy twine and rope, firecrackers, another flashlight, and tape. Nina took some candles and antiseptic ointment. Only Marko and Iris ended up with blades. He grabbed an army saber, she a reproduction of an Imperium short sword.

Johnny and Nina spent the rest of the morning interviewing Angus and taking photos of the burnt remains that used to be St. Egbert's School for Boys. Johnny kept hoping that the colonel or Rex might show up. They knew Johnny and Nina intended to visit the school.

It was out in front of an ugly building of gray stone that Johnny came across a cricket bat lying in the muddy grass. On the back of the bat a label had been burned into the wood: "Hawkins Super Smash." Below were the words "Deluxe Willow Bat." There was a name scratched roughly into the wood with some kind of indelible ink: BASIL HASTINGS.

After Johnny wiped it clean and swung it around to get a feel for it, he stuck it sideways in the flap of his camera bag. Not exactly a hickory Neuport Slugger baseball bat. That would have been perfect. But the Super Smash would have to do, if it came down to zombie bashing.

Angus fed the kids some stale bread and cheese for lunch, with cups of strong coffee. Johnny normally didn't care for the black brew, but he figured any stimulant he could get had to be a good thing. He grimaced when he drank it and got a little heartburn. But it definitely made him feel livelier.

Johnny kept looking expectantly across the athletic fields, hoping to see a small troop of First Border War ghost soldiers trotting toward them. But there was no sign of the colonel, the troopers, or Rex. And Johnny and his bunch couldn't wait any longer to be on their way.

Before they left, Angus marked up their map of MacFreithshire, showing the roads that would take them north to Blackcombe Bog. And he tried one last time to convince them to abandon their quest. But Johnny just thanked him and said they were going to push on.

As they tramped off the St. Egbert's grounds, heading northwest toward Blackcombe Bog, Angus hollered an ominous farewell.

"Don't say I didn't warn you. *It's your funeral!*"

CHAPTER 19

MARKO LED THEM UP A PAVED ROAD that curved through some hilly woodland, the stubborn fog still dogging their steps. It came and went with maddening unpredictability, as if it were a cat playing with a mouse.

Johnny would have felt a lot better if the colonel and some of his men were accompanying them. But he had to make do with what he had. So he suggested that Raj fly up ahead, to scout out any threats. It was difficult for the ghost boy to see in the fog, but he should at least be able to hear any ominous activity.

About an hour into their hike, Raj came zooming back out of the fog, looking scared. "Coming at us, fast," he warned in a desperate tone. "Zombies! We'd best get off the road."

They all scampered into a nearby woods, hiding behind an embankment covered with moss. Sure enough, within a few minutes Johnny could hear the clomping of heavy boots and low, guttural mutterings.

"Keep perfectly quiet," Marko whispered. "Not a peep."

Out of the fog to their left emerged one zombie, then another, and another, until a troop of eight revealed itself, moving along at a quick pace.

Although Johnny had caught glimpses of the bog zombies

during the attack in Royalton, this was the first chance he had to really study these creatures.

There wasn't a one who stood less than six feet tall, and they all resembled each other. Their faces looked like tanned leather, and the features on some of them seemed squashed or asymmetrical. Johnny wondered if that's what happened when the bog pressed down on them for hundreds of years. They wore no expressions at all—as if they weren't able to make even a tiny grimace.

They had on the same shapeless tunics and coats that the others had worn in Royalton. And they moved quickly. None of that slow, mindless staggering of movie zombies.

Now that Johnny had seen a bunch of them up close, he wanted to get their description back to the Special Ghost Service head-quarters. But how could he do that? All phone and telegraph services up here seemed to be out of commission.

Johnny was still pondering the issue as the last of the creatures disappeared into the fog. But the sound of boots was replaced with that of hoofbeats coming from the same direction—a rider still hidden in the mist. As the horseman came into view, Johnny near-ly broke Marko's order to stay quiet.

More than anything, he wanted to scream.

There, prancing along on his stubby war pony, was Burilgi. The eyeless Steppe Warrior who had tried to murder Mel on the Night Goose. Who had tried to set off the second etheric bomb in the ballroom of the Hotel Splendid.

Looking neither right nor left, the ghost warrior trotted quickly back into the fog, right behind his zombie foot soldiers.

This was not someone Johnny had ever wanted to see again. But the presence of Percy's hit man confirmed what Johnny had thought. Now there was no doubt whatsoever who was behind this whole, horrible mess.

"I hope my uncle can afford me a good funeral," Marko moaned. "There's no way I can keep you safe from these guys. We're walking into big trouble here."

"Yeah, it would help if we had some backup," Johnny replied, praying for a glimpse of even one member of the First Zenith Brigade. "But I think it's smart to move toward the bog. They're probably only using that area to dig up the bodies. I'll bet they're reanimating them somewhere else."

"But who's reanimating them?" asked Iris. "And how?"

"I can't tell you how," Johnny answered. "But a creep called Percy Rathbone is the one who's doing it. I'm a hundred percent sure it's him. He's the guy we came up against last fall, the guy who built the etheric bomb. He nearly killed us all."

After their zombie encounter, Johnny suggested that they stay off the road and proceed through open fields and woods, heading northwest. The fog continued to play maddening games with them. Thickening and lightening, lifting and settling. Johnny noticed something odd about it, though. Normally, a fog would make some kind of dew on the grasses and brambles that they were tramping through. This fog had no water in it. It didn't condense on his cold fingertips or in his nostrils or on his camera. What in heckfire could that mean? Here was another puzzle for Mel to figure out.

With Nina and her compass guiding them, they managed to cover a number of miles before dark. No more zombies crossed their path, though they did hear what sounded like an army truck convoy traveling in the distance.

It amazed Johnny how empty this countryside had become. Apart from a hog farmer, they saw no one. Why wasn't the Royal Army on patrol? Then he remembered the truckload of maimed and defeated soldiers they had seen yesterday. The zombies were apparently more difficult adversaries than the military had bargained for.

Johnny was marching tiredly right behind Nina, when she stopped dead in her tracks. He put on the brakes, too.

"Oh man," Nina groaned. "Everyone, hold it. I'm afraid we may have stumbled into a bog. Take a look around."

Johnny inched forward and put his foot into some slushy brown muck. "Soft gunky earth here, guys."

"I think you're right," Iris agreed. "Looks like there's bog on either side of us."

"Marko," Johnny said. "Turn around and we'll start heading back. Let's look for some solid ground to set up camp on."

"Gotcha." Marko was at the end of the line and pivoted, becoming the new leader.

Everyone began to move back in the direction they had come from. And for a moment or two, they went along without problems, until there was a squawk of surprise from Marko.

"Don't know what happened, but I seem to have come to a dead end here," he said. "Nothing but bog up ahead, and on either side."

"Did you follow our footprints?" Johnny asked, pushing by Iris.

"What footprints?" Marko snapped. "Look down."

Johnny did just that. The ground under their feet was dense with moss and spongy. Any footprints would have vanished within a few moments.

This was bad. What with the thick fog, they could be stuck in this bog overnight or longer. Johnny's idea to stay off the road didn't look so smart now.

"Does anyone see any other way to go?" he asked.

"No, nothing," Iris answered.

"It's like we're on an island in a bog," Nina observed.

Johnny turned around, looking this way and that, when

suddenly Marko was right in his face.

"I *knew* this would happen, Graphic. I said we shouldn't do this. You have no idea how dangerous it is to get lost in a bog. And evidently Nina isn't such a great guide after all. She doesn't seem to even know how to read a compass."

Though Marko was inches taller and pounds heavier, Johnny stuck out his chin and glared up into the older boy's eyes.

"Sparks knows exactly what she's doing with that compass," he growled. "It's not her fault that this bog isn't properly mapped."

"Yeah, well, we can all stop worrying about zombies killing us. We're all probably going to die here in the muck because of your stupidity."

At that, Petunia started to cry. Iris put her good arm around her dead sister and glared at Marko.

"You stop that right now, Marko Herne," she snapped. "We signed on to help Johnny and Nina find their way through Mac-Freithshire, and protect them along the way. But all you've done is tell them to stop and give up and go back home. How's that supposed to help?"

Marko looked like Iris's words had deflated him a bit. "Yeah, well, it's just that this is not my kind of territory. I know the city streets. I even know the main roads up here. But I don't know the bogs. And I don't see any way out of this."

"If we're lost in a bog, then wouldn't it be wise to wait for the fog to lift, so we can see?"

Marko blinked at Iris sheepishly. "Suppose so."

Johnny shot her an appreciative look. "I think we're all exhausted. Maybe both the fog and our heads will clear up by tomorrow morning."

They all found places to sit down. By the illumination of the two ghosts and one flashlight, they ate the canned pork and green beans that Angus had given them. Then they rolled out their sleeping bags and lay down to rest. But the ground was damp, and Johnny had a hard time staying warm. He would have given a hundred bucks for a wool blanket. Shivering away, he figured sleep was impossible.

Eyes shut but wide awake, Johnny had plenty of time to lie there and second-guess himself. They were here, lost in a bog, because of him. If he hadn't used that flashbulb back at the train, they would be traveling right now with the colonel and his men. And if he hadn't pushed to leave St. Egbert's so quickly, they might have avoided the zombies and been able to travel on the road.

What had happened to the Zenith troopers? Johnny shuddered to think that they might have been badly hurt during that battle after the train derailed. And why hadn't Rex sent out some of his scouts to find them?

Johnny's mind was working to unravel this mess when he noticed, through his closed eyelids, a light growing stronger and stronger. He peeked out of a half-shut eye and saw a green glow. Was it the colonel?

Hoping that the cavalry had finally arrived, Johnny opened his eyes expectantly.

But instead of cavalry boots, he found himself blinking at a green, semi-transparent pair of primitive leather boots, with many crisscrossed laces. His eyes moved a little farther upward to see hairy bare legs beneath a leather kilt with large metal medallions hanging down on it.

It was a strange, new ghost.

Staring down at him.

With his sword pointed right at Johnny's heart.

CHAPTER 20

TUESDAY, FEBRUARY 4, 1936

WICKENHAM

"YOU SAW *WHO* DOING *WHAT* in the library?" Grandmother gasped, her sausage-laden fork frozen in midair.

Everyone had gathered around the end of the long dining room table, starting on their breakfasts bright and early that morning. Grandmother was at the head of the table, of course. To her right sat Mel and to her left the professor. The serving maid had just set down a rack of cold toast and a pot of marmalade, and was scurrying out of the room.

"It was a man, a ghost," Bao said, floating next to Grandmother. The little girl was suddenly and distressingly aware that she might not be conveying good news. "He was looking at some papers. And then he used them to start a fire in the fireplace. He said he was warming up the library for you."

"Did he now?" Grandmother said darkly. "What did he look like? What was he burning?"

Mel and the professor looked every bit as shocked as Grandmother, and leaned in to listen to Bao's answer. She was acutely conscious of being the center of attention, and not in a pleasant way.

Bao began by describing the specter's heavy white parka and high boots, which were dripping water. He had a long, gloomy face and didn't look as though he liked to smile.

"I never saw him before. I asked if he lived here, and he said he used to, but he's been away for a while. Then he went out through a window."

Grandmother frowned for a moment. She slowly rose to her feet and marched out to the hallway. "Bao," she said over her shoulder, "please stay right where you are."

Grandmother returned a moment later with a small picture frame that she thrust at the girl ghost. "Did he look like this?"

Bao examined the picture in the frame and nodded at Grandmother. "Oh yes, it's the same man. He was very polite to me."

The old lady groaned and collapsed into her chair. "Oh dear. I'm afraid that Percy has paid us a little visit. And if he was burning papers, he may have destroyed some vital evidence."

"So he must think we're hot on his trail," Mel said. "And there must be some incriminating information in all this stuff. We'll have to search through the ashes in the fireplace grate to see if we can find any remnants of what he burned. But how did he find what he was looking for? There are dozens and dozens of boxes piled in the library. It's taken us days just to plow through one-tenth of them."

"Percy had nearly a photographic memory," Grandmother said. "When I had his archives brought down here, I made sure the servants kept the boxes in exactly the order Percy had left them. He would have known just where to look for things. I'm afraid all we can do is hunt for any signs of disruption amongst the material."

Mel shook her head in disgust. "That'll take forever. But I suppose there's nothing else we can do."

Bao followed everyone into the library, where they each took a different section of the room and began to dig through boxes. She felt badly that she hadn't known this man was Grandmother's son, that awful Percy Rathbone. But she had only seen Percy when he had been in a zombie body. She couldn't have known what he looked like as a ghost.

Now all she could do was patiently watch as her friends leafed through all those papers. She tried hard not to distract them. But standing beside Mel, she couldn't help asking a question.

"What did Grandmother mean when she said Percy had a photographic memory?"

Mel smiled down at her. "Well, you know what the pictures that Johnny takes look like. When Dame Honoria said Percy had a photographic memory, she meant that he could look at something, and never forget a detail of it. Just like he had a snapshot of it in front of him whenever he wanted it."

Bao felt a little bit confused about that. "You mean he could remember real good?"

"That's another way of saying it."

"I can remember real good, too. We played a game when I was little, and you had to remember every place that someone touched, and then go around and touch the same places in the exact same order. Here, I'll show you. I'll touch the exact spots in the room that Percy touched when I was watching him."

With that, the little girl ghost flew from the fireplace to a folder on one of the tables and back to the fireplace again and then to a window. Mel watched her in surprise.

"Dame Honoria, Professor DeNimes. I think I know one of the folders Percy was looking at," she said, staring at Bao.

It was a folder that Mel had examined the day before. She said it contained newspaper clippings from twenty years ago, back when Percy was a teenager. The stories were almost all about sports.

"But there was another article in here, way in the back," Mel said. "I remember it because it was the only one that wasn't about sports. It was a travel story from the *Royalton Times*. In fact, I remember it for another reason. The story was about Okkatek Island."

"That would have been long before Percy and your parents visited the place," Grandmother said. "I had no idea he was interested in Okkatek back then."

"Well, the article is gone now so we'll never know what clues it held. Darn it!"

Grandmother thought a moment. "Not necessarily. We simply need to find another copy of it. You said it was in with clippings from about twenty years ago?" She picked up the telephone on her desk and dialed a few numbers, waited a little, then said, "Tilda? This is Dame Honoria." There was another brief pause. "Very well, thank you. I need you to get me the Gorton's Little Pills headquarters in Royalton. You know the number."

Bao floated closer to Mel. "Who is Tilda?"

"Local operator," Mel replied.

A moment later, Grandmother was instructing some person to go to the *Royalton Times* newspaper office and request a copy of the old article. She gave the details of the newspaper clipping, and said that it was probably published about twenty years ago.

"You're to give this the highest priority," Grandmother said into the telephone. "And I expect to hear back from you later today. I want you to make notes on the contents of the article and, most particularly, anything having to do with ghosts and etheristics. Is that clear, Ned?"

Bao heard a tiny little voice come out of the phone. "Yes, ma'am, it certainly is."

Three hours later Ned called back. Bao watched with excitement as Grandmother picked up the hand piece.

"Hello? Dame Honoria here." There was a brief pause. "Yes, Ned, I'll make notes." Grandmother leaned over her desk and prepared to write. "Go ahead."

Mel and the professor came over and stood by the desk, probably hoping to catch anything Ned might say. Bao wanted to hear, too, and floated up above Dame Honoria.

"The author of the article was one Eustace Phipps, a prolific travel writer of the day," the tiny little voice said. "He toured all over Okkatek Island and sampled the tribal culture in all its variety. He ate the food, witnessed the music and the dance, commented upon the many gorgeous vistas, observed the wildlife, recounted the history, and so on. But I think the part that you may be most interested in, Dame Honoria, pertains to a week that he spent on horseback trekking through the northern mountains with a group of fellow adventurers.

"They were heading up to one of the high plateaus. Along the way, they passed a landmark called Morbrec's Cave. Legend has it that an ancient shaman of that region, one Morbrec, had died in the cave, of cold and starvation, after being driven from society. He was banished because people believed he had devised a way to bring the dead back to life.

"To this day, islanders won't go into Morbrec's Cave because they still fear his terrible power."

This Morbrec must have been very wicked if his own people cast him out, Bao thought. Could his evil power still exist after all these years? Had he survived as a ghost? And what if he was helping Percy?

She shuddered to think of it.

It meant things could get a whole lot worse than they were now.

CHAPTER 21

"THAT'S PURE SUPERSTITIOUS RUBBISH,"
Grandmother said as soon as she hung up the phone. "Percy would never believe in something as silly as an evil magical shaman, any more than he would believe in wizards and witches. And neither would I."

"I agree, Honoria," the professor said. "The Percy I knew and taught was every bit the scientist. Of course, he studied writings from ancient cultures as they pertained to etheric beliefs. But I always found him to be well-grounded in principles of scientific etherism."

Mel plopped down into a chair. "He certainly wouldn't have persuaded Mom and Dad to accompany him to Okkatek, if it had anything to do with magic and superstition."

"Maybe Percy is trying to misdirect our efforts," the professor mused. "Perhaps his late-night visit was a ruse."

As the others talked, Bao debated something in her own mind. Should she admit that she had made a mistake? If she didn't say anything, no one would even know. But the little girl felt she had to set the record straight.

"Mel," she said, tugging at her friend's arm. "I think my photograph remembering isn't so good. I forgot one place Percy touched." Then she flew over to a bookshelf on the wall and pointed to the left side of the third shelf from the bottom.

All looking very curious, Mel, Grandmother, and the professor went over to join the little ghost.

"This is where I keep books that contain reproductions of old manuscripts," Grandmother said.

Mel examined the books, which seemed to be arranged in order of height. "Look here, Dame Honoria. There's a small gap between these two books. Could there have been a skinny volume of something right here?"

The professor laughed out loud, looking a bit sheepish. "Yes, there was. And I'm afraid I'm the one who borrowed it. You see, the table that I've been working at over in the corner was a bit wobbly and it was driving me to distraction. I found a tiny little book to put under one of the legs. It didn't look like anything valuable, so I thought you wouldn't mind, Honoria."

The professor went to the table, stooped over very slowly—making a little groan under his breath—and pulled a well-worn but slender book from under one of the legs.

"What is it?" Grandmother said when the professor stood back up.

The professor opened the book. "It's called *Als Abhandlung über die Geister der fernen Meeren*. That means *Being a Dissertation upon the Spirits of the Distant Seas*. Written by a 16th century monk named Brother Konrad. I've heard of it. The original is in a museum library in Barovia." The professor leafed through it some more and stopped halfway.

"Wait a second," he said. "This page has been dog-eared. And there's a particular passage underlined." He cleared his throat and read. "Morbrec der Nekromant entdeckt die dunkle Kunst ..."

Grandmother snorted. "Athelstan, please. Neither Mel nor I

speak Barovian."

"I'll do my best, Honoria, but my translating may be a bit rusty. Here goes. 'Morbrec the Necromancer discovered the dark art of putting ghosts into the bodies of the dead and brought them to unholy life.'"

Grandmother grabbed the book out of his hand and examined it. "Look at this." She showed the book to Mel. "Percy made some notes in the margin: 'Remarkable. Must learn more.'"

Mel looked at Grandmother and raised her eyebrows. "Everything keeps pointing us in one direction."

Grandmother crossed her arms resolutely. "I believe we know what we need to do next. We have to go to Okkatek Island."

WHEN CORPORAL MARCHIANO appeared out of nowhere on the front staircase of Wickenham early that evening, Bao was surprised. She thought that he had gone north with the colonel and five other ghost soldiers, to keep an eye on Johnny and Nina. From the look on his face, it seemed that something was wrong. But Bao didn't think it her place to ask what. With a sense of dread, she led him through several walls and rooms, straight to Grandmother and Mel—who, as usual, were working away in the library after supper.

The corporal stiffened as straight as an arrow when he saw Mel, and he made a sharp salute. "Commander Graphic," he barked. "Corporal Marchiano reporting."

Mel's eyes widened and she looked very afraid. "Corporal, what are you doing here? What's happened?"

"The colonel sent me here from up north," the corporal said, looking very uncomfortable himself. "Sorry to bear you bad news. But the fact is, ma'am, Master Johnny and Miss Nina have gone missing."

"No!" Melanie moaned, shutting her eyes and slumping in her chair.

Grandmother came up behind Mel and put her wrinkly hands on the younger woman's shoulders. "Tell us what happened, Corporal. Every detail you have."

The corporal recounted how the train carrying Johnny and Nina had been knocked off the rails while traveling through a dense fog. Then there was a fierce battle. To be safe, the colonel had hidden Johnny and the others in the woods. But when he returned, after the fight had been won, the kids had vanished. The colonel and the men had been searching for them ever since, but the fog still hampered their progress.

"But I thought the SGS was going to provide escorts for them." Mel's voice was vibrating with frustration.

"That they did," Corporal Marchiano replied. "But the escorts, who were not very old themselves, have gone missing as well."

Mel stood up. "That settles it. We have to go and find them. Right now! I can't possibly sit here and arrange an expedition to Okkatek when Johnny could be hurt...could be prisoner...could be dying!"

Grandmother enfolded Mel in a hug and patted her back. "It would be pointless, my dear. You could end up getting lost yourself. Or worse yet, captured. If Percy's indeed behind all this, you know how happy he would be to put you out of commission. Permanently."

"But we have to do something!" Mel protested.

"Better that I call in some of my ghost associates." Grandmother went back to her desk and picked up the phone receiver. "Within twenty-four hours we shall have dozens of wraiths searching the wilds of MacFreithshire. We *will* find Johnny and Nina, I promise you that. And if anyone has hurt them, there will be hell to pay!"

Bao wanted to cry. It was so awful that Johnny and Nina had vanished. But, of course, being a ghost, Bao could not summon up a single tear. So she sniffled and frowned and thought furiously about what she could do to help. Wherever they were, Bao just hoped that her friends were safe and warm and not in any danger.

CHAPTER 22

TUESDAY, FEBRUARY 4, 1936

MACFREITHSHIRE

BLINKING AT THE GHOST WARRIOR'S sword with shock, Johnny slowly rose to his feet. He backed away on the spongy bog, keeping his eyes on the green-glowing apparition and the blade pointing at his heart.

"Hey, everyone, I think you'd better get up." Johnny's voice was shaking.

Soon, Nina and Marko and Iris were standing behind him. Johnny continued to stare at the ghost. This was one very old wraith. Maybe one of the oldest he had ever seen.

It looked like the guy had been a soldier of the Imperium, the empire that had conquered most of the Old Continent two millennia before. He wore a brass chest plate, brass wristlets, a dark red cape, and a fancy helmet with bird plumes coming out the top. He had a primitive-looking arrow sticking out of his neck. No secret about how this guy died.

And then there was the short sword—still pointed at Johnny. It looked sharp and dangerous. But maybe this ghost was just a ghost, without the ability to interact with the real world. In which case, his sword would be about as dangerous as a boiled noodle. Johnny could only hope so.

"Wha, wha, what do you want?" Johnny stammered to the warrior wraith.

The man had a narrow face, intense black eyes, and a dark stubble of beard.

"I am Centurion Quintus," he said. "And I guard these lands. Who gave you leave to pass?"

Johnny could understand him perfectly, even though the wraith spoke an ancient language. It still amazed Johnny that people who died and became caught in the ether acquired a sort of universal tongue. An ancient specter from the Imperium had no problem interrogating a twelve-year-old boy from the Plains Republic. And this guy definitely sounded as if he was seriously annoyed with the trespassers.

Behind him, Johnny heard a saber being pulled out of its scabbard. Marko was readying for a fight.

"We're lost," Johnny admitted, avoiding the question of permission altogether. "And we just want to get out of this blasted bog onto solid ground. We're going north to the Blackcombe Bog."

The ghost lowered his eyebrows and scowled. "People your age should not be journeying there. The place is crawling with abominations of dead flesh and vile spirit. I have seen them and destroyed them when I could. The gods do not allow such creatures to exist."

So, Johnny thought, someone *had* given Quintus the power to act in the physical world. That meant his sword could cut and kill. Johnny began to edge back a little farther, eyeing his cricket bat lying uselessly on the ground. He wondered if Marko had any experience fighting with sabers.

By this point, Nina had put on her etheric goggles. "We're going to help defeat them, Mr. Quintus," she said confidently.

"A small troop of children?" Quintus huffed.

Johnny knew they didn't have time to argue about whether kids could fight zombies. He had to find out if this character was friendly or not.

"We mean you no harm, Mr. Quintus," he said. "We want to leave this bog as much as you want us to. Could you just show us how to get out of here and heading toward Blackcombe Bog?"

The specter frowned. "If I lead you in that direction, I would be leading you to your doom. Should they take you, the abominations will show no mercy."

That's when Johnny figured they had nothing to fear from this ancient ghost. After all, he could have cut them to pieces as they slept. And now he was expressing concern about their safety.

"Don't worry," Johnny said. "We'll do fine with the zombies. But we sure could use your help finding our way out of here."

The ghost warrior nodded and sheathed his short sword. "Very well. I suggest that you sleep until first light. I will guard you. Then I shall lead you out of the bog, as you wish."

CENTURION QUINTUS was good to his word, and nudged everyone awake as the omnipresent fog began to brighten. Johnny had already tired of canned pork, but gobbled some down for breakfast. He did not want to be hiking on an empty stomach.

Everyone seemed relieved to be ending the unanticipated exile in the bog. Before they left, Marko pulled Johnny aside.

"Sorry I popped off about your girlfriend yesterday," he muttered. "Shouldn't have said all that. I guess I just needed some rest." He clapped Johnny on the shoulder and walked away.

That apparently was what passed for an apology from Marko.

Well, Johnny thought, *it's better than a punch in the nose.* And he was too surprised to say that Sparks *wasn't* his girlfriend—just his friend. Jeez, he liked Sparks a lot. But "girlfriend" sounded way too serious for a guy his age.

With Quintus leading them, they wended their way through the bog in close single file. Johnny fell in right behind Quintus, followed by Marko, Nina, and Iris. Raj and Petunia floated above them. It almost seemed that the centurion was taking them in circles, as they hopped from one piece of ground to the next. But less than half an hour later, Quintus announced that they were now all standing on solid earth—no mushy murk beneath their feet anymore.

"Well, Quintus," Marko said. "Thanks for saving our bacon, mate." He stuck out his hand to the centurion, who stared at it as if it were a dead fish.

Nina trotted over to Marko. "You've got to give him the Imperial salute. Only proper." She turned to the ghost, extended her right arm with fist closed, then brought the fist to the left side of her chest.

It was the first time Johnny had seen anything like a smile appear on Quintus's face, as he returned Nina's salute. Then everyone else saluted him in the same manner.

"I'm curious about one thing, Mr. Quintus," Johnny said. "Who's giving you your power to touch the real world?"

"I have been given the gift by nineteen different people during the centuries of my death. While they were alive, I could touch the real world. But after each of them died, I lost these powers until I found another. Sometimes I waited for decades."

This guy had seen twenty centuries of history, Johnny realized. *In person.* It absolutely boggled the mind.

"Presently I am in debt to a boy who now must be an old man,"

Quintus continued. "When he was only ten years old, he asked me to help his father defeat thieves and brigands. As long as that boy lives, so do I—so to speak.

"Now, I bid you farewell. The evil place you seek is to the north and west. The road is just over that hill. It will lead you there." He pointed to a prominent knoll some distance away, just visible through the lifting fog. "Follow it for eight or ten hours, and the monsters' camp will reveal itself. But take care to remain unseen. The creatures especially covet children."

Johnny recalled a disquieting image that had haunted him ever since Angus the groundskeeper had opened his mouth. Stews and pies made of kids.

Quintus rotated around and began to float away, back over the bog, when a tiny, whispery voice spoke up.

"Please, don't go, Mr. Quintus," said Petunia. "Come with us. Pretty please?"

Petunia's entreaty surprised Johnny, to say the least. But the little girl ghost made a lot of sense. What a great idea. It would be smart to have a fighting man along with them, now that Rex and the colonel and his men had been lost. Two swords and a cricket bat—especially in the inexperienced hands of Johnny, Nina, Iris, and Marko—probably wouldn't be much of a defense.

"We could sure use your help, Mr. Quintus," said Johnny, winking at Petunia.

Marko looked around at the others and nodded. "Wouldn't you like another chance to take a whack at those abominations, Quintus?"

The ancient soldier, his dark features scowling, turned and looked from Marko to Johnny to Petunia. The fact that he had even listened to them was a good sign. Slowly a predatory grin appeared on that dark, dangerous face.

"I don't know what 'whack' means, my young friend. I hope that it signifies an action similar to 'disembowel' or 'eviscerate' or 'decapitate.'"

Johnny jumped in. "It does if you want it to, Mr. Quintus."

Marko agreed. "As the only one here who is almost a copper, I have no problem with that."

Petunia floated right up to the Imperial soldier, looking him right in the eye. "So you'll come with us, Mr. Quintus?"

He grunted, but in a friendly sort of way. Then he did something quite unexpected.

He reached out and tousled Petunia's long blonde hair.

"You know, you look a lot like the little girl I left back home in the Imperium. Gone now these two thousand years. And as long as you have asked so respectfully, I shall agree."

QUINTUS LED THEM BACK to one of the country roads. In this position, they were more vulnerable to the zombies. But after their recent experience in the bog, no one wanted to travel through the wild land again. Johnny sent Raj to the rear and Quintus forward to warn them of any potential danger.

The moment their feet hit the pavement, they set off at a brisk pace. The road, to Johnny's relief, was constantly curving through little hills and dales, so they would be hard to see from any distance. The momentary lack of fog was a relief, but unfortunately it gave them less cover.

Not long into their morning march, Raj came racing up to them.

"They're coming up behind us, a bunch of zombies and their prisoners," he warned in his papery ghost voice. "Get yourselves hidden!"

Johnny and Nina found a spot behind an advertising sign that proclaimed, "Gorton's Little Pills—Good for the tricky tummy." The others found places nearby and they all waited.

The first thing Johnny heard was the clumping of boots, then the guttural voices. The next sound that hit his ears shocked him down to his bones. A kid's voice, a boy. Pleading.

"Please let me go, mister. Me mum'll be worried sick about me. Anyways, they haven't any money for a ransom."

Johnny looked around the side of the sign. A bunch of zombies were herding eight or ten children up the road. The kids were tied together. Johnny couldn't tell which one was asking for his mother. They all looked bedraggled, dirty, and hungry—and plenty scared. As soon as this dreadful parade passed out of sight, Johnny huddled with the others.

"They're going to eat them, aren't they?" Iris whimpered. "Just like Angus Snodgrass said."

"You don't know that," Marko said. "You've no way of knowing that for sure."

"But why else would anyone want to grab a bunch of whining, complaining children?" Raj asked, making quite a reasonable point.

"Well, whatever the zombies have planned for them," Johnny said, "I think I know what we have to do."

"Right," Marko said. "Follow those kids."

CHAPTER 23

RAJ AND CENTURION QUINTUS took turns tailing the zombies and their captives, then reporting back. Johnny and the others trailed well behind. Within hours the zombies and captive kids passed onto the Great Durstan Moor, heading due north through increasingly patchy fog. Johnny was not happy about this route, as they lurched off the road into the tall grasses, bracken ferns, and undershrubs. He remembered what it felt like to get lost in that bog, and worried about a similar fate out on this vast moor, the biggest in the Royal Kingdom.

A bit later the group stopped for a breather in a little vale that cut across their path—a good spot because it hid them from sight. Johnny took the opportunity to grab a few pictures of Marko, Iris, and Nina as they rested. Then he climbed a bit higher for a shot of the moor itself. He was leaning over, looking down into the viewfinder of his Ritterflex, through the little magnifying lens, when someone cleared his throat.

Johnny jerked upright and looked around. Just to his right was Quintus, gazing at him with that grim expression he always wore. He was standing at ease, with his legs spread and his hands gripped behind his back.

"Yes, Mr. Quintus?" Johnny said. "What's up?"

As a two-thousand-year-old guy, the dead soldier clearly didn't understand modern slang expressions. But he only made one grumpy sound, then started to talk.

"I have found the enemy's encampment," he said.

"You're kidding!"

There was a scowl darker than usual. "You don't believe me?"

Johnny really had to watch how he spoke with this wraith. "Sorry, of course I do. I don't mean to doubt you."

Quintus gave a mild "harrumph," then continued. "Apparently their track across the moor was a shorter path than the road."

"A shortcut?"

Another grumpy sound came out of the ghost's throat. But he did nod. "Yes, they were able to cut their journey short."

"So we don't have to stay on the moor much longer?"

"No, we do not. But as it is late in the day, I advise against approaching their camp until the new morning. Moreover, I have found a place for you living folk to shelter."

Johnny almost said "You're kidding!" again, but bit his tongue.

"That's excellent news, Mr. Quintus. Let's go tell the others."

IT FELT AWFULLY GOOD having a roof over their heads for the night, even if there were a few drafty holes in it.

Quintus had discovered an abandoned granary on the edge of dense forestland, built of rough, gray stone. It was about the size of Birchwood, Johnny's big brick house back in Zenith. It was cavernous inside, but way better than sleeping out in the cutting wind that had come up.

Before it became totally dark, Johnny explored the place and found bales of unused burlap sacking. He figured it was meant to hold the barley that was stored there.

"MacFreithshire is famous for its whiskey," Marko explained as they sat around the fire that Nina had made on the dirt floor. The smoke went right up through one of the holes in the ceiling. "They make it out of barley and send it around the world."

Raj rubbed his hands in front of the fire, as if he could actually warm them. "MacFreithshire whiskey ain't cheap. But they say it's awful good."

Johnny had once tasted whiskey, stealing a sip from Uncle Louie's glass. He had nearly spit the stuff out but decided to swallow, no matter what. The disgusting smoky flavor and an awful burn down the throat made quite an impression. He couldn't imagine that it would taste any better when he was a grown-up.

After they ate a meager supper from the last of the cans Angus Snodgrass had given them, the adventurers sat awhile around the fire. Johnny and Nina hunched cross-legged on the dirt floor. Iris sat in a rickety wooden chair, cradling the cast on her left arm. Marko perched on a small crate. Raj kept rubbing his hands over the fire. Petunia leaned against Iris, resting her head on her sister's right shoulder. Quintus had gone outside to patrol, keeping an eye open for marauding zombies.

Raj spoke up first. "Tell us about this Percy Rathbone bloke, Johnny. He sounds like a right nutter. Why's he making so many people and ghosts miserable?"

Johnny sighed and told how, ever since he was young, Percy thought that ghosts should be treated better than they were. "After all, his mom, Dame Honoria Gorton Rathbone, had always been a fighter for the rights of women. And I guess Percy wanted his own cause. He wrote a book about the rights of ghosts, but no one paid attention. That made him bitter and he became more fanatical. He built the etheric bomb, and I guess he planned to use the thing to blackmail some country into giving ghosts their own place to live."

"He even persuaded some of the top officials in the Plains Republic to help him," Nina added. "But I don't think they knew what he was planning to do with the weapon."

"He only managed to blow up one bomb before we captured him," Johnny recounted proudly. "But he still blew thousands of ghosts to bits. Not a good fate for a ghost."

Raj shuddered. "Don't even want to think about that."

"Unfortunately," Johnny said, "Percy escaped his zombie body and now he's at it again, making trouble here in MacFreithshire."

"But what's his problem?" asked Iris. "Why does he keep doing these things?"

Nina shrugged. "I think he's just a spoiled brat who wants a lot of attention."

Johnny smiled at Nina's simple reasoning. "I'm not sure anyone can say why anymore. Not even his own mother can figure it out. But I think he really feels he's doing something good for ghosts."

"He's convinced them that he can help get them out of the ether," Nina said. "That's why Burilgi and Checheg are so loyal."

"Who are they?" asked Raj.

"They're ghost Steppe Warriors," Johnny said. "And two of his most fanatic followers. They both tried to kill my sister. Checheg is a girl warrior, but she's as fierce as any man. Mel even chopped off her arm, but Checheg still won't give up."

"So," Marko said after a long silence, "how'd you get to be a news photographer?"

Johnny was caught off-guard. Before this, Marko had not shown much interest in the newspaper game. So Johnny told the story of his passion for news photography and about the things he had done since leaving school last summer.

Then it was Iris's turn to ask about Nina's history. She listened intently to that sad, sad story. Mother died in childbirth. Orphaned when her father was killed in an automobile accident.

"You poor dear," Iris said. "And here I am, with more family than anyone needs—four sisters and three brothers."

Nina stared at the fire. "It really hasn't been that hard for me. You can't really miss something you never had. And except for my dad, I never had a family."

Johnny looked surprised. "Hey, what about me? I'm practically your cousin."

"Oh, yeah. I forgot about my goofy almost-cousin." She gave Johnny a cross-eyed look and stuck out her tongue.

Johnny grinned and turned to Marko. "Your turn now. How did you get to be an official escort for journalists?"

For one of the first times since Johnny had met him, a slight smile appeared on Marko's lips. He wiped his thick, black hair off his forehead and nodded.

"Well, I live with my Uncle Oren, and he's a copper, an inspector with the Higgsmarket constabulary. Always admired the man and wanted to be a police officer myself someday. Took it in my head to be his eyes and ears out on the street, when I wasn't in school. My uncle's come to rely on yours truly in certain types of situations."

"You still in school, Marko?" asked Nina.

"Naw, Uncle took me out a year ago. Thinks someone my age should be learning a trade—my trade being police work." He puffed up a little. "Anyways, I know how to read and write and figure numbers. That'll do. Don't need school no more."

So Marko turns out to be a bit like me, Johnny thought. Out of school early and hard at work. Maybe the two of them had a tough time getting along because they were too much like each other. That was often the case with similar personalities.

Nina stared intently at Marko. "What about your parents?"

"Dad spent most of his time inside the bottle. MacFreithshire whiskey, in fact. Don't even know where he's at now. And Mum was always sick. I tried to take care of her, but she finally passed. I ended up in the orphanage. Having etheric vision didn't make me many friends there. The other kids thought I was a freak. By and by, Uncle Oren took me on."

There was nothing Johnny could say that would make any difference. And he didn't want to probe any further. Marko had lived a tough life, but it didn't seem he was looking for sympathy.

So Johnny turned the conversation to the two sister.

"Now Iris, does Petunia help you much?"

"I do!" Petunia exclaimed, zooming around and landing right in front of Johnny. "Even though I'm smaller, I'm still her big sister."

Everyone burst out laughing, but Petunia didn't seem to mind.

Iris chuckled. "And she constantly reminds me of it. You know, if she were alive, Petunia would be eighteen."

That hit Johnny like a ton of bricks. Petunia would be about the same age as Mel. A young woman with a whole life before her. What a horrible thing, for a kid to die so young. Life and death could be so baffling and unfair.

He pulled out his pocket watch and was surprised at how quickly the evening had gone. It had been fun talking and learning more about each other—it felt like barriers were coming down. Maybe things would go smoother from now on. At least Johnny hoped they would.

He couldn't stifle a huge yawn. "You know, guys, I think we ought to try to catch some zzz's. Tomorrow could be a long, dangerous day."

Finally, they were going to do what they had come here for. They were going into the lair of the bog zombies.

CHAPTER 24

WEDNESDAY, FEBRUARY 5, 1936

MACFREITHSHIRE

EVERYONE WAS UP by six the next morning, ready to roll.

One by one, they followed Centurion Quintus through heavy fog and brambly woods. He warned them to keep very quiet, in case the zombies had scouts in the area.

But Johnny was preoccupied with something else. He was worried that the fog would prevent him from getting good photos of the bog zombie camp.

Of course, he had to stay out of sight. He didn't want to repeat the disaster back at the train wreck, when his flashbulb attracted a zombie attack.

Johnny couldn't help but think that he might be the first and only photographer to capture these scenes. He could just imagine Mr. Cargill's reaction—especially when the *Zenith Clarion* scooped all the newspapers in the whole world.

His daydream of journalistic glory was interrupted by a whispered command from Quintus: *"Down on the ground, all of you!*

Low as you can get!"

The Imperial officer's voice carried a tone that made Johnny instantly obey. Since Nina couldn't hear Quintus, and couldn't read his lips without her goggles on, Johnny had to grab her and pull her down. Everyone else hit the dirt, too. And just in time.

Because not thirty feet beyond them, there came a pair of bog zombies hustling their way through the undergrowth. If the creatures happened to look off to their left, they almost certainly would see Johnny and his companions—even with everyone on the damp, mildewy ground.

Johnny held his breath as the zombies vanished behind some trees. He realized he had gotten so close to the ground that he had some of the forest dirt and dried leaves in his mouth. But instead of spitting them out and wiping his mouth on his jacket sleeve, he waited until he thought it perfectly safe. Better to eat crud than make any noise.

Slowly, Quintus rose from his hiding place beneath the soil. "All right, we are in the clear. Come along now."

Within ten minutes they were lying prone on a heavily wooded hill that overlooked what must have been a large farmyard. Johnny could see the foundations of several structures that had been destroyed or torn down. Two barn-like buildings were intact, however, and there was a large pen packed with hogs, oinking and squealing away. And in the distance, behind a screen of stately elms, stood a hulking old country mansion. The real estate, in itself, wasn't that remarkable. It was what was going on there that set Johnny's pulse zooming. He scanned back and forth with Nina's binoculars.

There were scores, if not hundreds, of bog zombies and ghosts milling around, standing in clumps, coming in and out of many tents. Their coalesced voices made a sort of grating rumble and nagging hiss in the air. Johnny spotted a troop of Steppe Warrior ghosts at the far end of the big farmyard. One of them was Burilgi, for sure. That eyeless mug was unmistakable. Johnny shifted the binoculars slightly to the left and gasped. There stood Checheg, the one-armed girl warrior.

How about that? he thought, his spine tingling. *The gang's all here.*

Johnny had to get a shot of this incredible scene. He rolled on his side and began to extract the Ritterflex from his camera bag. But before he could even open the viewfinder, someone slapped his hands and camera down into the dirt.

"Not now," Marko growled. "You'll have to show yourself over this ridge to get your shot. If just one of those zombies or ghosts happens to be looking this way, we're all goners."

"I wasn't gonna stand up," Johnny whispered angrily. If Marko had damaged his camera, that would be the final straw.

The others watched the confrontation in silence, looking a little alarmed.

"Listen, Johnny. I know you have to take risks to do your work. But you could get the rest of us killed, too. Like you nearly did after the train wreck."

Just last night, Johnny had thought that he and Marko were starting to get along better. But now the guy was on his case again.

Johnny was preparing to throw some choice words back in Marko's face. But then he caught sight of Nina shaking her head at him, scowling. He knew that look: *Don't do it,* she was saying. *Don't be stupid. Wrong place, wrong time.*

He took a couple of deep breaths and glared at Marko. "Okay. If I can't take my shots here, then where?"

Marko nodded, as if to say, *Glad you're being sensible.* He took a peek over the ridgeline. "I think over there, off to the left. You sneak down through the undergrowth and use the old farm equipment to hide behind. You get your shots, and then we all get out of here. This dump gives me the heebie-jeebies."

Johnny had to agree that Marko's plan was a good one. But before he took his pictures, there was an important piece of business to discuss.

"Nina," he said. "Can you locate this place on your map?"

"Yeah, I think so," Nina answered.

"You don't have to." Everyone twisted around and blinked at Raj.

He had been lying behind them on his belly, chin in his hands—like a kid listening to the radio on his own living room floor. He looked a little pained, though. He had been complaining about the stubborn headache he had.

"This here is Bilbury Hall, near the village of Digginsham. Former family seat of the old Earl of Pilt. Anybody who knows west central MacFreithshire will know where it's at."

Iris beamed at Raj. "You, my friend, are brilliant."

"Absolutely, mate," Marko agreed.

"The problem," Johnny said, "is how do we get this information back to the authorities, now that we've lost Rex Ward and our SGS guys?"

"And besides, we're miles from anywhere," Nina said. "It'd take a couple of days to even hike back to Chippington."

"But what other choice do we have?" Iris asked.

"I'll go."

They all looked at Raj again.

"I can fly back to Higgsmarket in a few hours, if I don't get lost in the fog. Then I'll just hunt around until I find the right blokes to tell. Maybe Captain Ward's back there already."

Petunia looked as if she was about to cry. "But you're my best friend, Raj. You can't go!"

"Don't you worry, Pet. I promise I'll be back before you know it."

Johnny knew Raj's idea was the best option that they had. "I think Raj is absolutely right. He should leave immediately. The sooner we get word through to the authorities, the better."

Marko nodded. "Agreed. Finding this lot of zombies is why we came. Be a waste not to finish the job proper."

With a few words of farewell, Raj slipped away down the hill, into patches of fog and out of sight. Johnny supposed he would soon be flying hundreds of feet up in the air.

Marko rubbed his hands together and grinned. "Now let's get Mr. Graphic his newspaper photographs."

WHILE THE OTHERS LAY HIDDEN twenty or thirty feet to the rear in the weeds and brambles, Johnny crept forward until he was underneath a giant, rusting steam tractor. Quintus had come, too. They were partly hidden in yet more nasty weeds and thistles. Johnny had never, ever worn filthier clothes than these. He could hardly wait to get out of them and into a nice, hot bath. But that might be a while yet.

From his vantage point under the tractor—right beneath the boiler and next to one of the giant iron wheels—Johnny could see zombies and ghosts milling around. It was a good spot to shoot from.

Quintus made one of his grumbling sounds. "If I only had my century here with us, we would make short work of this mangy Eldurian mob."

"Your what?" Johnny whispered. What was the wraith talking about? His *century?*

"My hundred men true and strong."

Of course! Johnny thought. *He's not talking about a hundred years. Quintus was a centurion. Made sense that his unit would be called a century.*

"The finest troop in the whole Ninth Legion," the ghost continued. "None fiercer, none braver. The Eldurians took us only with overwhelming numbers, and then by ambush. Five hundred against one hundred."

Now that sounded like a story Johnny wanted to hear. But first he had to get his shots. He flipped open the Ritterflex's viewfinder, peered through it, and focused to infinity. He pushed his index finger against the shutter button. *Click.* Then came *whiz-snap*, as he rotated the lever on the side of the camera forward to advance the film, then backward to cock the shutter. Johnny repeated the process three times.

Just as he was closing the viewfinder, he saw something appalling out in that farmyard of horror.

A group of zombies and ghosts was herding six kids across the open space. Those boys and girls looked awful—dirty, hungry, scared out of their wits. They were being pushed and prodded toward one of the barns. They were shoved inside through an open door, and Johnny heard more kids screaming from inside.

So *that's* where they're keeping them!

There was still no telling why the zombies wanted kids. Johnny was betting it wasn't to make meat pies. And it didn't make sense to kill them and zombify them. They were too small to make good fighters. What could the reason be?

Whatever it was, wouldn't it be great to spring all those kids and get them out of there? An idea began to form in Johnny's head, a totally nutty idea that he hoped the others might like as much as he did.

Out of nowhere, Johnny heard a girl yelp in shock and surprise.

As he turned around to look, he bonked his head on the bottom of the steam tractor's boiler. Stars formed before his eyes, and through them he saw his worst nightmare coming true.

A bog zombie.

Charging through the undergrowth, heading toward the farmyard.

With Nina Bain squirming and screaming under its right arm.

CHAPTER 25

HE HAD TO RESCUE NINA!

Johnny scrambled forward on his hands and knees, still beneath the old tractor. His only thought was tackling that zombie and freeing his best friend.

He made it only a few feet when someone grabbed his left leg and hauled him back under the tractor's boiler—like a fish being reeled in. Johnny was about to holler a protest. But a rough, semi-transparent green hand slapped onto his mouth with a *thwaaap*, muffling his angry words.

"Shut up, boy!" Quintus hissed in his ear.

Johnny struggled a little, his mouth still covered, but the ghost was way too strong.

"Don't be a fool," the centurion continued. "You can't save her. Not just yet. We have to get out of here. Now is the moment for withdrawal, not attack. One soldier and a gaggle of children have no chance against such foes."

Johnny watched, horrified, as Nina—still kicking and screaming in her captor's arms—disappeared into a roiling mob of bog zombies.

Then the most terrible, gruesome thought entered his mind. *They're going to kill her! Eat her! My best friend in the world! How could I have let this happen?*

"We go," Quintus growled. "Now."

Johnny barely managed to grab his camera and bag as the centurion dragged him back from under the abandoned steam tractor. A moment later, they caught up with Marko, Iris, and Petunia, who had retreated back to the hillock they'd started from earlier. Everyone looked shattered.

Infuriated, Johnny glared at Marko. "What happened? How could you let Nina get caught?"

Marko glared back. "Don't blame me! It was your stupid friend that put her own stupid neck in the noose."

Johnny wanted very much to punch Marko right in the nose. But he held back. "You're saying it was *Nina's* fault?" he asked incredulously.

"She was complaining about not being able to see what was going on," Iris explained. "I think she snuck off for a better view."

"She was such a nice girl," Petunia sighed. "I'm going to miss her."

Was a nice girl? Nina was still alive, and Johnny intended to snatch her back.

"That zombie just got lucky," Marko said defensively. "Must have stumbled across her in the weeds."

Johnny was still fuming. "Well, why didn't any of you try to stop her from going?"

Marko's shoulders slumped. "I didn't know she'd been grabbed until I heard her scream."

"So much for our crack security escorts," Johnny grumbled. "I thought your job was to keep Nina and me safe."

"Enough!" Quintus commanded. He looked like he was quite fed up with quarrelsome kids. "Vituperation doesn't help. We have to get out of here. The abominations may already have begun prying our secrets out of that girl, and it's not wise to stay. We need to make a plan for her rescue. But not here."

Johnny snorted and glared at everyone, even poor little Petunia. Reluctantly, he nodded.

"Let's go then."

HUNDREDS OF FEET BEHIND THEM, they could hear crashing and growling and hollering in the woods. The zombies had clearly figured out that there were more kids to be captured, and were on the hunt. Quintus led Johnny and the others quickly away from the environs of Bilbury Hall. After a couple of breathless miles, Johnny was the one who spotted a stone house on the bank of a small creek.

After they scampered across an open field, they nipped into the house. It looked as if it had been recently abandoned. From the photos on the shelves, Johnny figured an old couple had lived in it. There were shots of a white-haired woman and a bald man surrounded by what were no doubt their children and grandchildren.

Plenty of canned food in the larder suggested that this couple had left quickly, probably fleeing the zombie infestation. Johnny, Marko, and Iris silently ate a lunch of beef, potatoes, and peas, with soda crackers and evaporated milk. Johnny knew he had to keep his strength up. But just thinking about Nina made the food taste like cardboard. He had to force himself to swallow each bite.

Finally, Marko spoke up. "Right now, Raj is probably briefing the authorities in Higgsmarket. I say we sit tight and wait for help to arrive. The army or the police could be here in a day or two. Agree?"

Johnny was in a foul temper. He couldn't help but think that this was all Marko's fault. If he hadn't stopped Johnny from taking his shots of the zombie mob from the top of that hill, they wouldn't have snuck down below, near the old steam tractor and far closer to disaster. Nina wouldn't have been there, wouldn't have been tempted to crawl off for a better view. Of course, it was dumb of her to do so. She should have known better.

But what good would it do to tear into Marko now? The damage had been done. Johnny's best friend was in a terrible fix. If he lost her for good, he'd never, *ever* forgive himself.

He finally answered Marko. "That is, *if* Raj can persuade anyone to listen. He's just an unknown ghost kid. Why would they trust him? Unless he manages to find Rex Ward or Colonel Mac-Farlane, I wouldn't count on the cavalry riding to our rescue."

Marko didn't argue. "So what are our options?"

Johnny knew exactly what he had to do—no matter how dangerous.

"I'm going to sneak in there alone, and get Nina out. You don't have to come. You didn't sign up to risk your skin on a dangerous bet. Not fair to expect it of you. And Iris can't be much help with that busted arm of hers. I got Sparks into this mess, and I'm gonna get her out."

Petunia zoomed right up into Johnny's face. "Don't do it, please. They'll catch you and eat you, too."

Johnny gave her a smile. What a cute little ghost she was. She reminded him of Bao. "Sorry, kiddo. But I gotta do this."

"If it were me over there in that barn and I were alive, I would never want Iris to come for me," Petunia said.

Johnny understood what she meant. Someone whom you're very fond of would never want you to risk your own neck on her behalf. He guessed that's what love was all about. Not that he thought he "loved" Nina. But he liked her a lot. And he wanted to be best friends with her for the rest of their lives. But unless he acted quickly, Nina's life might not last too much longer.

He patted Petunia on the head. "It's okay. I promise to be careful."

Petunia frowned and floated back to her sister, pouting.

"Pet's right, you know," Marko said with a tone of discouragement. "No good can come of it."

Johnny's irritation flared again.

"Of course some good can come of it!" he snapped. "I can save Nina's life! And if I can't, I don't really care what happens to me."

Marko wouldn't look Johnny in the eye. Iris and Petunia glanced at each other, seeming quite uncomfortable at the fire in Johnny's words.

"There will be time for reproach another day," said a deep, papery-sounding voice.

Everyone turned to regard Centurion Quintus, who had been standing unnoticed in a dark corner of the kitchen. He strode toward Johnny. Halting a few paces away, the ghost regarded him up and down. Those ancient black eyes and fierce features almost made Johnny quake. He would never want to be on the other side in a fight against this guy.

"You cannot walk into that vipers' nest blind and helpless," the ghost warrior said. "Allow me an hour, two hours at most, to scout and spy. Perhaps I will find a way to free your friend, but with lesser peril. If I believe such an exploit would be suicidal, I will tell you honestly. You can trust me to never lie. I tell true, even when it disappoints."

"Listen to him, mate," Marko said. "It's your only chance to save Nina."

"Do what the centurion says, Johnny," pleaded Iris.

Even though he was hot to act, Johnny knew that doing foolish, impetuous things—like, say, rushing off from the group to get a better view of dangerous bog zombies—might end in disaster. He might be angry and impatient, but he wasn't stupid.

Johnny looked up into the centurion's grim face. "Okay, Quintus. I'll expect you back in two hours."

CHAPTER 26

WEDNESDAY, FEBRUARY 5, 1936
BILBURY HALL, MACFREITHSHIRE

BASIL HASTINGS SLUMPED against the wall in a corner of the dimly lit, odoriferous barn, contemplating his fate. He had no idea what these zombies intended to do with him and the other kidnapped children—roughly forty of them when Basil had last counted. But whatever the creatures had in mind, Basil doubted that he'd live to celebrate his thirteenth birthday.

He wondered how his two older brothers might feel when they heard about his demise. Maybe they'd regret those several occasions when they had put treacle inside his shoes and hid his favorite cricket bat.

But the person Basil felt most sorry for was his father, Lord Hurley of Evansham. Lord Hurley had lost his older brother Edward—the then-Lord Hurley—to an unfortunate drowning accident.

Basil's uncle had been only sixteen when he died, long before Basil was born. Poor Father, Basil thought sadly, to have lost an older brother so prematurely.

That was precisely the word he had been trying to remember! *Prematurely.*

And now Basil wondered whether he might be prematurely deceased himself one day soon.

The monsters had taken good enough care of the kids. It had been two weeks, so far. They had provided them with ample blankets to sleep on. And though the fare was simple—bread, cheese, porridge, and water—it was clear that keeping the kids alive and healthy was a priority.

But why had the monsters rounded them all up in the first place? Basil had eavesdropped on a few of their conversations, hoping to glean some information that could help. Rather than being inarticulate fiends, they had actually sounded like reasonably intelligent—if rather loathsome—individuals.

One time, a pair of them guarding the barn were having a long discussion about the peculiarities of their new bodies. And while they were grateful to have bodies "again," they found them to be clumsy and awkward, not nearly as much fun as what they'd had before.

"I miss me old self," one of them had sighed, in that rumbly-mumbly way of theirs. "But I died a long time ago, back in army days. Me first body would be dust by now."

"Well, I say we old warrior ghosts owe a debt of gratitude to good Lord Percy for showing us the zombie trick," the other had remarked. "Only way we could possibly get to be in the real world again in a real way. This body ain't great, but I sure like being able to eat again."

Basil was curious about who this "Lord Percy" bloke was. But none of the zombies elaborated. Undoubtedly, he was the worst villain of the whole lot of them.

Others had complained about dry skin and the need to grease

themselves constantly. Another was unhappy with its looks—and who could blame it?

Basil heard numerous conversations about centuries-old battles that he had studied in history class. He was pretty sure that inside each of these repulsive creatures was a spook that had once been a soldier.

Basil hated to say it, but they all sounded like pretty ordinary chaps doing pretty ordinary jobs. Still, he worried about what they intended to do with the kids. Maybe they were going to hold them for ransom. Maybe they were going to use them as slave labor.

Meanwhile, within the little prison, boys from St. Egbert's and other schools clumped together in one corner of the barn. And the youngsters from town and country did the same in another—though boys with boys, and girls with girls. Every now and again a schoolboy and a town boy would irritate each other enough to end up wrestling down on the dirt floor, perhaps throwing a few pitiful punches. Apart from the odd bloody nose and bruised pride, no harm was done. And it did let off a certain amount of steam.

The escapees Carson and Leith had ended up with Basil here in the local branch of hell. And he finally had the chance to find out how their escape had gone bust.

Leith shook his head in befuddlement. "Thought it would be easy. You know, just slip away quietly. Trying hard to not snap a twig or send a sparrow fluttering. And for a while, everything seemed tickety-boo. I bet we got a mile, at least. We came out on a country lane, and Goldsworthy and I had a bit of a debate about which way to go."

"You know how pigheaded Goldsworthy can be," Carson put in. "So he went his way and that was the very last we saw of him."

"And it turns out he was right," Leith groaned. "Carson and I promptly walked right into a mob of the monsters."

So as far as anyone knew, Goldsworthy was still banging around out there. Maybe he had alerted the police. Or maybe he had simply gone back home and was right now enjoying roast beef and potatoes.

Basil found life in stir grindingly boring. Unless one of the monsters came to grab someone. Or a new captive arrived. Then the place became a beehive.

So Basil felt a strong twinge of excitement when they brought a dark-skinned girl into the barn. "Brought" wasn't the right word. It was more like they tossed her in through the door, very nearly pitching her over onto her face.

She had on hiking clothes of brown tweed—with knee pants, not a skirt—and had curly black hair cut fairly short. She wore a very nice canvas backpack that looked jammed full. The moment she opened her mouth to cuss out the monster that had thrown her in, Basil knew that she came from the New Continent. Her accent was unmistakable. Which country, he couldn't say. Freedonia? Northland? Plains Republic? Who knew? Not the Old Dominion. No drawl or twang.

A few of the girls rushed forward to cluster around the new arrival and provide, Basil supposed, sisterly comfort.

But this was a very different sort of prisoner. She didn't act frightened or waste any time in tears. She almost looked like she had come here on purpose—though Basil couldn't imagine why you'd risk your neck in MacFreithshire these days. Still, he really wanted to talk to this girl. And not because he thought she was pretty—though she certainly was. Something about her struck a note of familiarity in Basil. But blast if he knew why.

Within minutes, the newcomer, who had introduced herself as Nina Bain, was walking about, looking for chinks in the barn through which to escape.

Basil thought it only polite to sidle up to the new girl and tell her that no chinks whatsoever had been located. He knew, of course, that sidling up to a girl would earn him a hazing from his mates—who were even now looking on and making kissing noises and smackings of lips.

"No good, I'm afraid," Basil said over the girl's right shoulder.

She pivoted around and blinked at him. "You've already tried it?"

Basil was a little surprised. She didn't even say, "How do you do?"

"We've all hunted high and low for a way out," he answered. "The only thing we've found is a sort of manhole cover over there in the corner. But we'd need a big wrench to loosen it."

"Well," Nina Bain said, "it doesn't hurt to have a fresh pair of eyes check things out, does it?"

Basil shook his head nonchalantly. "No, not at all."

Nina Bain continued to nose about one of the corners of the barn, paying particular attention to a barred window. Basil trailed behind her.

"You know," he said, "you look dashed familiar."

She peered at him, up and down. "Sorry, you don't."

"I know I've seen you before."

"It's possible. I mean, I had my picture in the newspapers last fall. Maybe even over here. Went on an adventure with my friends Johnny and Melanie Graphic."

Of course, Basil thought. The business of the etheric bomb out in the Greater Ocean. She was a very close associate of Johnny Graphic. Their adventures were well known among the boys at St. Egbert's.

"You're the girl who saved that flying boat from a crack-up in the ocean," Basil said in admiration. He gave her a friendly, expectant look, hoping for a nice chin wag about her exploits.

That's when one of the young ladies from Mrs. Vinson's Academy for Girls let out a shout of warning. She was the only young captive who had the ability to see wraiths.

"Ghost!" the girl hollered in her high-pitched voice. "Coming through the double door!"

Nina Bain muttered a few more cuss words under her breath, then whipped off her backpack. Basil couldn't imagine why.

Then the girl did the most remarkable thing. From inside the pack she plucked out a pair of highly peculiar aviator goggles, with wires and batteries attached to them. She slapped them on, then gazed toward the big double door.

A look of horror played across her face.

"Dogs in dishwater, *no!*" she whispered. "It's Burilgi!"

CHAPTER 27

THURSDAY, FEBRUARY 6, 1936

MACFREITHSHIRE

IN ADDITION TO HAVING ACUTE ANXIETY

when flying up in the sky on ghost horses, Johnny had a particular aversion to being confined in tight places. He tended to hyperventilate and panic and turn into, generally speaking, a quivering mound of hopelessness and misery.

So when Centurion Quintus described what he had found and what he thought represented the best plan for freeing Nina, Johnny gulped and slowly nodded, thinking, *no, no, no.*

But it was the only option they had. And Johnny had really meant it when he said he'd rather die—even in a tight, dark, cold place—than abandon his friend.

So, soon after midnight that evening, Johnny set out through the woods and fields, back toward Bilbury Hall—following Quintus's green, ghostly glow. Behind him came Marko, and behind him came Petunia Budd. The whole rescue mission depended on just the four of them. They had left Iris behind at the little cottage. There was nothing she could do, with that arm in a cast. But she had persuaded her "big" sister Petunia to go on the rescue mission. It took many repetitions of the "magic" word.

"Please, please, please, please…"

It was slow going in the dark, as they treaded carefully through patchy fog and brambly undergrowth. Off to the west, Johnny saw muted flashes of lightning when the fog allowed, followed a moment or two later by distant rumblings of thunder. So far, they had managed to hike around MacFreithshire without getting drenched. And Johnny earnestly hoped that they would stay dry tonight.

Arriving at the culvert that Quintus had found, Johnny could see the glow of zombie campfires just a few hundred feet away. The creatures' rumbly, grating voices were just audible. What, he wondered, did zombies chat about late into the night? "Well, I nicked me another black-haired boy. Now I just need a redhead with freckles for my collection. You got one to trade?" Or, "How does a feller unsquash his face and clean up proper-like after centuries under the muck?"

"Johnny Graphic!"

Johnny started and looked up into the dark, grim visage of Quintus.

"Sorry," Johnny said. "Daydreaming,"

"We are here," the ghost said. "Your torch, point it there."

Carefully shading the top of his flashlight so the nearby zombies couldn't catch sight of it, Johnny illuminated the thing he had been dreading.

It was the mouth of a tile culvert that opened onto the edge of the pond they were standing by. It was about two feet wide. Its purpose was to drain rainwater from the estate and farmyard, and feed it into the pond. A grown man might not fit inside it, but a boy would.

Lying in the mud next to it was a large, adjustable wrench,

which Quintus had earlier "borrowed" from an unguarded tool shed.

Johnny gulped, inwardly rebelling against the notion of climbing into that hole in the ground. Not being able to stand, turn around, stretch. He could only inch forward on his hands and knees, or go in reverse. A desperate voice inside his head kept chanting, *Are you crazy? Are you crazy?*

"As I instructed," Quintus continued, "you will go forward behind the girl ghost. She will light your way. To your rear, Marko will bear the wrench. Take the first fork to the left. This will lead you to the children's prison. Somehow, you must wake one or more of the prisoners, who will use the tool to remove the drain cover. At the right moment, I will make a diversion, drawing away the abominations."

Johnny knew the plan well enough. They'd gone over it a dozen times. But as is often the case with unpleasant tasks, the reality was altogether scarier than talk and theory. If they were going to do it, though, they might as well get on with it.

He nodded briskly. "Well then, full speed ahead. Please, Petunia, after you."

He figured the girl ghost was probably more agitated at being separated from her "little" sister than by the dangers of a midnight prison break. She, after all, could fly up and away whenever she wanted. Johnny and Marko had no such option.

"Okay," Petunia agreed.

"Ready, Marko?" Johnny asked.

Marko snatched up the heavy wrench. "Ready as I'll ever be."

Johnny blinked at Quintus. "See you back here, hopefully in about an hour."

Quintus gave Johnny an Imperial salute. "May the gods defend you."

"Sure hope so," Johnny groaned, returning the salute. "In you go, Petunia."

The little green ghost floated headfirst into the culvert. Johnny got on his hands and knees and climbed in, and he was soon a dozen feet along. He heard Marko come after him, the wrench he carried clunking on the inside of the tile enclosure.

Johnny tried to twist around, but it was impossible in the tight quarters. "Marko, can you maybe not make that noise?"

"I'll try," Marko replied, sounding unsure. "But I just barely fit in this thing."

Johnny crawled along—his hands and knees dragging through dirt and dampness and slime, his head bumping on the tile. He felt sorry for Marko, who had to feel even more cramped and trapped. Johnny at least had some elbowroom. And of course neither of them could turn around if they needed to. That was maybe the worst thing. If for some reason they had to retreat, they would have to crawl out of the culvert backward.

Even though he wasn't moving that fast, Johnny could feel his heart thump-thump-thumping away like a steam engine. Sweat was dripping down his forehead. That had to be the adrenaline. From all his adventures last fall, Johnny was well acquainted with it. To control it, he tried to pretend he was a crawling robot—just a machine that put one hand forward, then a knee, then the other hand and the other knee. Hand, knee, hand, knee, hand, knee…

Empty out the head, that was the trick. *If I can do that*, he thought, *I'll get through this culvert with no problem. We'll open the grate quick as you like, spring Nina and the other kids, and head for the hills. Say goodbye to this whole rotten nest of zombies and ghosts.*

But just then Johnny slapped his left hand down onto something furry and squishy and quite dead.

He let out a yelp. *"Eeeeyewww."* Without thinking, he tried to jump to his feet. But, of course, all he succeeded in doing was clunking the back of his head and mashing his shoulder blades into the culvert tile.

"What is it?" Marko snapped.

By now, Petunia had floated back to see what was wrong, coming in close enough to illuminate the object.

Still shaking, Johnny rubbed the back of his head and looked down.

A rat. Probably dead only a few days.

Oh, great! Now he had rat crud on his left hand. Who knew what kind of germs it was full of? He rubbed his hand violently on his left thigh, attempting to get every vestige of the critter off his skin.

"I touched a dead rat," he finally said, with a shudder.

Marko laughed. "Is that all? Let's get going."

They continued on, Johnny cringing whenever he put a hand down on the tile culvert. But he squashed no more dead rats. And, amazingly, he found himself getting used to the cramped quarters and the slightly rotten, mildewy smell.

A few minutes later they took the left fork in the culvert and soon arrived at an open space that allowed them to almost stand up and stretch. A couple of feet above their heads was a circular grate. This, according to Quintus, would be their entrance into the kids' prison.

"Pet," Marko said, "pop up there and make sure there're no zombies about."

Petunia floated right up to Marko, face-to-face, and frowned at him. "You forgot the magic word. Nice people use the magic word."

Marko rolled his eyes. "*Pleeeeaaase*, Petunia, make sure there are no mean, old zombies up there."

"Okay, Marko." The little ghost smiled and zipped up through the grate.

A nervous moment or two passed. If there happened to be a guard inside the barn, all of their efforts would be for naught. All that crawling through the miserable tube in the ground would have been pointless.

For just a second, Johnny shut his eyes—he was super tired. And when he opened them, there was Petunia, looking very pleased with herself.

"No ugly old zombies up there at all," she reported. "Just lots of children sleeping."

"Good," Johnny said. "And now we wake 'em up." He nodded at Marko, who hefted the heavy wrench he'd been carrying and knocked gently on the iron grate above. He did it three times, slowly.

Cloink. Cloink. Cloink.

Then again.

His heart in his mouth, Johnny waited. He hoped at least a few of these kids were insomniacs. It would be awful if no one heard that metallic clanging.

But someone did.

A single, whispered word came fluttering down through the grate.

"Hullo?"

"Hi up there," Johnny whispered back. "We're here to rescue you."

"You're here to *what?*" the disembodied boy's voice said.

"To rescue you, you dolt," Marko snarled.

"But how?" the boy up above asked, apparently not offended by Marko's rudeness.

It looked like Marko was about to say something churlish again, but Johnny put up his hand to silence him.

"We have a wrench," Johnny explained. "And you're going to unscrew the bolts holding the grate and everyone's going to escape through the rain culvert. Just go grab Nina Bain, and we'll get this show on the road."

"The girl in the hiking clothes?" the boy asked, his wide-eyed, dirty face now visible near the grate. "Curly black hair? With the weird goggles?"

"That's her."

"Sorry, mate. They took her away."

CHAPTER 28

"YOUR FRIEND WAS HERE less than half an hour,"
the boy above the grate said. "Then the pretty blonde woman came
in and hauled her off. There was a ghost with the woman, name of
Brillgy, or some such thing. I can't see ghosts, but he scared the
sap out of Miss Bain, he did."

What rotten luck! Johnny thought. Not only were Burilgi and
Checheg here, but so was Pamela Worthington-Smythe. He
wouldn't be surprised if Percy Rathbone himself was hiding out
nearby.

"Do you know where the woman took her?" he asked.

"Probably up to the big house, old Bilbury Hall, I should guess."

Johnny's brain started churning. They needed to get these kids
out of here. But they had to grab Nina before it was too late.

It seemed that Marko had read his mind. "We have to get moving, Johnny. Or we'll miss our chance to free this lot. Nina'll have
to wait. Nothing else for it, I'm afraid."

Johnny wanted to scream in frustration. But, of course, Marko
was right.

Johnny looked up again at the face above the grate. "My friend
here's going to pass up a wrench and you're going to undo the four
big nuts that are holding down this grate. Try not to make too

much noise. By the way, what's your name?"

"I'm Hastings, Basil Hastings. Of St. Egbert's School for Boys."

"Well, Basil," said Marko, "I'm Marko Herne. And my friend here is Johnny Graphic."

"I say," Basil responded. "It is indeed a pleasure to meet you, Johnny. You too, Marko."

"Now here's the wrench and good luck." Marko held the handle up through the grate, and Basil took it.

Success depended on several things, Johnny realized. Were the nuts that held the grate frozen or movable? And was Basil Hastings strong enough to move them? If he wasn't, was there another kid up there who had the muscle power?

Up toward the grate floated Petunia, whose green ghost glow helped Johnny to see Basil's efforts.

Basil adjusted the wrench—a big, heavy plumber's wrench—to fit the first nut. Then he spit on his hands, sucked in a lungful of air, and began to push the wrench handle in a counterclockwise direction. He made a sound deep in his throat. A kind of *"Eh-eh-eh-eh-eh…"* Johnny knew that the kid was straining with all his might to loosen up that tiny bit of metal.

But nothing happened. The wrench, and therefore the nut, didn't budge.

"Once again," Basil muttered to himself, inhaling deeply.

"Try jerking it," Johnny suggested.

"Okay." Basil repeated the process, with some jerking motion.

This time there came a little metallic *errrrk* sound, and the wrench moved an inch.

Johnny almost cheered *hurray*. But Basil had more work to do before they celebrated. And Johnny hoped the kid didn't rupture a muscle in the process.

Basil pushed again and there was another, longer *errrrrrrrrk*.

The wrench went five or six inches. He kept pushing, the wrench rotating around two times. The first nut jumped free and made a crisp *claaank* as it bounced off and through the grate, onto the culvert tile right in front of Johnny's feet.

"Brilliant, Basil!" Marko exclaimed. "One down, three to go."

"You've got 'em on the run now, buddy," Johnny said with a giant grin. This whole plan might work out after all! He snatched up the nut and stuck it in his pocket—a special souvenir from a dangerous adventure.

The next two nuts were even easier, now that Basil had mastered that jerking force. Just one tiny piece of metal stood between all those kids and their freedom. *Piece of cake*, Johnny thought.

Basil pushed and jerked and pushed and jerked, but the fourth nut would not budge. Johnny could hear him panting, could imagine his heart thumping like a drum in a big band. Basil tried again and again, but it was futile. The nut was frozen.

That's when someone else arrived up above.

"Oy there, Hastings," a boy said. "What're you doing?"

Still panting, Basil stood up. "Some chaps..." More panting. "...down below..." Pant, pant. "...trying to rescue us." A whoosh of breath going out. "Have to get the grate off. Can't convince this fourth nut to let loose."

At least three boys' voices spoke at once. Johnny couldn't make out what they said. Finally one voice took charge.

"Chaps down in the piping? No crazier, I suppose, than getting kidnapped by zombies," the unseen boy said. "Here, let me have a go."

The new arrivals all took a turn but not one could persuade the stubborn nut to rotate. Basil Hastings, having finally caught his breath, said that he'd try again. Then someone else arrived on the scene quite unexpectedly.

Centurion Quintus.

The boys up above obviously couldn't see him when he floated down through the grate, right in front of Johnny and Marko.

Before the ghost could say anything, Johnny groaned. "They can't budge the last of the four nuts."

The scowling wraith snorted. "There is one more effort to be made."

He floated back up and provoked a little yelp from the boy holding the plumber's wrench, when he firmly yanked it away.

"What the…?" the boy yipped, rather too loudly.

"Shut up," Johnny barked. "It's a ghost trying to help you."

"Well why didn't you warn us?" the boy whined.

"Well, *sor-ry*," Johnny snapped back.

Ignoring the arguing boys—the way a big dog ignores a pair of buzzing flies—Quintus knelt down with the wrench he had purloined, fitted it to the last remaining nut, and began to push in the counterclockwise direction. He grunted with the effort.

By this time, Johnny could hear more kids up above, muttering and talking. Obviously, they'd been wakened by Basil and his friends, and by the metallic noises. He just hoped they had the good sense to keep as quiet as possible. Too much activity in the barn so late at night might prompt a visit by their captors.

That's when Johnny saw something almost miraculous. Quintus managed to turn the wrench ever so slightly—the muscles in his forearms bulging and quivering with the effort—and there came a very quiet *reeeeeech* sound. Had he done it?

The ancient ghost took a fresh grip on the wrench and pushed with all his might, moving the handle a good three inches.

With a nod of satisfaction, Quintus finished loosening the nut in a few slow but steady turns of the wrench. It rattled down through the grate, just like the first one. Quintus set the wrench down, lifted the grate—which Johnny figured had to weigh seventy or eighty pounds—and set it aside.

"Now," Quintus said, floating down in front of Johnny and Marko, "I shall provide you with your diversion. The abominations shall become rather preoccupied very soon."

"Just don't do anything to the big house, okay?" Johnny said. "Nina may be in there."

Quintus nodded. He zoomed up through the opening where the grate had been, vanishing in a wink.

As he did, a flash of light came from up above, and almost instantaneously a deafening BOOM of thunder.

It seemed that the stormy weather Johnny had noticed out to the west had arrived. And with it, probably there would be rain. It suddenly struck him that in a few moments they were going to be sending dozens of kids through a tight, dark culvert that might start to fill up with rainwater. They had to get a move on!

Johnny looked up and saw Basil Hastings peering down at him.

"Go wake up everyone," Johnny barked. "Tell them if they want out, they're going to have to crawl through the culvert. We've gotta do this as quick as we can."

"Ummm," Basil said, "that culvert might fill up with water. Oughtn't we to wait?"

"The longer we wait, the greater the risk is that we'll be discovered. We gotta move fast."

"If anyone's scared of going," Marko added, "tell them they'll just have to stay. To the daring goes the victory."

And sometimes, Johnny reflected, the daring get themselves killed. But now wasn't the time to mention that possibility.

"Carson, Leith," Basil said. "Go wake up as many as you can. Tell them what's up. Tell them if they don't go, they may never see their families again."

Within a minute, kids started jumping through the now-open hole in the barn floor. Johnny and Marko tried to catch them as they dropped down, but it was still a bit of a jolt when they landed on the tile floor of the culvert. One by one, white with dread, they went crawling off down the culvert, back in the direction from which Johnny, Marko, and Petunia had come not more than twenty minutes before.

Johnny counted eleven kids who had crawled off. Up above, Basil Hastings announced that a dozen more were ready to go. A few had refused to come, petrified of a long crawl in pitch-blackness to an unknown fate.

But that was life, wasn't it? Sometimes all a fellow had was a bad choice and a worse choice.

Finally, Basil and his two friends, Carson and Leith, dropped down. All doing their best to look brave, they crawled away, jabbering at each other to keep their spirits high.

Then it was Marko's turn to go, with Johnny and Petunia bringing up the rear.

Though there had been flashes of lightning and thunder from up above, only a trickle of water had come into the culvert so far— just enough to get a kid's knees wet.

But just as he was about to crawl back into that cramped, awful place, Johnny noticed something that made his blood run cold.

The water had begun to flow more rapidly and to rise—two or three inches in just the last minute.

If it kept rising at this rate, Johnny could well end up like that repulsive rat he had mashed with his hand coming in.

Waterlogged. And quite dead.

CHAPTER 29

JOHNNY CRAWLED AS FAST AS HE COULD, trying to keep up with Marko, who moved quite quickly on his hands and knees. To help him see, Johnny asked Petunia to fly up in front of him. What sense did it make to light the space behind him rather than the space ahead of him? She happily obliged, but only after Johnny used the "magic word"—which he had forgotten about in the panic of the moment.

The little ghost zoomed forward, right through him, giving him that odd tingling sensation that he always got when a ghost passed through his body. There, up ahead ten or twelve feet, in her green ghost light, he saw Marko's rear end and the bottoms of his shoes rocketing along—well, rocketing as fast as one could rocket in a dreadful culvert. The air was filled with the sounds of splashing hands and knees.

They made good progress for a couple of minutes. Then Johnny noticed that the water, which once merely covered his hands, was now halfway up his forearms. The downpour outside must have intensified. He could hear and feel the thunder still booming, right through the culvert and the ground it was buried in.

But they were moving along nonstop, and Johnny had every reason to believe that they would make it to safety before the culvert totally flooded.

Creeping along, he was looking down, assaying the water's rise when, quite unexpectedly, he ran right into Marko—who had stopped dead in his tracks.

"What in heckfire is wrong, Marko?" he exclaimed. "Get a move on!"

"Would if I could," Marko snapped over his shoulder. "Someone's jamming things up. Don't know who. Hastings is right in front of me."

"What's going on up there?" Johnny bellowed. "We can't stop. The water's rising and we'll drown like rats." He'd been thinking a lot about that dead squashed vermin.

"Who's plugging up the works?" Marko shouted, his angry voice echoing through the culvert.

"Not me," came Basil Hastings's reply.

"Not my fault," said Leith out of the dark up ahead. He sounded every bit as peeved as Marko.

Johnny expected to hear next from Carson, who had been the first of the three captive boys to scurry into the culvert, there in the last moments. But not a peep did he utter.

"Carson, are you there?" Basil shouted.

"He's here, sure enough," said Leith. "His fat rump is right in front of me. Get a move on, Carson!"

Carson finally spoke up. "Leith, stop pushing me," he whined.

"Carson, what's the problem?" Johnny hollered.

Carson's voice, quavering and thin, reverberated back down the culvert.

"I can't do this! I can't do this! We're going to die. Let me through, Leith. I have to go back. *Let me go back!*" And there came the sounds of two boys struggling in a very confined space.

There wasn't room in the culvert to turn around, so Carson

must have been trying to back up, while Leith pushed forward. Whatever they were doing up there was the opposite of a tug-of-war, Johnny thought. A push-of-war?

"The water's rising, Carson," he shouted, now feeling panicked himself. He looked down. Illuminated by Petunia's green ghost glow, the flow was almost up to his elbows. "It'll take more time to go back than to go forward. Just get moving and everything'll be okay."

There were some more scuffling sounds from up ahead. "Ow! That hurt!" Leith yelped.

"You've got to go forward, Carson, or we'll all drown," Basil yelled. "For heaven's sake, move it!"

For a brief moment, all that Johnny could hear in the culvert was the sound of four boys panting furiously. Then he had an idea. Petunia had retreated behind him, and he whispered back to her, over his shoulder, telling her what he wanted her to do—*pretty please*. She didn't think it was a nice, polite thing. But when Johnny said they could all die without her help, she reluctantly agreed. Provided Johnny would apologize afterward. He said he would. *Happily*.

Now pretty much in the dark with Petunia gone, Johnny waited with sodden, crossed fingers. It took about ten seconds.

There came a loud squawk of shock and outrage up ahead. From Carson.

"Ow! What's happening? Who's there?"

Johnny heard some scuffling noises, and Carson exclaimed, "Get it off me, dash it! Stop that!"

In the near-blackness Johnny couldn't tell if his idea was working. But one thing was certain—the water was coming higher.

Out of the murk Leith yelled, "The blighter's moving! Carson's going forward!"

Johnny said a silent *thank you* to Petunia. He had told her to yank on Carson's hair and box his ears a few times. It must have worked.

There was another brief, nervous silence. Then Marko barked, "I'm moving, Johnny! So is Basil. Come on!"

Johnny began to crawl, fast as he could. He was scraping his hands, banging up his knees, and whacking the back of his head as he went along. But he didn't care. There were bandages and iodine in the bag he'd left at the end of the culvert.

The only thing he could think about was the water that now rushed along just below his chest. In a way, the current was helping, pushing him forward.

But if any of those kids ahead got jammed up in the culvert—well, it would be a watery grave for everyone who tumbled into them from behind.

Johnny had no notion of how long it had been since he, Marko, and the other three boys had started crawling through the culvert. Five minutes? Fifty minutes? Five hours? Time had compressed and distorted. His journey in this terrible tile tube seemed as if it had become his entire life. There was only forward progress and rising water. Everything else was meaningless.

The water now reached up to his chin. Soon it would cover his mouth, then his nostrils. And then it would all be over. Johnny had read that drowning was an easy, peaceful way to die. But somehow he didn't think that filling up his lungs with water would be all that pleasant.

Still, it shocked him when he swallowed a mouthful of filthy rainwater. All he had to breathe with now was his nostrils. He twisted his head upward and sucked in air through his nose, then scampered furiously forward. When he tried to breathe that way again—nose up toward the culvert top—he inhaled water.

This was it!

Dead at only twelve and three-quarters!

He flailed and struggled and tried to scream out how unfair this all was.

Then, like a popgun shooting out a cork, the raging water spat Johnny right out of the culvert mouth onto the muddy bank of the drainage pond.

Coughing up water and fighting for breath, he scrambled to his feet. Someone grabbed him by the arm and hauled him aside, out of the force of the torrent.

Johnny blinked at his rescuer. A muddy, dripping boy in a grimy suit coat and trousers grinned back at him, then grabbed his hand for a vigorous shaking. "It's me, Johnny," the boy panted, wearing what looked like a drunkard's grin. "Basil Hastings."

The rain was still bucketing down. The only light they had came from the buildings that Quintus had set on fire. The other kids who had escaped stood nearby, speechless. Except for being drenched and exhausted, they all looked fine.

Then someone clapped Johnny on the shoulder. It was Marko.

"Good job, Johnny Graphic," the black-haired boy said.

Johnny nodded at him. "Nice work, Marko Herne."

THEY WERE ALL LUCKY that the night wasn't cold. Because if it had been, many of the kids—including Johnny— might have suffered from hypothermia and shivered themselves to death, as their body temperatures plummeted. The top order of business now was getting everyone's clothing dried out. They had to find a place to hide.

Johnny and Marko led them away from Bilbury Hall, just as the rain was stopping. In the distance, Quintus's diversions kept the bog zombies and ghosts occupied, as various buildings around the estate burned merrily, even in the rain. While they were tramping away, an explosion went off somewhere. Then there were random poppings of firecrackers, sounding a lot like gunshots. Johnny had given the centurion every firecracker Angus Snodgrass had provided.

By dawn, Johnny and all the others had made their way back to the little cottage where they'd left Iris. The zombies would almost certainly come looking for the escaped kids, so it was vital that they quickly get out of the area. The plan was for Iris to lead the escapees east toward the sea. Logically, this was not the best direction. But they figured that's what the zombies would think, too. Percy's foot soldiers would assume the kids would hightail it south, in the direction of Chippington—where rescue was more likely.

The next order of business was rest. Quintus had found a safe spot in the woods for everyone to catch some sleep, with the centurion and Petunia standing guard. Iris and her troop would head out as soon as the kids were ready. Then, at nightfall, Johnny, Marko, and Basil would attempt to rescue Nina.

On his late-night rampage, Quintus had discovered where they were keeping her. But he warned Johnny that freeing his friend would be even more perilous than the great culvert escape.

CHAPTER 30

THE DRIVE TO ROYALTON had taken over three hours. Bao and Evvie had decided to ride inside the automobile, so they could chat with Grandmother and Mel.

They arrived at Twinings Square and the headquarters of the Royal Society of Etherists, or the RSE, a bit after noon. Grandmother intended to use this group to help in the hunt for Johnny and Nina. She informed Bao that she was a "past president" of the RSE, whatever that meant. Grandmother and Mel planned to spread the plea for help far and wide. Through the RSE, they could reach out to hundreds of specters, rather than just dozens.

But that meant that Grandmother and Mel would be busy for most of the afternoon. Evvie, who had come along expressly to go look at the house he had grown up in, asked Bao if she wanted to accompany him. Grandmother said yes, Bao could go. Just so long as they both were back by four o'clock in the afternoon.

Not having Grandmother or Mel along meant that if Evvie— whose actual name was Edward Arthur Fotheringay Samuel Hastings—should encounter any members of his family, well, there would be no communication. Not unless someone in the house could see ghosts.

Bao and Evvie floated out of the RSE headquarters and into Twinings Square, which contained a little park full of garden beds and some kind of statue of a warrior on a horse. It was a foggy day, and a light drizzle was coming down.

"All right now, old girl," Evvie said, as they hovered over the busy street, "we go off this way." And he pointed to the left. "Hope my sense of direction has survived after twenty-five years in the jungle."

There was a time when Bao wondered why her friend called her "old girl." She was, after all, just a little girl who hadn't lived very long. But, as Evvie pointed out, she was also a girl who had lived, as far as they could tell, many, many centuries ago. And that would make her either a "very old young girl" or a "very young old girl." In either case, "old girl" seemed perfectly proper. In fact, Bao had grown proud of the nickname.

They soared up this street and down that avenue, making a number of turns. Evvie seemed to know exactly where to go.

Bao had never seen more people—both living and dead—in one place in her life. The living were jammed together down on the street, bustling along on the sidewalks, through the fog and rain. All kinds of people, of all ages and all colors. Many of them carried umbrellas and huddled against the damp and cold.

The ghosts were equally diverse. Some were friendly and waved at the two visiting wraiths. Many along the way seemed gloomy and indifferent—a common condition for ghosts. A few were even hostile, making rude gestures and shouting curses.

Finally, after a half hour of zooming along over the tops of what Evvie called "double-decker omnibuses," the two of them turned onto a short, dead-end street off a main road. Evvie said it was called Marcelline Place. There were several tall brick houses on it, sitting snugly next to each other.

Through the haze of the fog, Bao could see lights glowing warmly in many of the windows. The homes looked cozy and welcoming. The sight of them made her nostalgic for the fires of her home village. For the laughing and talking and joking that went on around those ancient flames. For her *own* family.

"These were our city digs," Evvie said, pointing to the biggest of the houses. "We had two country homes, too. But we lived here mostly. Father had his duties in the House of Lords, you know."

Bao nodded earnestly. She did indeed know. Evvie had told her many stories about his young years, and how he had become Lord Hurley at the tender age of fifteen. When he died, only one year later, his younger brother would have become Lord Hurley of Evansham.

Evvie hovered before the house, as if he hadn't quite decided to enter it.

"What's wrong, Evvie?" asked Bao.

"A little nervous is all. First time home in a quarter century."

"But maybe no one will even be able to see us."

Evvie nodded, but he still didn't move. Finally, he spoke.

"I'm worried that everyone is going to be heartbroken about my nephew's abduction. I'm not sure if I want to see them that way."

Bao understood but didn't know what to say.

At last, Evvie shrugged. "Well, nothing for it, old girl, but to pop in and have a look about. Come along, Bao."

And in they flew through the front brick wall.

The place was much more modest than Wickenham—the furniture plainer, the artwork less striking. But it looked like people really lived there, with knitting left on a sofa and a book open on the arm of a chair.

All of a sudden, footsteps clattered in a hallway. A young woman in a black uniform appeared in the room where Evvie and Bao were hovering. Evvie waved and said hello, but the woman couldn't see them.

"You know, Bao," he said, "I'm not certain any of my family even lives here anymore. They could have sold the old place after I died."

Bao noticed that Evvie's face looked a bit forlorn when he said that. But then it brightened up again.

"Guess we might as well go upstairs and find my old room."

They floated up the narrow staircase at the side of the front foyer. Bao followed Evvie to the third room down the hall on their left.

"Oh, look!" Evvie beamed as he saw the ragged sign on the door. "It says, 'The Lair of Basil Hastings. Enter at Your Own Peril.' So the family still does live here."

"Is Basil your brother?" Bao asked.

"No. I think he's my nephew. Perhaps the one who got himself abducted."

They went into the room and looked around. There were books galore, sporting equipment, posters on the walls, tiny aeroboats hanging from the ceiling, and a glass box filled with water and populated by colorful little fishes.

"The bed's neatly made up," Evvie observed. "The place is unusually tidy for a boy's room. Doesn't look like anyone is in residence at the moment. Makes sense, since Basil is almost certainly off at school. But I wonder why no one else is around."

He pondered briefly, then said, "Aha! It's about teatime for the Hastings family, I'd guess. And anyone who's home would be down in the conservatory."

Evvie led Bao down the stairs and out to a room at the back of the house. It had glass windows all around. Green, luxuriant plants crowded it. The space reminded Bao of the jungle at the bottom of her mountain.

In the middle of the large room was a small, glass-topped table. Around it sat a man, a woman, and a very old, white-haired lady in a chair with wheels.

"Ahemmm." Evvie cleared his throat loudly.

There was no reaction.

He floated down for a closer look, right into the middle of the table. He studied the man closely, from inches away.

"My good heavens," Evvie finally said, shaking his head. "I don't believe it. It's Roger. My little brother Roger. Lord Hurley. But he's gotten fat and bald and old. He used to be skinny as a stick and capered about like a monkey."

He stared a moment more, then twisted round to look at the younger woman.

"Don't know her, Bao," he said. "His wife, I suppose."

As Evvie turned his gaze to the old lady, she suddenly spoke.

"So we have no word at all of Basil," she said, her voice fluttering with emotion and age. "Taken from St. Egbert's over two weeks ago. No sign of him. When we lost your brother, our dear Edward…"

Evvie let out a choking sob and zoomed back up to Bao.

"I know that voice," he panted. "It's Mother. What's happened to her? *What's happened to her?*"

"She's alive, Evvie," Bao gently answered. "She got old. That's what happened to her."

Evvie nodded despondently.

Down below, Roger Hastings—the current Lord Hurley—glared at the old lady. "Just because Edward never came back from his dratted jungle expedition, it doesn't mean Basil won't be coming home. We're not giving up hope."

"The authorities are doing everything they can, Mother," the younger woman said, her voice also trembling. "They're searching high and low through MacFreithshire. All we can do is wait and pray. He'll be safe, I'm sure of it."

"This is terrible," Evvie muttered. "My nephew has been abducted. My brother and my mother have become old. So old! And there's nothing I can do for them."

"But at least you got to see your mother again," Bao replied sadly. "I wish I could be in the same room with my mother."

Evvie gave her a sympathetic look. "You know, old girl, you're quite right."

And quick as a wink, he zoomed down close to his mother and gave her a kiss.

The old lady put her hand up to her cheek and gasped.

"What is it, Mother?" her younger son asked. "Are you all right?"

"The oddest thing, Roger," she said with a look of bemusement. "It felt like a butterfly just kissed me."

CHAPTER 31

IT WAS LUCKY that there were few clouds in the sky that night. By the light of a quarter moon, Johnny and his comrades made their way on the slow sneak to Bilbury Hall, keeping their eyes peeled for any potential danger.

Iris had already left with her band of escaped kids. Carson and Leith had volunteered to help her herd the exhausted youngsters out of harm's way. Petunia had reluctantly agreed once again to stay and help Quintus with any ghostly duties.

After inching along the edge of the yard, Johnny, Marko, and Basil quietly slipped into Bilbury Hall's eight-car garage. Quintus and Petunia floated in behind them. Through a crack in one of the big overhead doors, Johnny saw a zombie guarding the back pantry entrance of the hulking old mansion. They'd have to figure out how to deal with that palooka. Quintus had said there was no other way for them to get into the place. The front entry of the great house was guarded far more heavily.

For weaponry, Johnny carried the cricket bat. Basil had delightedly recognized it as his own—the one he had dropped the night of the zombie raid on St. Egbert's. He was happy to loan it to Johnny for the duration of the crisis. For his part, Basil carried an ax that he had come across on their hike in. Perhaps one of the zombies had left it behind. Marko still wore the army saber that Angus Snodgrass had loaned him back at the school.

Johnny stared out through the crack in the garage door, wondering if anyone was searching for them. By now, Mel and Dame Honoria had surely been notified of his and Nina's disappearance. What must they be thinking? Mel was probably going nuts with worry.

And where were the colonel and Zenith troopers? Normally, they would have had no problem tracking Johnny down by now. Maybe it was that weird fog, which seemed to upset the ghosts' equilibrium.

"Pssst…"

Johnny nearly jumped out of his filthy hiking duds. Marko had crept up behind and surprised him.

"What?" Johnny whispered.

"Quintus says we'd better move soon, or forget it till later."

For Johnny, that wasn't an option. Wait another day, and Percy's goons might have taken Nina away. But he had just come up with an idea that could make their job easier.

The long garage they were in housed six automobiles, including a black Morton Monarch much like Uncle Louie's car. There were also several motorcycles in a far corner. One of them, a small bike, was a Chapman Hellcat. Johnny had gawked at a Hellcat at the motorcycle showroom in downtown Zenith not a month before, and had actually climbed up in the saddle. It was one nifty machine.

He grinned at Marko. "I have an idea. And it might just work.

That is, if I can teach Quintus and Petunia a little something about modern transportation technology."

JOHNNY, MARKO, AND BASIL climbed out of the back garage window they had come in through, then crept behind the inward-curving hedgerow that bordered the garage. The dense hedge hid them from sight, until it ended about twenty yards farther on. When Johnny peered around the thick vegetation, he had a clear view of both the front of the garage and the back of the mansion, where that single bog zombie stood guard. Johnny withdrew and let the two other boys have a look.

"Any minute now," he whispered, "it's gonna get interesting."

"I hope it works," Marko said.

Basil nodded calmly. "It'll work. Yeah, it'll work."

They didn't have to wait long.

An automobile engine roared to life behind the closed garage doors. Headlights flared through the glass windows inside the building, illuminating the tarmac and the back of the big house. And with a snarling roar, a great, blue-colored Lindt limou-sine lurched through one of the doors, smashing wood and glass to pieces. It surged out onto the driveway—bits of debris clinging to it—and headed straight for the back of Bilbury Hall. Straight, in fact, for the zombie standing there, wide-eyed and frozen to the spot.

In the driver's seat, gripping the wheel like grim old death, glowed a green Imperial soldier, some twenty centuries dead. Johnny could have sworn that Quintus was grinning ear to ear, though he couldn't be sure.

At the very last second, Quintus swerved to the left, missing the zombie by a few feet. He sent the limousine bounding across the turf and back onto the driveway, circling around the far end of the house and out of sight.

"Pretty good driving, for a beginner," Basil laughed.

"That it is. But he had a good teacher." And at that, Marko clapped Johnny on the shoulder.

Johnny was too preoccupied to even notice. "So where's Petunia?"

As if to answer him, another car engine rumbled to life inside the garage, and headlights flared. There was a grinding of gears and that black Morton Monarch smashed out through another door—though more slowly than Quintus's rapid exit.

Johnny figured that if Petunia could get the car started, operate the clutch, and get into first gear, it would be a minor miracle. And, by heckfire, she'd done it!

Now Petunia drove slowly and majestically in the opposite direction of Quintus, around the other end of Bilbury Hall, her blonde locks barely visible above the wheel. Her course wobbled a bit, but she managed not to run into anything.

After appearing immobilized by shock, the mesmerized zombie guard finally loped off after her.

"Yes!" Johnny exclaimed. "Time to go!"

The three boys dashed out from behind the hedgerow, making a beeline for the back pantry door. No one was in sight. Breathless, they tumbled into an entranceway lined with shelves, which were stacked with canned and bottled foodstuffs. No electric lights were burning, just a few oil lamps and candles. From there they tiptoed into the vast kitchen—shadowy and forbiddingly festooned with dozens of hanging pots, pans, and implements.

Quintus had made sure that Johnny understood exactly where he had to go. What the ghost couldn't tell him—and what worried Johnny most—was how many zombies and ghosts roamed the inside of the mansion. There was no easy way to answer this. The boys would just have to take their chances.

Johnny looked around at Marko and Basil, who were following behind him. "Okey-dokey, guys," he whispered. "Time to draw weapons."

Marko quietly pulled his saber from its scabbard, and Basil gripped his axe slightly higher on the handle. Johnny reached behind his head and withdrew the cricket bat from his backpack. Without a word, he tiptoed out of the kitchen and into one of Bilbury Hall's back corridors.

The coast was clear. No one in sight. Go right after about fifty paces, Quintus had said, then left. That brought them into the dining room—a grand space very much like that at Dame Honoria's Wickenham—and then into a wide corridor. Johnny peered around in the dim light of several more oil lamps. He looked both ways and spotted the main entrance hall and the staircase. "C'mon," he whispered.

No one was about. Johnny wondered if the big automobile commotion outside had drawn away all the zombies and ghosts. If it had, it meant they could get to Nina quickly and spirit her away in a hurry. *That* would be terrific.

But up on the second floor, his hopes were dashed.

Peeking out at the top of the stairs, Johnny clearly saw what they were up against.

At the far end of the hallway, down to the left, a zombie and a ghost stood guard before the bedroom in which Quintus had said Nina was being held. The zombie, a long-dead Eldurian bog man, was awfully big. Who knew what kind of wraith was inside that ancient corpse? And the ghost was a Steppe Warrior.

Johnny told Marko and Basil what he'd seen, then whispered, "Any ideas?"

Marko gulped. "Basil here can't even see the ghost warrior. So what we need to do is divide their forces. I borrowed this coming through that big hallway downstairs." He pulled a small ceramic vase from his pocket. "I'll throw it down the hallway, away from those blokes. If Mr. Tall, Dark, and Gruesome comes this way…"

Johnny assumed he meant the bog zombie.

"…then Basil and I go after it. And you charge the ghost. And if the ghost comes, vice versa."

Johnny liked the plan. Because Basil would have no chance against that Steppe Warrior wraith.

Marko was about to heave the vase when Johnny heard voices coming from the end of the hallway. He signaled Marko to wait, then looked out again.

Strolling out of Nina's room came Pamela Worthington-Smythe and a green-glowing specter in dripping cold-weather gear.

Percy Rathbone!

The couple, she holding the ghost's arm, walked slowly toward them.

CHAPTER 32

"WE'VE GOTTA HIDE!" Johnny whispered. "Back down the stairs!"

The three boys scampered down the steps as quietly as they possibly could. Johnny hid on the far side of a tall cabinet, while Basil slithered under a table and Marko ducked into a broom closet.

From his hidey-hole, Johnny could hear Percy and Pamela chatting. But only a few words were audible.

"…Royalton…"

"…surprise…"

"…the next step…"

"…filthy headache…"

"…Wickenham…"

And "…Mummy…"

Then someone—it sounded like a ghost—interrupted them, announcing that there had been a disturbance outside. Automobiles hijacked. Damage done. Percy angrily asked a question or two, then the voices receded.

When the coast seemed clear, Johnny fetched Marko and Basil, and they went back upstairs. The bog zombie and ghost Steppe Warrior were still on guard. So Johnny, with a deep gulp, told

Marko to toss the little vase.

Marko stepped out into the hallway, wound up like a Zenith Blue Sox outfielder, and threw the object as far as he could. There was a shattering noise. Marko nipped back out of sight.

Then everything happened very quickly.

The zombie came lumbering down the hallway, right past the staircase, not even seeing them crouching on the steps.

Marko and Basil charged after it, as Johnny ran in the opposite direction, winding up his cricket bat for a stinging hit the very instant he got close enough. What Johnny didn't anticipate, as he surged forward, was the Steppe Warrior drawing his bow out of thin air and nocking an arrow. The bowstring twanged.

It was sheer dumb luck that Johnny's bat happened to be directly in the path of that arrow—which made a solid *thoinnnk* in the hard willow wood.

The Steppe Warrior didn't have time to re-nock or draw a blade before Johnny was on top of him. Johnny swung the bat and caught the ghost flush on the side of his head.

Splaaat!

While the Steppe Warrior writhed on the rich carpeting of the hallway, groaning in agony, Johnny drew the bat back for a golfing kind of swing. Only with the ghost's head serving as the ball.

Just as he had back in Jadetown, when he was being chased by a ghost warrior, Johnny was prepared to smash this wraith into a miserable pulp. Even if it were the last thing he ever did.

But the ghost—his merciless, flat features a picture of perfect pain—seemed to know that he'd already lost this particular fight. He put his hands up, a sign of surrender. As livid as Johnny was, he'd had enough. He lowered his cricket bat. At that, the wraith warrior scrambled backward and dove through the carpeting as if it were made of water.

Johnny glanced back up the hallway to see how Marko and Basil were doing. He watched the two slowly backing away from the hulking bog zombie. Waving saber and axe, Marko and Basil were holding on but appeared to be giving ground. Johnny wanted to help them, but first he had to see if this had all been worth the effort. Was Nina in this bedroom?

He threw the door open. "Nina?" he barked. "Are you here?"

The room was as dark as ink. Johnny couldn't see a thing. "Sparks? *Sparks?*"

He heard some soft moaning straight ahead and he groped his way toward it, quickly ramming up against what felt like a bed. He reached around and found a leg, which he squeezed and shook.

"Wha... Hullo..." came a groggy, hoarse voice. A girl's voice.

"Nina, is that you?"

"Yeah, uh-huh." There was a little pause. "Johnny?"

Johnny bent over and hauled his friend to the edge of the bed. He pulled her upright and gave her a pat on the shoulder. He could feel her wobble, and she almost toppled over backward as he stood her up. She sure didn't seem as if she was ready to make a run for it. Somehow he had to get her moving.

"We have to vamoose *right now*, Sparks," he urged. "Marko and Basil are trying to put that zombie guard out of commission. This is our only chance."

"Don't feel real good." Nina leaned against Johnny. "Kinda dopey. Just wanna sleep."

Even allowing for the late hour, Nina shouldn't have been so disconnected. Johnny hauled her toward the door. "Sorry Sparks, can't sleep now."

"My right arm's numb, Johnny. Can barely feel my fingers."

Johnny stopped in his tracks, anger flaring inside him. "Did they hurt you? Did they torture you?"

"Don't think so. Can't remember much." She swayed on her feet. "Don't forget my pack. The goggles are in there. It's by the bed."

Johnny leaned his friend against the doorframe, hoping she wouldn't fall over. He dashed back to the bed and felt around beneath it, quickly finding the bag. A few seconds later he was dragging Nina down the hallway.

It surprised him to see Marko dueling away with a ghost, not a bog zombie. It was some kind of sea raider from a millennium ago. Blades clanked against each other again and again. But where had the zombie gone?

Then Johnny noticed a dark form sprawled down near Marko, with a small, roundish shape nearby. A body with a detached head. This ghost must have been inside the bog zombie, animating it. Marko liberated it when his saber severed the head. And just like the bog bodies back in Royalton, this one had shrunken and shriveled.

Johnny and Nina made it almost as far as the staircase when Basil popped out of the deep shadows.

"I'd better go help Marko," Johnny panted.

"No." Basil shook his head. "Marko said he'd hold this blackguard off, then follow after us in a few minutes. Anyway, he says this ghost hasn't much spunk, now that he's out of his bog body."

Johnny was torn. He knew he had to get Nina out of there, or risk her being captured again. But it just seemed plain wrong to leave Marko to battle it out without any help. For better or worse, he decided what to do. He hoped he wouldn't regret it.

"C'mon then," he said, leading Nina down the staircase. Basil followed close behind. They retraced their earlier steps all the way back to the pantry, ducking briefly into an alcove when a zombie came loping by. The coast was clear outside. But they couldn't go as fast as Johnny would have liked, because Nina's feet were still dragging.

They went into the garage through one of the smashed doors and straight to a sporty coupe, a red Allister. This and the cars the ghosts had taken were the only vehicles for which they had found keys.

After lifting the garage door in front of them, they climbed into the Allister—Johnny in the driver's seat, and Nina and Basil squeezed into the back. The idea was to start the car and wait for Marko to appear at the pantry door. But when Johnny attempted to get the auto going, it simply wouldn't catch. He tried again and again.

Basil climbed out of the rear seat and plopped down next to him. "Listen, Johnny, you've got to get Nina out of here. Pronto. These villains seem to have some special interest in her."

Johnny agreed, though he wondered why Percy had suddenly focused his attention on Nina. Without goggles, she didn't even have etheric vision. What kind of threat was she to him?

"Here's an idea," Basil continued. "I'll stay here and keep trying to start this motor."

"So I take Nina on foot?" Johnny didn't like that idea, with all those zombies and ghosts stirred up like a hornet's nest.

"Not exactly," Basil said. He nodded his head toward a far corner of the garage.

Johnny looked in that direction.

"The Chapman Hellcat?" he exclaimed. The mere idea astonished him.

"Can you pilot the thing?" Basil asked.

Johnny had ridden a small motorcycle that Uncle Louie had been working on, over some of the trails up off of Great Lake. He knew how to start it, shift it, and brake it. In fact, he was pretty good at riding a cycle. "Yeah, I think so, Basil."

His new friend grinned at him. "Then what are you waiting for?"

"And what about you and Marko? You know how to drive?"

"Oh, yeah," Basil answered. "Never told any of my mates at St. Egbert's, but my dream job is race car driver."

Within a minute, Johnny was straddling the cycle, Nina standing behind him.

"Before we go, Sparks," he said, "put on your goggles. I want you to be able to see any ghosts that might cause us trouble."

"Okay. I'll be on my guard." And she proceeded to don the eccentric eye gear. It seemed that finally she had woken up, suddenly full of nervous energy.

First, Johnny kicked the starter over a few times with the fuel and ignition switch off, just as Uncle Louie had taught him. Then he turned on the fuel valve, the choke, and the ignition switch. He twisted the throttle a couple of times and found the compression stroke. It took him only two kicks to awaken that glorious, thrumming Chapman engine. He was happy to see the bike had a full tank of gas. Then he gestured for Nina to climb on behind him. She hopped on and grabbed onto his waist.

"Can you hold onto me with that sore arm?" he asked.

"Yeah, it's better now. Not so numb. I'll be okay."

With a jaunty wave to Basil—back in the Allister coupe, still trying to get it started—Johnny and Nina rolled out of the garage and onto the driveway. Johnny didn't have the headlamp on, to avoid being noticed by the dangerous denizens of the place. He figured they could travel a bit with just the light from the quarter moon.

He was almost giddy with relief. It seemed that they were getting away clean.

But when he looked straight ahead, he gasped.

Two bog zombies had lurched out of the darkness at a bend in the driveway. And they were charging right toward the motorcycle.

CHAPTER 33

AS THE TWO ZOMBIES CHARGED, both from the left, Johnny twisted the Chapman Hellcat in the other direction. He managed to keep the cycle upright, then goosed the accelerator to zoom past the two attackers. But as he sped by them, they began to raise the alarm.

Johnny spotted a clutch of zombies up ahead on the long, winding driveway, milling around what looked to be a still-smoking, smashed up limousine—the Lindt that Quintus had hijacked. It had gone right into a big oak tree, but there was no sign of the ancient specter.

The zombies, of course, heard their comrades shouting, as well as the drone of the Hellcat, and turned around to see what was happening. They started to move toward the rapidly approaching cycle in a kind of zombie scrum.

Johnny knew what he had to do, even though it would bring him and Nina perilously close to the big pond in front of Bilbury Hall.

He figured that by swinging up onto the lawn—muddy and brown this time of year—he would be able to run this latest gauntlet. But he could see that one of those zombies looked especially fleet of foot.

Keeping the motorcycle going while shouting over his shoulder wasn't easy. But Johnny had to.

"See that bozo coming?" he yelled.

"Yeah, the thing's awful fast," Nina bellowed back.

"Grab the bat out of my pack and get ready to wallop it a good one."

Johnny could feel Nina snatching up the cricket bat as he swung right, near to the spot where the lawn dipped down into the water. Another few inches too close and the tires might slide out from beneath them, pitching them into the pond. Then their gooses would be cooked for sure.

In the rearview mirror on the handlebars, he saw a tall, dark form coming up behind them—almost faster than the cycle. Even as he gunned the Hellcat forward, he heard Nina scream. Not a scream of fear, but of power. The scream you make when you want a little jolt of extra energy. He felt her swing the cricket bat.

There was a sodden percussion of something very hard hitting something very meaty. Then came a bellow of pain and outrage.

"Gotcha!" Nina shouted.

Johnny steered the cycle back off the lawn. Soon they were zooming down the straightaway that took them through an open, wrought-iron gate and onto a narrow public road.

There wasn't a zombie in sight. Johnny flipped on the headlamp, and they zoomed down the curving country lane.

"Great job with that joker, Sparks!" he shouted to his friend.

"Thanks," Nina yelled back. "Managed to smash its knee. Folded up like an accordion."

Johnny felt her wedging the cricket bat into his pack.

"I heard some stuff when I was held prisoner," she shouted. "It might be really important."

"What is it?"

"I think they're planning a big attack real soon. I overheard Pamela. She said their people were in place and awaiting the order to move. She mentioned that Royalton would never be the same."

Johnny had heard Percy mention Royalton, too. Something was up. They had to alert the authorities before Percy could put his plan in motion.

They sped along for about ten minutes before Nina yelled in Johnny's ear. "Do you know where we're going?"

Johnny realized that he didn't. He had just wanted to get away from Bilbury Hall. As far and as fast as possible.

"You still have that compass, Sparks?"

They stopped by the side of the road. Nina consulted her compass in the light of the cycle's headlamp. They were traveling north, but that's all they knew. Johnny had left the map back in the Allister automobile with Basil.

"We have to get headed south," he said. "But I want to avoid Bilbury Hall. I don't want to go near that nest of nasties ever again."

Nina looked back in the direction they had come from. "I remember we went past a road on the left a few minutes ago. We could go back and see where it leads."

Johnny agreed. He was pretty much fresh out of ideas—it being so late and he being so exhausted. It was nice to have Nina's gray cells back in action.

Beyond his poor sense of direction and weariness, Johnny had another worry rattling around in his noggin. Had Basil and Marko managed to get out? Johnny still felt guilty about leaving them.

So it was a fine coincidence when, as they roared back in the direction they had come from, Johnny saw an automobile heading toward them, its headlights ablaze.

Could it be Marko and Basil?

The car sped right by them, going at least fifty miles per hour—a good pace on a country road like this.

Then Johnny heard a squealing of brakes. He slowed the Chapman motorcycle, braked to a stop, and turned it around to have a look. It took him a few seconds to recognize the very same red Allister two-door he had left Basil Hastings in. A head popped out of the passenger's side window. It was Marko Herne!

"Wrong way, Johnny," he hollered. "They're after us. Mounted ghost cavaliers. Follow us. I know where we are, and I know someone who can help us."

"Understood," Johnny shouted.

Marko's head disappeared back into the vehicle, and the car sped away.

Johnny and Nina tucked in right behind the coupe. Though Johnny snatched quick looks in the rearview mirror, he saw nothing behind them but darkness. A troop of ghost warriors would be glowing green.

But wraiths on horses could go a lot faster than either a motorcycle or a car. Johnny was expecting that kind of trouble to come from the direction of Bilbury Hall. So what happened next caught him totally off-guard.

Charging across an empty field beside the road came three mounted cavaliers, waving swords and shouting things that were undoubtedly unfriendly. The ghosts apparently didn't have bows and arrows, or Johnny and Nina would already be looking like pincushions.

Johnny could see absolutely no way that they'd survive this encounter with just a cricket bat and a Chapman Hellcat cycle. The ghosts' horses were fast and there was no room for Johnny to really maneuver the motorcycle.

"Nina!" he bellowed. "Hang on tight!"

The first of the cavaliers was closing in on them, his saber lifted up, ready to strike.

At the last instant, Johnny swerved slightly to the left. As the Chapman changed course and slowed, he could literally feel the air move—the saber blade slashing an inch or two over his head. Out of the corner of his eye, he saw that first ghost warrior fly off to the left, overshooting. But the other two were not far behind him, and they looked ready to strike.

Now that Johnny and Nina had slowed, they were sitting ducks. Then, out of nowhere…

BOOM! BOOM!

There was a frightful shriek.

It sounded like the high-pitched grinding of metal on metal.

The second cavalier had dropped his saber and was dragging his hand across his shoulder.

Johnny was astonished. What just happened? He glanced up the road, where the two-door coupe had slowed to a crawl.

Standing out on the running board, gripping the open door with his left hand, was Marko. In his right hand he had a big semi-automatic pistol, smoke wafting out of the barrel. He aimed it again, and the weapon barked twice.

The third cavalier yelped in pain and flew off to the side, aborting his attack. The wraith glared at Marko, then at Johnny and Nina. If looks could kill, Johnny figured they would all be dead.

Johnny stopped the Hellcat, and he and Nina climbed off. Basil put on the brakes, as well, and Marko hopped from the running board, gun at the ready.

They were out in the middle of nowhere, with ghost cavaliers on both sides, glowing ominously.

Johnny was having a hard time taking these spooks seriously. With their frills and ruffles and feathered floppy hats, they looked practically like overdressed floozies. But he knew they had a reputation as fierce fighters in their day.

"Why aren't they charging?" Nina asked.

"Licking their wounds, I guess," he replied. "We'd be in a huge fix if Marko didn't have a gun."

"I thought that bullets didn't hurt ghosts."

"Oh, bullets hurt 'em, all right. Smarts like the dickens. So I figure our attackers here have never eaten lead and it stunned them a bit."

By now, Marko and Basil had trotted over to join them.

"Nice shooting, Marko," Johnny said admiringly.

Basil nodded in appreciation, as well. "Good thing Marko found that gun in the glove box. Quite the sharpshooter, isn't he?"

Marko looked a little surprised himself. "My uncle's teaching me how to shoot. Says I'm a natural."

Nina, as she so often did, brought the conversation back to reality. "Guys, in case you haven't noticed, we're still surrounded. And I don't think they're too happy with us."

Then, to Johnny's great relief, reinforcements arrived.

Leaping out of the ground in front of him came Petunia. And right behind her came the Centurion Quintus, his short sword in hand. He gave a quick Imperial salute and turned to face the mounted cavaliers.

His arrival and Marko's semi-automatic were enough to discourage the three attackers. One of them, apparently the leader, made a hand signal. They turned their horses around and galloped away, up into the sky.

"Quintus, I've never been gladder to see anyone than you," Johnny said with a huge smile.

"After I left the horseless cart, I found the child here," Quintus said. He patted Petunia on the head. "And we came after you."

But Johnny's smile was fading. "Now what do we do? We're to heck and gone in the boonies, and we have important information to get back to the authorities."

"I think I know how to get you south in a hurry," Marko said. "If you two are ready for a dicey new adventure."

Johnny almost hooted. Hadn't they had a whole bunch of dicey adventures already? How much worse could one more be?

CHAPTER 34

JOHNNY PULLED THE HELLCAT OFF the country lane, following the Allister onto the narrow drive. It wended through an orchard and some woods, before spilling out onto a broad courtyard. There was a rustic, low-slung stone house on one side and a couple of large metal sheds on the other. An oil lamp flickered in one of the house's windows.

Johnny stopped the Hellcat right next to the coupe and held it steady while Nina climbed off. Then he dismounted and put out the kickstand.

"So where are we?" he asked, as Marko emerged from the car.

"Haven't been here since I was a kid," Marko answered, looking around. "Spent a few weeks mucking about the place one summer."

"And you were quite a handful!" came a booming voice.

Everyone spun around to see a stout, bewhiskered, ruddy-cheeked man of about sixty emerge from the front door of the stone cottage. He wore a blue bathrobe and a white nightcap, and he was barefoot. He had a shotgun in the crook of his left arm.

Next to him was a large, growling mutt of indeterminate breeding.

Johnny couldn't blame him for greeting them with a shotgun and a dog. Considering the shenanigans that had been going on nearby, a guy had to play it safe.

"You young scamp," the man said, giving Marko a terrific scowl. "Why haven't you visited since then?"

Marko just grinned, striding up to the old man with his hand outstretched for a shake. But the fellow pulled Marko into an exuberant embrace, his expression transformed with a beaming smile. The big dog jumped around them both, bouncing and barking like a jumbo puppy.

"Everyone," Marko said, "this here is my farmer uncle, Ezra Herne. The dog's Brownie. Uncle Ez, these are my mates—Johnny Graphic, Nina Bain, Basil Hastings. We've a couple of ghosts with us, too. An Imperial centurion named Quintus and a little girl named Petunia Budd."

"A dirty, exhausted crew, if ever I've seen one," Uncle Ez observed. "Let's get you cleaned up and in the sack. Morning'll be here pretty soon, and you can tell me your story over breakfast. I'll bet it's a doozy."

BY THE TIME JOHNNY AWOKE from a very deep slumber, everyone else was assembled around the kitchen table. Uncle Ez handed him a plate of scrambled eggs, cold toast, and fried kippers. A cup of strong black tea arrived next. Between bites, Johnny and his friends told Uncle Ez all about their adventures and close brushes with calamity in MacFreithshire.

The old boy's jovial features darkened. "Whoever set these monsters loose on poor old MacFreithshire needs a comeuppance, I say. I've only avoided disaster myself by sheer dumb luck. None of them have found this place, or they'd have faced my shotgun and Brownie's teeth."

Johnny explained how he and Nina had stumbled onto important information about a potential attack on Royalton itself. They had to get word back to someone in authority, before it was too late.

"I got my telephone hookup just last year," Uncle Ez said. "But the blasted thing cut out last week. Don't know when it'll get fixed. I've an old two-way radio that I haven't used in a while."

Johnny looked at Nina and his eyebrows shot up. "Maybe you should give it a look, Sparks. If we could send a radio alert, that'd be great."

"You betcha," Nina said. "Do you have a directory of frequencies that I could try?"

Uncle Ez led her and Marko up into the attic. But they were gone for only a few minutes, returning with glum expressions.

"The battery's dead," Nina sighed. "And Uncle Ez doesn't have a fresh one."

"Actually, I was thinking about Uncle Ez's biplane," Marko said, plopping back into his chair. "That was my idea last night. Uncle Ez is an old army air corps sergeant. Loves to fly. This is how I figured we could get you south in a hurry."

Uncle Ez shook his head. "The biplane's in pieces all over the hangar."

"Oh, rats!" Basil groaned. "Now there's no way to get word to Royalton in time."

Johnny felt sorry for Basil. He knew that the kid's family lived in Royalton, and maybe was in danger because of Percy's possible attack.

"All is not lost, though," Uncle Ez reassured. "There's still Thumper."

"What's Thumper?" Johnny asked.

"It's my gyrocopter."

"Ummm, what's a gyrocopter?"

"Well, young man, you know how an airplane is lifted by its two main wings?"

Johnny knew that and nodded.

"A gyrocopter," Uncle Ez continued, "is lifted instead by unpowered horizontal rotors. Then it's thrust forward by a front-mounted engine and propeller. I designed and built my own and have had it airborne for over two hundred hours. I call it Thumper."

"Why do you call it Thumper?" It seemed like a pretty silly name for a flying machine.

Uncle Ez grinned slyly. "You'll soon find out."

"So you can get us to Royalton?"

Uncle Ez looked at Johnny over the cup of tea in his hands, and shook his head. "Afraid not. Thumper will only do about two hundred miles on a tank of petrol."

Johnny deflated. Royalton was nearly four hundred miles away. And there was no guarantee they could find a fuel source en route.

"How about Gilbeyshire?" Nina asked.

Johnny wanted to slap himself. Of course! If they could get to Wickenham, Dame Honoria could get word quickly to the king's people—and they could spread the alarm.

Uncle Ez thought for a moment. "Well, just barely. With a good tail wind. Where in Gilbeyshire?"

"A country house called Wickenham," Johnny said.

"Let me get out my air atlas and we'll see."

Uncle Ez vanished for a minute and returned with a large, paperbound book that contained a detailed map of the Royal Kingdom, showing every known airfield and landing strip, as well as flying boat ports. He pulled a pair of bifocal spectacles out of the pocket of his blue workman's coat, rested them on his nose, and studied the map of Gilbeyshire.

"Ah, here it is. The village of Blackfield, near Wickenham. And there's an airfield not five miles away." He looked from Johnny to Nina, then to his nephew and Basil. "Yes, it can be done."

"That's fantastic!" Johnny exclaimed. "When can we leave?"

"Three or four hours to prepare and fuel Thumper," Uncle Ez said. "No more. We'll have to weigh you and Miss Bain. Any excess poundage will need to stay here. "

THUMPER THE GYROCOPTER sat out on the edge of Uncle Ez's grass landing strip, which had to be at least a mile long. The flying machine was tied down, with blocks under the wheels. Uncle Ez was walking around her, doing his final pre-flight inspection. Marko, Basil, and Brownie the mutt observed the proceedings intently. The time was about one o'clock in the afternoon.

Because of weight considerations, all Johnny would be able to bring on the flight was himself, his camera, Basil's cricket bat, and the dozen rolls of film that he'd shot in MacFreithshire. The only extra items Nina could take were her etheric goggles, which she hung around her neck, and her notebook. There was only one passenger seat in Thumper. So though it would be cramped and uncomfortable, Nina would have to make the journey sitting in Johnny's lap. Or vice versa. Johnny wasn't sure which spot would be more embarrassing.

Everyone shook hands and said goodbye. Johnny was actually sorry to leave Marko and Basil behind. Despite his early crankiness, Marko had proven a brave, stalwart companion. And Basil was simply a good kid. Johnny wouldn't mind spending more time with him.

As soon as the gyrocopter took off, the two boys would set out in the two-door coupe to find Iris Budd. With good luck, she would have gotten all the escaped kids to safety by now.

Quintus and Petunia had already left on the mission that Johnny and Nina had devised for them. They were making for Wickenham, to warn Mel and Dame Honoria about the potential attack on Royalton. With two pairs of couriers heading south, there was a better chance that the warning would get through.

"Now, Miss Bain," said Uncle Ez. "I know from the papers that you're a pilot, and a ripping good one, to boot."

Nina grinned at him and shrugged modestly.

"So I need you in the cockpit when I prop Thumper. After it's going, we'll stick you in back."

Nina agreed enthusiastically and climbed up into the cockpit. This arrangement meant Johnny had to get into the back seat and eventually have Nina sit on his lap.

"Set the magneto, Miss Bain," shouted Uncle Ez. After she flipped the switch, he spun the propeller counterclockwise, but it didn't catch. It took three more tries, before the engine roared to life. Then Nina climbed out of the cockpit and onto Johnny's lap in back. Since the flight might be cold, she had borrowed a black, hooded wool jacket from Uncle Ez. Johnny made do with an ugly purple-and-green sweater.

Uncle Ez climbed up on the wing, hopped into the cockpit, and gave a thumbs-up to Marko and Basil. The boys let loose the tie-downs and removed the blocks from under the wheels.

Johnny and Nina waved to their friends as Thumper rolled forward, picking up speed. Up above, the big horizontal rotor began turning.

It struck Johnny, bouncing along the airstrip, that the aircraft wasn't lifting off the ground. And, looking around Nina, he could see that the trees at the end of the strip were approaching rather rapidly. As his eyes widened and he held onto to his friend's arms, he hoped that he wasn't reliving what had happened that rainy night last October out on the Treport River—the near miss between floatplane and pine trees.

With absolutely no warning, the gyrocopter leapt into the air several hundred feet short of the tree line and climbed at a steep angle.

They were up. They had made it clear of the trees. Good ol' Thumper. Good ol' Uncle Ez.

For half a minute Johnny enjoyed the flight, enjoyed the Mac-Freithshire landscape spreading out beneath him. As far as he was concerned, he didn't have to come back here *ever again*. He'd had quite enough of the place.

Then, appearing out of nowhere, a grim wall of dense fog rushed toward them and enveloped the gyrocopter.

Johnny could barely see Uncle Ez up in the pilot's seat, or the ends of the gyrocopter's big rotors off to either side. They were practically in a bowl of gray soup, blinded and unable to see where they were going.

CHAPTER 35

"WHERE'D *THAT* COME FROM? " Johnny yelled.

Almost simultaneously, Uncle Ez let loose a string of expletives. "Blast!" and "Blimey!" and "Oh, darts and daggers!"

"Not fog! Not now!" Nina moaned.

Uncle Ez twisted around and bellowed at his two passengers.

"Have to take Thumper up above this muck. And hope that we fly beyond it."

Nina turned to Johnny. "If this fog doesn't clear up, we won't be able to land," she explained. "We need a visual on any landing strip, and for navigation, too."

"And if we can't get a visual?" Johnny gulped, thinking he might know the answer already.

"Then we fly until we run out of gas. And we crash. And die."

So yet again, out of the frying pan and into the fire. It seemed that every time they turned a corner, there was another rotten corner that needed turning. What Johnny would have given to be back home in Zenith, listening to Captain Justice on the radio, and being an ordinary kid.

That rotor up above was awfully loud. *Thump-thump-thump-thump...* It was now pretty clear where the gyrocopter's nickname had come from.

Johnny felt Thumper climb, as the air was getting colder and colder. With their luck, they'd probably fly right into a driving rain. So when they crashed, they'd be all soaked and chilled, in addition to being dead. But it was all out of his hands anyway. There was still the chance, though, that Quintus and Petunia would get through and alert Mel and Dame Honoria about Percy's plot.

It wasn't exactly comfy being jammed into the rear seat with Nina. Talk about a tight squeeze. And she was getting kind of heavy. His legs were starting to go numb. He could barely move, besides. Of course, it probably wasn't much more pleasant for her.

When this was all over, Johnny wanted the two of them to make a pledge to never admit that this lap-sitting thing had ever happened. If word ever got out, they would never hear the end of it.

With nothing better to do, Johnny shut his eyes and tried to doze awhile. Wouldn't do any good to get all panicky. But sleep didn't come. Not a big surprise.

Johnny started daydreaming about taking up the quest again for his lost parents—if he lived that long. He thought about the good times he and Mel and their mom and pop had had together. The trips. The family projects. The fun and games at Birchwood. He remembered how they often went to eat at Tony Weller's restaurant, where Johnny usually got the tenderloin steak burger with its delicious mushroom sauce, or the Monte Cristo sandwich. And they would talk and talk and talk, the four of them, in the middle of this busy bustling eatery, yakking out loud about school and hobbies and work and...

Uncle Ez's voice yanked him out of his reverie.

"We're over twelve thousand feet now. I'm heading roughly south by southeast. That'll get us closer to Blackfield."

Johnny wasn't enjoying the watery mist that was accumulating on his face, his hands, his clothes. Apparently it was real fog, not that dry stuff that had been plaguing MacFreithshire.

Just a couple of days ago he had been cold and miserable after nearly drowning in that dreadful culvert. And here was the water, coming at him once again. Not just blinding him, but soaking him. At the risk of being morbid, Johnny wondered which would be worse. To die by water? Or by flame? Well, naturally, the answer was that it's best to live forever.

Nina had put her etheric goggles on. Johnny didn't know why. Maybe it was to keep the mist and wind out of her eyes—the aviator goggles' original purpose. Or maybe she thought if the goggles could help her see ghosts, they might help her to see through fog. Johnny wished they could, but he knew better.

"We just hit fourteen thousand feet," Uncle Ez shouted over his shoulder a bit later. "Not much more room upstairs, I'm afraid. Have enough petrol for another hundred miles."

A moment later, they popped up through the top of the massive cloud and fog bank. "I can see the end of the clouds off ten or fifteen miles," Uncle Ez announced.

That was music to Johnny's ears. They'd be able to observe the ground again, and maybe get back on track. And if the gas was running out, they'd have a decent chance to find some place to land.

His attention had been toward the ground. But Nina urgently nudged him with her elbow and pointed skyward. "Look."

Johnny blinked up into the blue, cloudless sky stretching above them to infinity. It was so much brighter than being in the fog that, at first, he couldn't see much. The light overwhelmed his eyes.

Then he saw what Nina had seen.

"Holy maroley," he said, his jaw dropping.

Soaring along, faster even than the gyrocopter, were hundreds of ghosts, scattered off into the distance. Many were mounted on horses. Others flew under their own power. And they all seemed to be warriors. From the Middle Ages. From the Dark Age. From more recent centuries and wars. Scattered among them were sea raiders and Steppe Warriors and cavaliers.

We've flown right into the middle of a regiment of ghosts, Johnny realized. It had to be the force that Percy was sending to attack Royalton. And down below there were probably a whole bunch of bog zombies heading toward the great city.

Johnny had to get down on the ground *now* and sound the alarm. This was real proof that an attack was on the way.

"Uncle Ez," he hollered. "We've got to land as quickly as we can. We've got to tell people what we're seeing."

Uncle Ez twisted around as best he could, looking puzzled. "What're we seeing, then?"

Johnny had forgotten that Uncle Ez didn't have etheric vision. He had no idea they were surrounded by deadly combatants.

"There's a ghost force all around us," Johnny said. "And I think they're heading for Royalton. Take us down first chance you get."

Uncle Ez nodded, then gave Johnny the thumbs-up sign.

"Uh-oh," Nina said rather loudly.

Johnny's blood was cold already from the fog, but it cooled a few more degrees upon hearing her utterance.

"What?" he asked dismally.

"Over to the left. Is that who I think it is?"

Johnny twisted his head. There, a hundred feet away, was a Steppe Warrior charging along, seemingly oblivious of the gyrocopter. It looked an awful lot like Burilgi. If it was him, and he should happen to see who was sitting in this rear seat, they were utterly defenseless.

"Nina, you're right. I think it might be Burilgi. Pull up your hood and slump down, like you've fallen asleep. I'm gonna do the same. With any luck, he won't even notice us. And take off your goggles—they're a dead giveaway." Nina did just that.

Johnny leaned against the side of the aircraft facing away from the Steppe Warrior. He would wait a moment, then take a peek. By then, Burilgi should be gone. The ghost, after all, was flying faster than the gyrocopter.

Johnny counted up to sixty seconds. Then he slowly moved, still keeping his face hidden, until he could see off to the left.

He managed not to jerk in surprise. If he had, it would have been the end.

There was Burilgi, not forty feet off Thumper's port side, galloping along, regarding the aircraft and its occupants with a certain curiosity. Of course, Uncle Ez wasn't aware of those empty eye sockets coldly studying him. But Johnny and Nina had to convince the warrior wraith that these wet, chilly passengers were unworthy of his interest. Lucky, Johnny thought, that Nina was wearing the black, hooded jacket. Burilgi couldn't even see her face.

But the Steppe Warrior came in closer yet. Johnny thought that those bleeding eye sockets revealed some glimmering of recognition. The specter seemed to know who they were!

A scowl formed on Burilgi's flat, cruel face. He began to withdraw his sword from its scabbard.

Johnny was frozen in place, unable to do anything but watch that curved blade reveal itself. There was nothing he could do to defend himself and Nina. Without even thinking, he held on to her even tighter. Twelve and three-quarter years wasn't a long time to be around, but at least he'd packed it with a lot of neat adventures. It could've been worse. And they wouldn't die alone.

Just as Johnny was saying his final goodbyes to the world, their rescuer—who had no idea he was rescuing anyone—came dashing out of nowhere, right up to Burilgi. Another Steppe Warrior.

The two ghosts exchanged a few words. With the noise of the rushing wind and the thumping rotor above, Johnny had no idea what they said to each other. But it caused Burilgi to re-sheath his sword, give one contemptuous look in Johnny's direction, and charge forward with the other ghost. They easily outpaced the gyrocopter and flew quickly out of sight.

"I think we're okay," Johnny told Nina. "You can straighten up."

"What happened?" she asked breathlessly. "I feel practically blind now without my goggles."

Johnny told her. He was about to inform Uncle Ez that they had just had a very close call when he noticed that the gyrocopter was descending. There was clear visibility beneath them, the rolling green landscape stretching out ahead.

Uncle Ez twisted around and shouted back to them. "We've had a bit of luck. I can see Chapswith Castle down there, with its oval moat. Blackfield and Wickenham aren't too much further."

CHAPTER 36

FRIDAY, FEBRUARY 7, 1936

WICKENHAM

GRANDMOTHER HAD APPOINTED BAO the official ghost greeter at Wickenham. All morning long the little wraith haunted the grand entrance hall and front staircase, waiting for ghosts who flew in to report on their searches through Mac-Freithshire for Johnny and Nina. Whenever a new ghost turned up, Bao would look at him or her eagerly, hoping to see a happy or encouraging expression. But most of what she got were grim and downcast looks.

She always asked, "Any sign of Johnny and Nina?"

No one ever said yes.

In the small sitting room where Grandmother questioned her ghost searchers, all Bao heard was that *this* district or *that* village or *those* farms had been thoroughly gone over, with fine-tooth combs. And no sign of the two missing youngsters had turned up.

The mood in Wickenham certainly hadn't improved the evening before, when Colonel MacFarlane and his troopers had finally come back from the north. The colonel blamed himself for losing the two youngsters at the train wreck, and no one could persuade him otherwise.

At lunch Bao listened as Grandmother, the professor, and Mel discussed the weird headaches and stomachaches that ghosts up north were reporting. They wondered if the ailments had anything to do with the mysterious fog that kept appearing and disappearing. Mel ominously suggested that Percy had somehow upset the balance of the ether, causing these effects.

"Maybe by reanimating so many dead bodies," she said, "Percy has caused some part of the ether to intrude into the physical world. What if he has created some kind of connection between the two universes?"

The professor raised his index finger. "That's an interesting idea. Percy may be drawing a sort of miasma from the ether, which we perceive as the fog. And, being of the ether, it affects the residents of the ether—the ghosts."

"Exactly," she said. "The irony is that Percy may not even realize the unintended consequences of his actions."

Dame Honoria shook her head and groaned. "Sometimes I wonder if he's doing all this just to torment me. I often think that I should never have made him eat all those prunes when he was little."

The ghost searchers that continued to arrive were of all different sorts and sizes. Bao had rarely seen such a variety of wraiths. But they all had one thing in common—none of them had found a trace of Johnny or Nina.

As badly as Bao felt about this—because she still had a hopeless crush on Johnny, and Nina wasn't too bad a person—she felt sorrier for Mel. The young woman took the loss of her brother and Nina very hard indeed. Even a letter from her friend Danny Kailolu failed to lift her spirits.

Later that afternoon Bao asked the colonel if she could ride along on his patrol up in the sky. She thought some company might help to take his mind off his worries about Johnny and Nina. And she loved flying with him and Buck.

Bao sat in front of the colonel on Buck and gazed up, down, sideways, backward, and forward, on alert for anything suspicious. She did see lots of ghosts. But there were always ghosts flying around up above Wickenham—just as ghosts flew around everywhere. The ones Bao saw were the local wraiths "mooning about," as Mel liked to say.

Several thousand feet in the air, trotting along on Buck, Bao could see great distances. Even though it was still wintertime in the Royal Kingdom, the rolling hills down below looked green and rich. She could only imagine what her father, a farmer of rice and other crops, would have given for land like this, rather than the sparse, hard ground and small paddies he had to work with back home.

The sun peeked through puffy white clouds, but far to the north a dense fog bank covered the land. Off over Bao's left shoulder came a strange mechanical sound—a distant, barely audible *thump-thump-thump-thump*. She twisted her head around and squinted back in that direction. It was some kind of flying machine, but not like any she had ever seen.

"What is that?" she asked the colonel.

The bearded officer took a look over his left shoulder and shrugged. "Don't know, Miss Bao. Shall we go have a look?"

"Yes, please, let's."

They galloped in a broad semi-circle back toward the peculiar aeroplane.

Bao could see that the thing was quite different from the flying boats that she had ridden on. It was small. And it had no great wing to hold it up in the air. Instead, the aircraft had some kind of giant blade going around up above, while a smaller blade spun in front. There was a bearded man in flying goggles in the pilot's seat. Bao saw a passenger. Or maybe it was two passengers.

Suddenly, the strange flying machine banked away and started to descend.

"I think he's making for that landing strip down below," the colonel said. "And we had better go check him out."

CHAPTER 37

IT'S NOT THAT JOHNNY DIDN'T like Nina. But he was getting awfully sick of being crammed into the little cockpit with her jammed onto his lap. Fortunately, their flight south was almost over. Uncle Ez was heading for a broad, grassy stretch down below—the Blackfield aeroport.

"We have to get to Wickenham in a big hurry," Johnny yelled in Nina's ear. "Dame Honoria can phone her contacts about the attack on Royalton. Maybe we're not too late." But when he thought about those flying ghost warriors they had encountered, he feared that time may have already run out.

They came in over what looked like a vineyard, then flew almost on top of a large herd of cows, and finally settled down on the long grass strip with hardly a jolt or joggle. They rolled to a stop close to a hangar that resembled Uncle Ez's back in Mac-Freithshire. By this time, the big rotor up above had stopped turning. Uncle Ez killed the engine and clumsily got himself back on solid ground.

Nina climbed out of the back seat. Johnny followed, hanging his Ritterflex back around his neck. He could still feel the pins and needles in his legs and feet when he hit the ground, but at least he didn't collapse in a heap. He checked to make sure all his film rolls were safely in his pockets.

Uncle Ez cupped a hand to his mouth. "Anyone at home?" he hollered.

The door of the nearby cottage—brick below and thatched roof above—swung open.

Johnny cringed a little, half expecting some angry farmer with a shotgun to emerge. Instead, a tall woman in knee pants and heavy wool sweater came out, wiping her hands on a red towel. She stared at Johnny and his friends, then at Thumper. A toothy smile broke out on her weathered, freckled face.

"Low on petrol, are we?"

It turned out the woman was a flier herself, proud owner of an old army air corps biplane. She and Uncle Ez instantly struck up a conversation about the gyrocopter. They were so deep into their discussion that Johnny had to interrupt them by tugging on Uncle Ez's arm.

"Excuse me," he said. "But we need to get to Wickenham as quickly as possible."

"Maybe we can lend a hand," said a voice from above him.

Johnny jumped about a foot, then looked up. There, hovering in midair, were Colonel MacFarlane, Bao, and Buck.

"Am I ever happy to see you guys!" Johnny exclaimed. "Can Nina and I hitch a quick ride to Wickenham?"

AFTER SAYING GOODBYE to Uncle Ez and his new lady friend, Johnny and Nina hopped aboard Buck. The colonel flew them straight back to Wickenham, with Bao zooming along beside. When they arrived, the two youngsters jumped off the ghost horse and raced up the front stairs and into the stately old house.

With Bao in the lead, they went in through the entrance hall, past all those glorious paintings, then turned down the long hallway to the library. The door was open and all three of them burst in. The room smelled like a used bookstore, like old paper.

"Grandmother, I found them!" Bao shouted.

Dame Honoria, hunched over her desk, looked up. When she saw Johnny and Nina standing there, her long, gloomy face lit up like an electric bulb.

"You're alive!" she gasped. "You're alive! Melanie, see who's here!"

Mel, with dark circles under her eyes, blinked up from her desk. Then it was her turn to look amazed. "You're safe!"

Not that he didn't expect it, but Johnny quickly found himself smothered in Dame Honoria's firm embrace, while Mel was hugging Nina. Then the two older women exchanged their victims for another round of hugs—but fortunately very few kisses. Dame Honoria got two or three in, on Johnny's forehead.

By now, Professor DeNimes—who appeared to have been sleeping at his desk—had joined the scrum. He slapped Johnny on his back and said, "Good job, old boy, good job."

Johnny grinned at the professor. "Real glad to see you, too."

The onslaught of affection took another moment to run its course. Then Mel grabbed Johnny by the shoulders and looked him straight in the eyes, in that big-sisterly way of hers. Johnny knew what was coming.

"Where have you two been? We've been worried sick about you. Why didn't you get word to us?"

"It's been a week since that train wreck," Dame Honoria said.

"And it's as if you both vanished from the face of the earth."

"You haven't seen an Imperial centurion ghost and a little dead blonde girl, have you?" Johnny asked.

Mel looked baffled. "What in the world are you talking about?"

"Guess you haven't. But now we've got some real important intelligence that you have to get to the authorities."

Then, in a torrent of words, Johnny and Nina told about what they'd seen up at fourteen thousand feet not an hour earlier. And how Percy and Pamela Worthington-Smythe themselves had made menacing mention of Royalton. And how if you put everything together, it seemed that a massive ghost assault on the capital might be imminent.

"We even sent two ghosts here to warn you, in case we didn't make it," Johnny continued. "That's the centurion and the girl ghost. Guess they got lost or something." Johnny hoped that Petunia and Quintus were okay. He'd feel awful if anything happened to them. And what about Raj? Had he gotten word through to the SGS about the zombie camp at Bilbury Hall?

Dame Honoria marched over to her telephone, talked to the local operator, and waited for a line to Royalton. She first spoke to the home secretary's assistant, and gave him Johnny and Nina's report. Then she called her contact in the royal household. She quietly and urgently repeated what Johnny and Nina had told her, then listened. She said goodbye, set the hand piece back in the receiver, and marched back to Johnny and Nina.

"We are to report immediately to the king at Castle Henry," she said gravely. "In person. Johnny and Nina, I'll have the upstairs maid draw two quick baths for you and lay out changes of clothes. You appear to need them. We'll leave as soon as you're spick-and-span, and ready to go."

CHAPTER 38

BEFORE THEY LEFT WICKENHAM, Johnny had a quick visit with the colonel and the soldiers of the First Zenith Cavalry Brigade. To a man, they were impressed with his tale of flooded culverts, zombie battles, and the gyrocopter flight. Johnny had his back slapped more than a few times.

Some of the ghost troopers' stories were equally hair-raising. The battle of the derailed train had been fierce and terribly treacherous in the fog—where the danger of mistakenly attacking a comrade was ever present. By the time the colonel and his men, assisted by SGS agents and army soldiers, had driven off the zombies and their ghost allies, it was too late to find Johnny and the others, though they searched and searched.

Sergeant Clegg kept apologizing, but Johnny blamed it on the confusion of battle and his own stupid decision to shoot off a flashbulb. For their part, the ghost troopers felt that there was something about the fog that, as Private Boo put it, "took the sap right out of a feller."

By the time they started for Castle Henry, it was dusk. Johnny, Nina, Mel, and Dame Honoria spent the drive catching up on the past week's events. Johnny wanted to know about Uncle Louie. Mel said she had sent word to him about the kids' disappearance.

He was supposed to arrive at Wickenham the next day, to help with the hunt.

The report of Percy's late night visit to Wickenham's library caused Johnny's jaw to drop. That scoundrel sure got around. But Johnny was excited to learn that the clues Percy had unintentionally provided all pointed to Okkatek Island—the very spot where Johnny's parents, Lydia and Will Graphic, were last seen. Mel and Dame Honoria had already made plans for an expedition there in a few weeks.

Word of Ozzie Eccleston's fate—shipped in a wooden box to Old Number One—gave Johnny a good laugh. He'd like to see the guy try to mooch a free hamburger on an abandoned tropical island.

The two-hour drive went quickly, interrupted only by munching on sandwiches and sipping of tea from thermoses.

The long limousine finally rolled to a stop at a checkpoint manned by soldiers of the Royal Army. A lieutenant with an improbable baby face peered into the back of the auto in a self-important manner. Dame Honoria explained that they had been summoned to meet with the king, on a matter of national security.

Looking at the odd group, the young officer rolled his eyes and shook his head.

"Madam," he said, "I'm sure his majesty would enjoy a chat with you, but I'm afraid he's rather busy this evening."

"Lieutenant McKenzie," a man's voice barked. "What is going on here?"

As if he had some kind of powerful spring down his spine and legs, the lieutenant jumped to attention, rotated to face someone whom Johnny couldn't see, and snapped off a very crisp salute.

"Some civilians, *sir*. I've told them they cannot be admitted to Castle Henry under the present circumstances, *sir!*"

"Have they identified themselves, Lieutenant?"

"Yes, *sir!* A lady called Dame Honoria Rathbone and her companions, *sir!*"

"Lieutenant, you are dismissed. I'll handle it from here."

"Yes, *sir!*" The young officer snapped off another salute and strode away.

Then a somewhat familiar face appeared in Dame Honoria's open passenger window. It took Johnny a second or two to remember the man.

"Brigadier Stafferton!" he exclaimed.

It was the fly-fisherman from the day of their first visit to Castle Henry. He had been at the same creek where they had enjoyed their picnic lunch. The convalescing brigadier had told Johnny that he was waiting for his next assignment, which was top secret. Now Johnny knew what that assignment was.

"We've been expecting you and your friends, Master Graphic," the brigadier said. "Please follow me."

They trailed behind the brigadier's olive-drab vehicle and parked next to it, by a single-story, wood-frame building off to the west of the big mansion. Everyone filed into a cramped office filled with cabinets, desks, and several soldiers banging away on typewriters. In the corner was a fancy shortwave radio setup, which caught Nina's eye in a big hurry.

The brigadier sat down behind a gray metal desk and invited his guests to pull up chairs opposite him. "Tell me first about what you saw in the sky this afternoon, then everything else."

Dame Honoria cleared her throat. "I was under the impression that we were to speak directly to his majesty."

"His majesty regrets that he will be unable to meet with you this evening," the brigadier explained. "For purposes of his personal security, we have placed him in a secret and safe location within the castle. We have a whole regiment deployed around the perimeter, nearly a thousand men. Circumstances have changed since you were in touch with his assistant earlier today. Whatever intelligence you provide will be relayed to him promptly."

Johnny and Nina recounted their shock and horror up in the air when they saw the flying ghost force. Then they told about their various encounters with Percy and his henchmen—particularly what Nina had heard and seen while being held captive in Bilbury Hall. Johnny noted that Nina had been able to dispense with one of the bog zombies by smashing it in the knee. The soldiers here, he said, might want to know about that tactic.

The baby-faced lieutenant rushed into the office. He saluted his superior. "Reports from pickets, sir."

"Yes, Lieutenant McKenzie?" the brigadier said.

The lieutenant gulped and steadied himself. "Sir, we're being surrounded. Zombies and ghosts by the hundreds. On all four sides of Castle Henry. The major requires you at the command post immediately!"

CHAPTER 39

IT WAS AS IF JOHNNY and his companions didn't exist.

The brigadier jumped to his feet and snapped at the radioman in the corner, hunched over his equipment. "You heard the lieutenant. Notify the Ministry of War that we're threatened with attack. And the rest of you—to your posts!"

Then the brigadier and the lieutenant led a hurried exodus from the cramped office. Except for the radioman, all the soldiers working there headed outside, grabbing rifles that were leaning against the wall by the door and snatching battle helmets from pegs. No one even gave a backward glance to the civilians left behind.

Dame Honoria groaned. "It looks like my darling sweetums has thrown us into the soup again!"

Johnny noticed that, at last, Dame Honoria was pronouncing her former term of endearment for her son with a tone of sarcasm. He felt sorry for her. What must it be like to have your own flesh and blood become a megalomaniac? For a few seconds, he tried to imagine Mel as a dark force of evil. The thought was so ridiculous he almost laughed out loud.

Nina was rubbing the temples of her head with her fingers. "Maybe those ghosts we saw this morning weren't even heading for Royalton."

"Maybe Percy has been after the king all along," Mel said.

Johnny had a very scary thought. "Or maybe Percy has enough ghosts and zombies to attack several places at once."

"Well, we can't let him capture the king," Mel declared. "Snatching the head of state would give Percy incredible power to extort concessions."

Johnny stood up and started to pace. "So what can we do to help?"

"These are professional soldiers, Johnny," said Dame Honoria. "Not too likely they would appreciate having women and children manning the battlements with them."

"But we have far more experience fighting zombies and ghosts than any of them," he protested. "They need to know that zombies have weak knees and you can finish them off—at least release the ghost inside of 'em—by decapitation. And Sparks could tell them her idea about the zombie skin."

Johnny looked at Nina for confirmation and noticed that she appeared uncomfortable, almost sick. He knew that her right arm still hurt a bit and was sometimes numb, from whatever had happened to her in Bilbury Hall.

"Are you okay, Sparks?" This had been the day from hell, and it looked like it would stretch long into the night. Nina probably wouldn't have a chance to rest anytime soon.

"I'm all right," she answered. "Just a little pooped."

"Tell them about seeing the bog zombies and the potion," Johnny urged. "It might be important."

Nina turned to Dame Honoria and Mel, who both looked quite

interested. "Before they took me upstairs to the room where they held me, I saw them doing something kind of weird in the kitchen at Bilbury Hall."

Dame Honoria nodded encouragingly. "Yes, my dear, go ahead."

"Well," Nina began, "they had tubs of some kind of thick cream or soft wax. The zombies took it, and rubbed it all over their faces, hands, arms, and legs. And it was as if it made them more flexible. After they put it on, they kind of stretched, as if they'd been stiff or something."

"Hmm, I wonder," Mel said.

Dame Honoria raised her eyebrows. "Are you thinking what I'm thinking?"

"Well, it does seem a bit obvious. Those corpses have been in the bogs for a thousand years, under the cold, damp pressure of the peat. What if, when they come up into the regular atmosphere, their skin starts drying out? What if they need some kind of lubrication to stay limber?"

"Yes. If their skin dries out too much, it would be very difficult for them to move, much less make mayhem."

"Did you see them doing anything else, Nina?" asked Mel.

"No," Nina replied. "Some of them started to take their clothes off, to put on more of the cream, I guess. That's when I pretended to pass out. I didn't want to see any of those naked, wrinkled-up, disgusting dead bodies."

"Very understandable," Dame Honoria observed.

"There's one other thing," Mel said, almost to herself. "The reason those bodies were so well preserved is that the bog environment prevented bacteria from decomposing them. Wonder what would happen if they were exposed to a solution of some type with a high bacteria count."

Johnny could almost see the wheels turning around in his sister's head. What was she coming up with?

"It's important that we tell the brigadier what Nina saw," Dame Honoria intoned. "There may yet be time to act upon her information."

JOHNNY WAS AFRAID the brigadier would forget all about them, seeing as how he had his hands full commanding the defense of Castle Henry. And they did sit in the office for a while, darkly communing with their own thoughts. Johnny paced. Mel hunched over in her chair, chin in hand, probably pondering some kind of anti-zombie tactic. Dame Honoria had shut her eyes, pretending to sleep. And Nina just looked beat, drooping in her chair.

So far they had heard no gunfire, no sounds of conflict. Johnny figured that meant the ghosts and zombies surrounding the great estate had avoided contact with the brigadier's troops. But just after midnight, Lieutenant McKenzie came rushing in.

"The brigadier said that he saw the ghost soldiers from the First Border War when you arrived this evening."

"They're just outside," Mel said. "Colonel MacFarlane and the boys."

The baby-faced lieutenant looked immeasurably relieved. "The truth of the matter, miss, is that while we have some lads from the Special Ghost Service and a handful of regular troops who can see ghosts, we are a bit short in that department. I am confident that we can handle the, uh, zombies..." He shook his head as he uttered that word, as if his military training had never prepared him for such a situation. "But we surely could use the help of your dead friends to defend against any ghosts that we may be facing. And your good selves, as well, if you're willing to go into harm's way."

About time we were asked to help, Johnny thought. "We've been in harm's way pretty much steadily since the beginning of October, Lieutenant. Ghost assassins, midair battles, blindness, the biggest bomb ever…"

The lieutenant seemed a stoic sort of guy, but even he looked a little shocked at Johnny's litany of perils. "You saw the etheric bomb?"

"Nearly got killed by it," Johnny said.

"Some of the things we've seen and done have to remain top secret for many years to come," Mel added. "That's the honest truth. We'd get in big trouble if we told you anything more."

"Of course. Now come with me."

They all trooped out of the office, across the courtyard, and into a large army tent that smelled damp and mildewy. The brigadier was in there, talking intensely with a group of soldiers—officers, sergeants, and enlisted men. When he saw Johnny and the others, he waved them to come over.

Lieutenant McKenzie snapped off a salute. "Our friends here have agreed to your request, Brigadier."

"Good, good, thank you all," the brigadier said. "Now, these lads can see ghosts." He gestured at the soldiers he had been talking to. "With your permission, I would like to divide up your Border War troopers and place them with these men. We're going to attempt to cover the entire perimeter of Castle Henry. That is about three miles of line. The mission is to minimize any infiltration of ghosts. Will that be agreeable?"

Mel and Johnny turned simultaneously to the colonel, who had followed them in.

"You heard the man, Colonel," said Mel. "Is that okay?"

"That would be absolutely splendid, Commander," the colonel answered. "The boys are itching for another go at the enemy."

"And the rest of you can do tremendous good," the brigadier

continued, "by taking places at observation posts along our perimeter. I'm promised reinforcements by morning, but we need to hold Castle Henry until then."

This time Dame Honoria answered for the group.

"You can count on us, Brigadier. But before we leave for the... Well, for the *front*, my young friend here, Miss Nina Bain, has interesting tactical intelligence about some of our adversaries' potential vulnerabilities."

CHAPTER 40

SATURDAY, FEBRUARY 8, 1936

CASTLE HENRY

JOHNNY WAS HUDDLED in a hastily dug foxhole with Lieutenant McKenzie and Sergeant Clegg. Off to either side were other soldiers in other quickly excavated hollows in the open field south of Castle Henry. They all had weapons, of course. Sabers, bayonets, and rifles. A machine gun off to the right. And Clegg had his double-barreled Old Equalizer.

For his part, Johnny would have to rely on Basil's cricket bat. But now he had a good idea how to use the thing, and he intended to whack a few zombie knees.

Tall light poles scattered around the estate cast dim illumination over the grounds. The bounteous stars above offered a bit more visibility. Not much to see by, but probably enough to reveal any hulking shapes charging at them.

As for the enemy ghosts, Johnny and Sergeant Clegg would scan for their telltale green glow, then warn the soldiers if they spotted any. It would be hard for any attacking specter to hide his glimmer.

The first sign of action came on toward one in the morning. Johnny had dozed off for a while when Sergeant Clegg woke him with a nudge to the shoulder. "Ghost lights out there," the Zenith trooper whispered. "A half dozen of them. Coming in toward us slow and steady. Behind them, some bog zombies, I think."

Johnny told Lieutenant McKenzie about the incoming forces and where they were. The officer called over to the machine gun crew and said something like "commence probing fire at your eleven o'clock." Johnny understood that to mean a bit to the left and across the field. He had heard nothing from other posts around the perimeter—no shouting, no gunfire—so this would be the first action of the night.

Suddenly the machine gun stuttered a dozen shots at the spot Johnny had described, red tracer bullets slicing through the night. The racket was loud and shocking. Then the gun repeated itself— *tat-tat-tat-tat-tat-tat-tat.*

There were guttural shouts and barks of anger from across the field. The machine gun had stung the advancing wraiths a little, it seemed. It was hard to shoot ghosts when you couldn't see them, but a spray of slugs gave you a decent chance of hitting them a few times. The point was not to stop them, but simply delay them a bit.

"The ghosts have retreated," Johnny reported, surveying the field with the binoculars that McKenzie had given him. "The zombies, too."

That was when a machine gun erupted off to the north. Another probing attack, Johnny supposed. Then silence.

He thought about how nerve-wracking it would be to live the soldier's life. Waiting. Wondering. Anticipating the next attack. And just when you start to relax, BOOM. You're caught off-guard. Never knowing when your number would be up.

It made sense to conduct these kinds of random attacks, he figured. You caused your enemy to feel jittery. And jittery foes might make bad decisions.

But if Johnny had been in Percy's position, he would have sent the entire force of zombies and ghost warriors at them all at once. That type of attack probably could overwhelm the defenders in a single wave.

What happened next made him wonder if Percy had somehow figured out how to read his mind. For out of the darkness on the other side of the field came ranks of ghosts, charging forward. Some on horseback, others on foot, still more flying under their own power. Behind them loped the zombies, waving axes and bludgeons and other brutal-looking hand weapons. There must have been hundreds of them.

Johnny warned the lieutenant, who shouted to his machine gunner. The terrible weapon clattered to life, making a deafening din.

But the bullets seemed to have little effect this time—the ghost warriors kept coming. Johnny was sure they would be overrun until the very last second, when the wraith force retreated once again. What was the enemy up to? Were they just testing the king's defenses?

Lieutenant McKenzie began talking on his portable radio unit, briefly explaining the situation. He listened for half a moment. "Yes sir," he said into the hand piece. "Understood." Then he jumped to his feet and shouted, first in one direction, then the other. "Pull back to the next position, lads." Johnny could hear soldiers up and down the line relaying the order.

They were making a tactical withdrawal. Not retreating, Sergeant Clegg told Johnny, but going to a position where they could more easily delay, or perhaps even defeat, their adversary. Johnny wasn't sure if this would work, given that the adversaries were ghosts and zombies. But it seemed the best chance they had of surviving this night alive, until reinforcements arrived.

He darted back up a narrow lane with several dozen soldiers, his cricket bat in hand, the binoculars bouncing on his chest. Up on his ghost horse, Sergeant Clegg brought up the rear, ready to keep any pursuers away with his Old Persuader. They all made for the big barns.

Johnny joined Nina in one of the structures. All the lights were out. Dozens of horses could be heard moving nervously about in their stalls, snorting and whinnying. The place reeked with a weird, sour smell.

Electric pumps and hoses had been set up by the open windows. A dozen Castle Henry workers, in their blue workmen's coats, stood ready by the pumps. Several soldiers gripped the hoses and spray nozzles.

The king's workers were mostly older than the soldiers, and certainly far older than Johnny and Nina. But behind those weatherworn faces and gray hair, Johnny saw pure grit and determination. He figured they were as outraged as anyone at such an attack on his majesty, and were willing to give their lives to defend their monarch.

It was a waiting game now. Johnny told Nina about the skirmish in the field. Soon the real fight would start—the all-or-nothing attempt to destroy the attacking bog zombies for good. He could tell that Nina was pretty jumpy from the quaver in her voice.

"I just want this over and done with, one way or the other," she said. "My arm hurts like the dickens and I have a splitting headache. I'm exhausted. I feel like I can't think straight anymore."

That's when Lieutenant McKenzie, standing near one of the pumps, told them to hush. "I have a report of incoming hostiles heading this way. We mustn't reveal ourselves."

Johnny quickly buttoned up his lip, and so did Nina. It would be awful if their yammering tipped off the bad guys.

The soldiers inside the stable had fixed bayonets to their rifles, ready to charge out into the midst of the enemy. Johnny looked at the soldiers—many of them not much older than him—and wondered who would live and who would die. Because this would surely be a terrible, treacherous hand-to-hand fight.

"Here they come!" the lieutenant shouted. "Get ready!"

Johnny and Nina stared out the window from several feet back, so they wouldn't be seen. Johnny's heart was beating so loudly that he worried the zombies might hear it. This was it, the moment of truth for the plan that Nina's inside knowledge had inspired.

"Nina," he whispered urgently. "Put on your goggles. Quick. There may be ghosts around, too."

Just as she secured her etheric eyepieces, one, then another, and another, and several more hulking figures loped toward the barn.

"NOW!" Lieutenant McKenzie bellowed.

Four electric pumps thrummed to life.

Within a couple of seconds, sprays of liquid were showering out onto the bog zombies.

Johnny couldn't help himself and rushed to the window for a better look, with Nina right behind him. The zombies had stopped in their tracks, looking confused—their leathery faces and hands dripping, their cloaks and coats soaking.

The creatures just stood there, silently. A few of them looked down at the cobblestones covered with soapy bubbles.

Then the remaining three pumps came to life. They sprayed the zombies with a second liquid—this one creating a terrible stench.

CHAPTER 41

THE AIR FILLED with the frightful, keening noise of something inhuman screaming in agony.

In the courtyard, zombies were scratching and clawing at their faces. Almost all the attackers who had gotten soaked were hopping about, ripping off their clothing, trying desperately to wipe the fluid they'd been sprayed with from their skin. Axes and swords and cudgels clattered to the cobblestones.

But even as the doused zombies fell to the ground in agony, a second wave of zombies came up behind them. And there was no more solution in the pumps. The next part of the fight would be man-to-zombie.

Lieutenant McKenzie pushed the stable doors open. "*Now, boys!*"

Several dozen Royal soldiers poured out to meet the new assault. As the horses in their stalls whinnied with terror, Johnny and Nina rushed to the stable door and stared out at the melee of man and zombie. Just in case, Johnny had Basil's cricket bat in hand, and Nina a short sword she had borrowed from Dame Honoria's collection.

Soldiers and zombies traded blows. Axe versus rifle and bayonet. Sword versus sword.

CLASH and CLANG!
SMASH and BANG!
THUD and THUMP!
BOOM and BUMP!

Men and zombies fell to the cobblestones. It was impossible to know who was winning. Everything was jumbled and shadowy—a confusion of violence.

But one thing was for sure. If the first wave of zombies hadn't been knocked out of action—and they were still writhing helplessly on the pavement, practically scratching their skin off—the fight might have already been over.

By now, the lieutenant's platoon had managed to disable many of the newer zombie attackers with their slashing, stabbing bayonets, which proved effective at keeping axes and cudgels at a distance. The tide appeared to be turning.

Already, Johnny had seen several ghosts pop right out of the "dead" bog zombies—erupting out of the slashed and punctured skin. It appeared that many of the ghosts animating these ancient corpses had had enough of the fight. They flew straight up into the night sky and disappeared. Johnny wondered if they had been duped by Percy into thinking that they were invincible and invulnerable. But now that they were being beaten, fewer and fewer of them remained in the fight.

"Johnny!" screeched Nina.

Lurching out of the shadows to their right came a zombie. It lifted a heavy cudgel as if it meant to smash in their brains.

Trying to decoy the zombie away from Nina, Johnny spurted out of the barn and straight into the courtyard. Then he nimbly changed direction, cutting right. The zombie tried to follow, but the cobblestones were wet and very slick from all the liquid that had been sprayed out there. The creature's hard, hobnailed boots slipped out from beneath it and it went down with a resonant *thuuud*.

It scrambled upright again, an expression of grim determination on its distorted, leathery face. Then it came after Johnny, who scampered like a demented monkey, trying to dodge the creature. He flitted right, left, and backward, just out of reach of that nasty-looking cudgel. A few swings came awfully close, one grazing Johnny's left shoulder and smarting like the dickens.

The zombie finally stopped its pursuit and headed back to the barn, no doubt to see if it might have better luck attacking Nina. Johnny saw an abandoned mace lying just over by the stable wall. He managed to grab it and heave it at the zombie. It hit the back of the thing's left foot.

"I'm over here, you dumb old blockhead!" Johnny shouted, hoping the mace and the insult would draw the zombie away from Nina.

It did. Faster than Johnny expected.

The zombie charged at him full speed, cudgel hefted as if to crush Johnny's skull. For a second time, though, one of Johnny's agile moves left his adversary down on the cobblestones, this time in a puddle of sprayed liquid. Its cudgel had rolled a couple of yards away, out of reach.

As the creature struggled to get upright again, Johnny rushed in and delivered a terrifically hard *whaaack* of his cricket bat to its left knee. His undead adversary howled with pain and tried to grab for its cudgel. Then Johnny hit the hand that was doing the grabbing.

The zombie was a stubborn one, though, and kept trying to get back into the fight. Johnny's blows to knee and hand had certainly hurt it, but not put it out of commission altogether. But having to put its hands into the spray liquid seemed to be causing it even greater distress, as it tried frantically to wipe them on its filthy tunic.

"I think that guy's a little mad at us, Sparks," Johnny panted as Nina came to help him. "Better if we don't stick around."

"Back in the stable, then?" Nina replied. "Hide with the horses?"

"Best idea you've had all night."

They backed away, keeping their eyes on their tormenter, which was still preoccupied with the condition of its hands.

To their left, they heard running footsteps. It was Lieutenant McKenzie, rushing toward them, his army saber held out in front of him. He approached the zombie, which looked up helplessly.

Johnny almost felt sorry for the repulsive old thing.

The lieutenant whipped his blade downward and to the left. The zombie's homely head was suddenly dangling from its shoulders by a scrap of skin and gristle.

Not a second later, the green figure of a ghost spurted up and out of the zombie's body, which collapsed in a heap. The specter seemed confused, frantic, looking for something.

Johnny was thunderstruck. It wasn't some ancient warrior after all. It was a teenaged boy dressed in the ragged clothes of a nineteenth century street urchin—a beggar or pickpocket, most likely. Then the boy ghost caught sight of Johnny and flitted over like a hummingbird.

"I didn't wanna hurt no one," the boy ghost said, his nose just inches from Johnny's. He had a round face and freckles, like Johnny, but black hair sticking out every which way. "But I wanted to be *real* again. Terrible bad. I wanted to be flesh again. So I took that rum old thing to live in. It wasn't much, but it was all I had."

He made a head nod in the direction of the ruined bog zombie that sprawled on the cobblestones. "Trouble is, the living won't let us be. Your lot don't want us ghosts to be real again. That's why we're fightin' for our rights, for our place in the real world. Good ol' Lord Percy's told us so, and we believe him. It's not over, boy. Not by a long shot. Just you wait."

Johnny was speechless. He didn't know what to say. This ghost—which a couple of minutes ago had been a frightening monster trying to beat Johnny's brains into jelly—almost sounded sensible.

"Here's a little thank-you present, mate," the ghost smirked. He snapped back his right arm and punched Johnny in the nose.

Johnny tumbled backward into the stable, onto something squishy and smelly. He rubbed his throbbing beak, and there was blood on his fingers. Looking up, he saw Nina. But the urchin wraith had vanished.

Nina grabbed his hand and hauled him to his feet. "I think that kid didn't like you very much," she said with a grin.

"Dah feelig's mooojel," Johnny said.

"Here's a handkerchief for your nose."

"Thaaags, Sbargs." Johnny blew some blood out into the beige linen and waited for the twinkles in his vision to fade away.

Then it struck him.

There was no more noise from the courtyard. No sound of blade on blade, of cudgel on flesh.

He and Nina stepped out of the stable and saw soldiers standing over dozens of bog zombie remains. Johnny wasn't sure what to call a corpse that had come back to life and had "died" again. But whatever the word was, these were it.

Lieutenant McKenzie walked over to join them. "I never thought I'd be so grateful to a group of civilians. But without your idea for the spray solutions, many good men and women might have died. And this realm might have lost its monarch."

"You've got Nina to thank for being such a sharp secret agent,"

Johnny said. "Without her clue, we might never have figured it out."

"It just made sense," Nina said, reprising her idea. "If the zombies' skin needed to be oiled or greased, then *degreasing* them would make their lives, so to speak, more difficult. And what dissolves grease? Ordinary washing detergent."

Johnny beamed at her. "It was a swell idea, Sparks."

Nina shrugged and smiled back at him. "Well, the second round of spray was Mel's idea, and it was pretty clever, too. She figured the bacteria in liquid fertilizer would cause the zombie skin to start decomposing."

"And they had a good supply of the stuff around here," the lieutenant laughed. "Worked a treat, didn't it? The old things are discombobulating right before our eyes. But before we claim a victory, we'd better find the brigadier and your companions. It sounds as if the fight has moved to Castle Henry itself."

CHAPTER 42

LIEUTENANT MCKENZIE ORDERED several of his men to tend to casualties—three soldiers had gone down with ax and cudgel wounds, another had a concussion from slipping on the cobblestones. Amazingly, no soldiers had been killed. Then the lieutenant led Johnny, Nina, and his remaining troops the two hundred yards to the king's grand country house.

The fight had indeed come together there. The brigadier and his soldiers were battling to keep a troop of bog zombies from storming the front entrance. Hundreds of men and zombies engaged in desperate hand-to-hand combat.

Helping the soldiers in their efforts were workmen from the estate. Armed with buckets, the workers rushed toward the creatures, dousing them with the remaining liquid.

Up above, Johnny saw that another battle was being fought.

Ghosts on horseback and free-flying wraiths were soaring in and out of the royal mansion—dueling with swords, shooting arrows and guns, and wrestling each other as they tumbled through the air. There were Steppe Warriors and cavaliers battling marines from the Great War and cavalrymen from the Peninsular Campaign. Sergeant Clegg, his sawed-off shotgun in his right hand, had joined the battle, chasing after what looked like a sea raider.

And Johnny spotted Colonel MacFarlane high above Castle Henry, crossing swords with his old foe, Burilgi the Steppe Warrior.

Staring skyward at the skirmish through her goggles, Nina whistled in astonishment. "Well, that's something you don't see every day."

"Come on, Sparks. Let's see if we can get inside. Maybe we can help protect the king."

They threaded their way up the circular drive in front of Castle Henry, past the grand equestrian statues and fountain, and up the central stairs—dodging soldiers and bog zombies as they went. Inside the royal mansion it was practically a madhouse.

Ghosts were dueling and fighting all over the place. Glorious antique furniture had been upended. Glassware and china smashed to smithereens. Paintings knocked askew on the walls. Priceless sculptures tipped over and broken. Tapestries slashed, crumpled on the marble floors.

Johnny and Nina huddled by a huge, heavy rosewood china cabinet for several long minutes, as a Steppe Warrior dueled a dead army officer—an SGS man whom Johnny had seen on the train north out of Higgsmarket. If he and Nina had tried to move forward, they would have gotten sliced and diced.

"Got any plan in mind?" Nina asked, peering around the corner of the cabinet to see how the duel was going. "How did you figure we could help protect the king?"

Johnny didn't have a good answer. "I guess I just thought we would wing it."

All of a sudden there was a terrible crash of breaking glass and porcelain. Johnny and Nina stuck their heads out into the passageway, around the corner of the massive china cabinet. One of the ghosts had missed a strike and instead smashed a glass door in the cabinet—wrecking a number of valuable figurines.

Now the two ghost combatants had moved a few dozen feet away, to the right, toward the end of the hallway. They were still fighting fiercely, sword to sword, but the SGS man seemed to be gaining the advantage.

Nina gestured to the left. "Let's go this way."

They tiptoed out and away and were almost back down to the spot where the main floor hallway joined up with the central atrium. Up above hung a huge, golden chandelier. The marble floor had patterns of colorful stone embedded in it, in a large circular design.

"If I were a king, where would I hide out?" Johnny pondered, gazing around.

"If you were a king," Nina whispered, "I'd want to hide in another country."

Johnny gave her a mock scowl. "I betcha he's downstairs in the dungeon," he speculated, not knowing if all castles came with dungeons.

"No, actually he's not," said a papery voice right behind them.

Johnny spun around.

No one was better at sneaking up on a guy than a ghost. And Corporal Marchiano was a particular master of ghostly surprise. The Zenith trooper was always sneaking up on Johnny back home at Birchwood.

The boy and the ghost shook hands and exchanged greetings.

But Corporal Marchiano was not alone. Rex Ward was with him, along with Private Boo and a couple of living people—obviously servants—in tailcoats and white ties. One of them was Oates, the man whom the king called his "ghost eyes."

"Hey, Rex," exclaimed Johnny. "You're okay! It's so good to see you."

"And you, too, Master Graphic." Rex took Johnny's hand and

shook it vigorously.

"Do you know if the king is okay?"

Rex whispered in Johnny's ear. "Look carefully at the gent there." He gave a head nod in the direction of the smaller servant in the tails.

Johnny did just that, wondering what the ghost was on about. Then it hit him.

It was the king!

In the guise of a servant.

The king winked at Johnny, as if they were secretly sharing a very good joke.

Johnny winked back, then whispered to Rex. "You're sneaking him out?"

"Too many blasted hostile ghosts flying through every room," Rex sniffed. "We have to move him to a safer location."

"Then let's get out of here, guys. C'mon, Sparks."

Rex Ward took the lead, heading for the main door that Johnny and Nina had entered through. The king and Oates came next, with Marchiano and Boo on either side of them. Johnny and Nina brought up the rear.

"You're awful quiet, Sparks," said Johnny as they walked out into the night.

"Got a stinking bellyache, too," she replied, her voice thin and shaky. "A good night's sleep would do me wonders."

"Bet it would," Johnny agreed, figuring his friend was just out of sorts. Who wouldn't be? "This'll be over soon, and you can snooze around the clock back at Wickenham."

From the look of things, the fight outside was as good as done. Bog zombie bodies were sprawled all around, and hundreds of royal soldiers stood guard. Up in the sky, the fighting specters had vanished. Johnny wondered how Colonel MacFarlane and Sergeant Clegg had fared. He sure hoped they were okay.

"Your Majesty!" came a stouthearted shout from out by the grand fountain.

It was Brigadier Stafferton, trotting toward them, with Lieutenant McKenzie right on his heels. Both officers jerked to a halt and snapped off crisp salutes.

"Thank heavens you're safe," the brigadier exclaimed. He hastily added, "…Your Majesty."

"I was exiled in the wine cellar with all my best clarets," the king said with a wry half-smile.

"We seem to have taken the field," the brigadier said. "But better safe than sorry. Don't know if the hostiles will counter-attack. We have an armored car and convoy at the ready."

Johnny was impressed by how unruffled the king seemed. He'd just been through a horrible night and the threat of assassination. But he stood there, gazing around, as if he'd never quite seen Castle Henry before.

Then he regarded his rescuers. "First, I should like to thank Brigadier Stafferton and his fine troops. To my loyal Oates, my ghost eyes, a hearty note of gratitude." Oates bowed from the waist and shook the king's hand. "To my ghost friends, whom I can't see, a tip of the hat."

The king's gaze turned toward Johnny and Nina. "And I'm eternally obliged to Master Graphic and Miss Bain."

Remembering the etiquette, Johnny bowed from the waist and shuffled over to shake the king's rather limp hand.

After Nina curtsied, she approached the monarch of the Royal Kingdom with an oddly harsh, cold expression.

Johnny spied a glint of something in her left hand. Something metallic and pointed.

Nina had a knife!

With a terrible grunt, she began to jab the blade toward the king's stomach.

Arms outstretched, Johnny leapt toward her.

"Noooo!" he screamed.

CHAPTER 43

JOHNNY WAS ONLY AIRBORNE for a second and a half. His hands shot out in front of him as he prepared for impact with his suddenly insane friend.

He hit Nina with a solid *thuuud* that made his shoulder explode in pain and his already bruised nose zap him with the nastiest throb imaginable. The full force of his ninety or so pounds drove her sideways, as she let loose a ghastly, ear-piercing scream that hardly sounded human.

They both landed on the pavement. Johnny banged his knees and elbows, and scraped the side of his face on the macadam road surface. He saw Nina sprawled in front of him. And for the briefest moment, he worried that he might have knocked her out.

But that thought quickly evaporated as she twisted around like a scalded cat and rose up, coming at him with the very knife she had intended to use on the king. Johnny managed to roll to one side as the blade whizzed by his right ear, barely missing him.

Nina's momentum carried her forward and she tumbled to the pavement again. Taking a deep inhalation of air, Johnny jumped on top of her and grabbed her knife hand with both of his, attempting to bend her wrist and make her drop the weapon.

But he had no idea she was so strong. She was overpowering

him, bit by bit, and Johnny watched as the knife edged closer and closer to his chest.

What in the world had turned Nina Bain into a mad and murderous maniac? It made no sense at all. Only a few seconds had passed since the nightmare began, but it felt like an eternity.

By now, the brigadier, Rex Ward, Corporal Marchiano, and Private Boo had descended on the two of them, dragging them apart. Boo wrenched the knife from Nina's hand and tossed it aside, while Corporal Marchiano clamped an arm around her neck and tried to subdue her. She fought him ferociously, but wasn't strong enough to break free.

Johnny felt as if his whole world had turned upside down.

His best friend *an assassin?*

It was absolutely, positively, utterly *nuts!*

Nina was the most solid, most dependable, most honest, most upright person he had ever known. She could be a bit of a pain about it, in fact. Whenever she caught him making a tiny cheat or cutting a corner—which he occasionally felt entitled to do—he could count on a good chewing out.

What would bring her to the lunacy of trying to murder one of the most important people in the whole world?

Nina was writhing and twisting, screeching away about being let go. Claiming that she'd done nothing wrong. Protesting that the king deserved to die for the horrible way his country treated ghosts and zombies. She was spouting profanities, too, which was not at all her style.

Johnny wondered if the horrible strain and dangers of the last few days had finally gotten to her—sent her right round the bend. Her face was so contorted with rage that she hardly looked like Nina Bain.

That's when Dame Honoria and Mel rushed onto the scene.

Johnny didn't know where they had been during the battle. But from their soaked clothes, he figured they had been splashing some zombies.

"What on earth's happened?" Dame Honoria huffed.

"Sparks went crazy," Johnny said. "Tried to stab the king. I don't know why." Then he shrugged helplessly and threw up his hands. He felt almost like crying.

Corporal Marchiano still had Nina in a tight grip, as Mel walked up to her. "Why did you do it, Nina?" she asked. "*Why?*"

For some reason, seeing Mel's face—right through the etheric goggles that she still wore—seemed to calm Nina down. She took a few deep breaths and looked around at the circle of people and ghosts surrounding her. "I suppose they'll throw me in prison."

The brigadier had been standing close by, with a dark expression on his face. "I'm afraid we don't take kindly to attempts on his majesty's life, Miss Bain. You'll have a trial, of course. Unless you throw yourself on the mercy of the court. Or successfully make a plea of insanity. But the outcome is clear. The rest of your life will be spent in Heathmoor Women's Prison, or a madhouse."

Naturally, that's what would happen. Johnny just couldn't imagine that ol' straight-arrow Sparks would get herself into such a pickle.

Quite unexpectedly, the king walked up and regarded the girl who had tried to kill him. He looked amazingly calm and collected, considering what had just happened.

"I think of myself as a good judge of character, Brigadier Stafferton, and this doesn't seem the same young lady I met last week in my orchid house. The same young lady who showed me her miraculous ghost goggles. And the same young lady who provided us with valuable intelligence about the zombies."

He looked Nina straight in the eyes. "Something has happened to Miss Bain. *But what?"*

Johnny, and clearly everyone else, was asking the exact same question. He didn't think an answer would come as quickly and dramatically as it did.

Nina's face abruptly went empty and expressionless, and her body limp. Only the steady grip of Corporal Marchiano kept her from collapsing in a heap.

A luminous green light appeared in her slack, open mouth, and a sinuous, jade-colored form slithered out of it, like a serpent. All in a matter of a few seconds.

The ghostly, twisting thing was briefly amorphous, but then expanded and coalesced into a shape that was instantly recognizable.

Checheg! The one-armed Steppe Warrior!

Johnny began to yell a warning, just as Mel did.

The king was only a few feet away and he couldn't even see the threat.

With a snarl, Checheg let her ghost dagger fly.

And just as she did, Johnny saw a flash of green in the dim light of the new dawn, coming out of the sky.

It was Colonel MacFarlane. Diving like a hawk.

The instant he landed, there was a frightful *thunk* of blade burying itself into flesh.

And for a split second Johnny expected to see King Robert the Seventh die right before his eyes.

But instead, the colonel had taken the dagger. It was lodged in his chest, the handle still vibrating from the violence of its flight.

"Grab her, boys!" the colonel bellowed.

From out of nowhere came four troopers of the First Zenith Brigade. Lieutenant Finn, Sergeant Clegg, and Privates Moody and Schultz fell upon Checheg like a pack of wolves onto their prey.

The girl ghost howled and struggled and bucked and kicked and bit and scratched. But to no avail. The four Zenith troopers had her good and proper, each gripping one of her limbs. And before Mel or Johnny or anyone had the chance to say a word, off they flew with Checheg.

"Where are they taking her, Colonel?" Johnny asked.

"To a proper punishment, I should think," the colonel said, regarding his newest wound. "They're sick of that Steppe Warrior, as are we all."

He peered down at the knife handle, yanked it out, and tossed it aside. The weapon evaporated like fog in the sun. The blade was gone, but the wound would be there in his chest forever. Never to heal.

"What are they going to do with her?" Mel asked. "I didn't give any order."

"I think that's why they took her away in such a hurry, ma'am," the colonel said. "They might have been afraid you would order her released. Out of compassion. As we once did back in Zenith, after she attacked you in the middle of the night. There can be no more mercy for such a dangerous ghost."

"But we have to find out how she did what she did. How did she possess Nina? If ghosts can possess living people, then I'm afraid everything has changed."

"It would be the worst possible scenario," groaned Dame Honoria. "Every living human could be hijacked."

Johnny understood exactly what she meant. What if that person next to you at home or at work or at school seemed to be himself or herself, but somewhere inside was a ghost just waiting to take control? Like the brain snatchers in the Captain Justice stories. It meant you couldn't trust anyone. You couldn't believe anyone anymore. You would always be afraid.

"Excuse me, ma'am," the colonel said to Mel. "But just to clarify. That blasted Steppe Warrior will still be able to answer your questions. However, she won't be able to do much else."

CHAPTER 44

BAO HAD WANTED to go with Grandmother to visit the king's castle last night. But Grandmother had told her that she had enough to worry about on this trip, without having to keep an eye on a little girl ghost. Bao had frowned and pouted, but Grandmother, as usual, wasn't moved by such antics.

As everyone drove off in the big black automobile, Bao had watched from an upstairs window, feeling forlorn. Professor De-Nimes had stayed home too, but he was busy all evening down in the library, going through more of Percy's papers. And Evvie had said he wasn't in the mood to play—he was still feeling melancholy after seeing his mother and brother.

So the night had dragged on more slowly than usual. Bao had plenty of time to imagine all the fun Grandmother and Johnny and Nina and Mel were having at Castle Henry. The king would serve them tea and cakes, like he had the time Bao met him. And probably they would play wonderful games.

Finally it was morning. Bao sat on the front entrance staircase, chin on hands, staring out at Wickenham's magnificent landscape. She figured that sooner or later, Grandmother's auto would appear on the driveway.

But instead, she saw two wraiths floating up the curving road to the front entrance. And when they got closer, Bao could see that they weren't locals. She knew most of the area's ghosts by now.

These were strangers. A young girl and some kind of ancient soldier. A very odd pair, indeed.

Then Bao remembered. Johnny and Nina had sent two ghosts from the north, bearing news of the possible attack. An old warrior and a little girl with blonde hair. This must be them. But why were they so late?

"Welcome to Wickenham," Bao said, as the two wraiths floated up to the entrance. "I'm Bao. You must be Johnny and Nina's friends."

The warrior, who wore a feathered helmet and a kind of leather skirt, thumped his fist up to his chest and back out. Bao didn't know how to respond to that.

"I am Centurion Quintus," the warrior said. "This girl is Petunia Budd. And we are indeed comrades of Johnny Graphic and Nina Bain, with whom we lately campaigned in the north. We've come to report on events since they left us."

"We're late because we got lost in the fog," the girl Petunia said with an exaggerated frown. "Did Johnny and Nina get here safe?"

Bao told the new arrivals everything that had happened since Johnny and Nina had reappeared. Then she showed the two specters into the great house and asked them to stay in the sitting room off the entrance hall. She warned them that it could be a long wait before everyone returned from the king's house. But they didn't seem to mind. Ghosts, of course, were used to waiting.

For some reason, the pretty little blonde ghost eyed Bao as if she were some strange, peculiar object. Bao sniffed at her and left the sitting room, thinking, *I bet she doesn't have an important job like I do.*

A few hours later, an old automobile pulled up at the front entrance of Wickenham. Four living people piled out of it, along with one boy ghost. This time the butler Gilligan and the professor joined Bao to greet the visitors.

A black-haired boy with a swagger in his step was the first to speak up. Bao wasn't sure she liked him. He acted very important.

"How do? I'm Marko Herne. This is my Uncle Ezra Herne, my new mate Basil Hastings, and my associate Iris Budd."

Bao noticed that the pretty redheaded girl had her arm in a cast. And she had the loveliest violet eyes—though one of them had a bruise around it. Bao wondered if the girl had been in a fistfight with a zombie.

"The wraith is Raj Gupta, an ace secret ghost agent," Marko continued. "We've come to see Johnny Graphic and Nina Bain. And I believe a couple of our ghost friends should have gotten here by now."

"They have, sir," said Gilligan in his ever-even tone. "They are waiting for Master Graphic, Miss Bain, Miss Graphic, and Dame Honoria in the sitting room. Would you please follow me?"

As soon as he entered the entrance hall, with all its paintings and sculptures, Marko whistled. "These are some fancy digs, aren't they?"

Iris looked all around as well, agog at the sight of Grandmother's house. But Basil didn't seem too impressed. The ghost boy came next, followed by Uncle Ezra. Bao remembered the man. He had flown Johnny and Nina back home on that strange flying machine.

Gilligan brought them all into the sitting room, where they

joined Quintus and Petunia. The instant they made eye contact, the living girl and the ghost girl rushed at each other and embraced. Iris showered kisses on Petunia's blonde head. "I was so worried about you," she exclaimed. "But you're okay. You're okay!"

"I missed you lots, sweetie," Petunia replied, hugging Iris for all she was worth. Then she turned and looked at Bao. "This is my little sister," she explained.

Bao watched, happy for the girls, but kind of jealous, too. She wished her little sister was still around. It had been centuries, but she missed her very much.

When the sisterly reunion trailed off, Gilligan promised the living guests and the professor some refreshments and food.

"Excuse me," said Uncle Ezra, "but do you have a telephone I can use?"

Gilligan nodded. "Please come this way, sir."

BECAUSE BAO HADN'T HEARD many details about Johnny and Nina's adventures up north, she stayed with the professsor and the guests, standing silently in the corner of the sitting room. No one seemed even to be aware of her.

The first account came from the boy ghost called Raj. He explained how he had flown away from some place called Bilbury Hall to a town called Higgsmarket. He had spent many hours searching for someone to tell about the zombie camp at Bilbury. And finally he did. At first this person wouldn't believe him.

"The bloke was in the Special Ghost Service and he thought I was just some kind of dead street waif," Raj said with a scowl. "But when I mentioned Johnny and Nina and Marko here, he had to pay me some attention. Took me to an officer who sent ghost spies back to Bilbury to check out my story. Well, they ended up sending in hundreds of army and SGS forces to take back the hall. I went with them, and it was a heck of a fight. No sign of that scoundrel Percy Rathbone and his bird, Pamela Whatsername. And they were able to save all the children who hadn't escaped. No one was hurt. Just a few scratches, bumps, and bruises."

That's when the food and drink arrived, as well as a friend of Uncle Ezra's, a woman called Bess Tippett. Bao remembered her, as well, from when Johnny and Nina arrived in the flying machine just the day before. They had landed on her grass airstrip.

"How did you find Iris?" Petunia asked, while everyone was eating. Marko repeated her question to Uncle Ez, who could not hear the girl.

"After I got back from flying Johnny and Nina south in ol' Thumper," the aviator explained, "myself and Marko and Basil got in the auto and headed toward Bilbury. We knew it wasn't entirely safe, but we had to locate Iris. At a roadblock, an army bloke told us about a refugee center that had just taken in a bunch of kids. And that's where we found her." He winked at Iris. "Didn't we, luv?"

"Did indeed, Uncle Ez," Iris affirmed. "Carson and Leith and I were never so happy as when we saw those soldiers. They loaded us on lorries and took us to the camp. It warms my heart to think that all those kids are heading home now. No more zombie nightmares for them."

After being mostly silent, Professor DeNimes spoke up. "I say, Centurion, I should so like to know a little about your history. Which legion did you serve in? What campaigns did you fight in?"

Quintus's expression brightened, and he floated over and sat next to the professor. He began to tell him about all the action he'd seen in "the glorious old Ninth."

Which was *incredibly* boring, as far as Bao was concerned. She went over and stood behind the children, who were talking about much more interesting things.

"When I'm done here," said Basil, who couldn't see Bao standing next to him, "I'm heading home to Royalton for a rendezvous with the parents and sibs. We managed to get a phone call through to them during the drive down here."

Iris beamed at him. "Well, I expect Lord Hurley of Evansham will be delighted to have his youngest son safely back at home."

Bao's eyes widened. That was Evvie's other name. She summoned her courage and spoke up.

"Lord Hurley's here at Wickenham."

Marko, Iris, Petunia, and Raj looked at her quizzically.

"What do you mean, Lord Hurley's here?" asked Marko.

That got Basil's attention.

"He's here," Bao insisted. "He's a ghost. He's my best friend."

Marko told Basil what Bao had said.

Basil seemed dubious. "Ask her how she knows him."

Marko did just that. And Bao briefly told how she had met Evvie and how they were nearly blown up together. Which Marko, in turn, related to Basil.

The St. Egbert's School student looked quite astonished. "Well, I'm flabbergasted. That's got to be my dad's big brother. The chap who drowned in the Roobuco River. And he's here? Ask her, the ghost, to please go fetch him. I've dreamt about meeting Uncle Edward ever since I was little."

Bao went and found Evvie and brought him to the sitting room. A smashingly good introduction was made between uncle and nephew—with the help of Marko and Iris.

"Uncle Edward" told how he had recently visited the family home in Royalton, but was unable to make contact.

"Well," said Basil, "we'll just have to arrange a proper reunion, won't we, Uncle? Grandmother will be over the moon to talk to you again. So will Father."

Basil and his dead uncle chatted for hours, until their "translators," Marko and Iris, went hoarse.

CHAPTER 45

JOHNNY, MEL, AND DAME HONORIA piled into the town car and drove away from the king's estate at about four o'clock in the afternoon. And as unlikely as it would have seemed a few hours earlier, Nina left with them.

Johnny had been worried sick that she'd be in jail forever. After all, dozens of people and ghosts had witnessed her attempt on the life of King Robert.

It was touch-and-go, nerve-wracking.

Brigadier Stafferton—who had seemed to Johnny to be such a nice guy—had insisted that Nina be charged and hauled off to jail immediately, to await her trial. When Johnny saw the look of helplessness on his friend's face as the police came to take her away, it cut right into his heart.

Johnny had protested emphatically that it wasn't Nina who had committed the crime. It was the wraith Checheg, who had somehow possessed and commandeered his friend. Dame Honoria, in her most imperious voice, had argued that it would be a grave injustice to prosecute the child for anything—that she deserved a medal instead. Mel had pointed out that, more than anyone else, Nina was responsible for the defeat of the bog zombies. She had provided the essential clue that led to victory.

But the brigadier had said that, as much as he appreciated their opinions, he was bound by the laws of the land to take Nina into custody.

Then, quite unexpectedly, the king himself had spoken up.

In that soft, small voice of his, he made a very eloquent case for Nina's release. Although he couldn't see Checheg, his manservant Oates had described the horrifying scene of the Steppe Warrior rising out of Nina's mouth like a puff of poison gas. With Checheg finally dealt with by the Zenith troopers, the king said he felt no further threat to his wellbeing.

And he pointed out that the country, and perhaps the world, was still in grave danger from rogue ghosts. Nina, being the only living person they knew of who had been possessed by a ghost, would be far more valuable aiding Dame Honoria and Melanie in their efforts than sitting in a frigid jail somewhere in the Royal Kingdom.

The brigadier had finally relented, with the proviso that Nina make herself available for questioning before she left to fly home to the Plains Republic. Nina assured him she wouldn't go anywhere until she had revealed every last detail about her stay at Bilbury Hall.

Johnny had even been allowed to take a few shots of the battle scene before cleanup took place. The grounds were littered everywhere with bog zombie remains, shrunken and lifeless, no longer a threat now that the ghosts had vacated them.

The brigadier gave assurances that the corpses would be returned to the north and given honorable re-burial in the bogs they had come from.

"These bog men, these warriors were victims, too," he had said. "Their graves in the bogs were desecrated for the sole purpose of giving Percy Rathbone a ready-made army. They deserve to again rest in peace."

In the aftermath of the Battle of Castle Henry, Colonel Mac-Farlane had watched Johnny like a hawk. He explained that he still felt awful about losing Johnny and Nina the day of the train wreck. He blamed it on that odd, heavy fog that blanketed the northern areas. "We don't get weather like that in Zenith," he remarked. "Strangest thing is, it seemed to make me feel muddled and uneasy. The boys, too. I really didn't start feeling normal again until we arrived at Wickenham."

Just before their departure from Castle Henry, the king had taken Mel aside and said a few words to her. She explained in the car that he had asked her to send him a pair of etheric goggles. He was "awfully keen" to see ghosts whenever he felt like it. And "cost was no object." But Mel had already decided that they would be a gift, in gratitude for the king's spirited defense of Nina.

Back at Wickenham, Johnny was delighted to be reunited with his MacFreithshire companions. Over a delicious supper whipped up by Dame Honoria's cooks, everyone caught up on the news. Johnny didn't mention it, but he knew that Marko, Iris, Basil, and Uncle Ez would be receiving a special letter of commendation from his majesty. And the SGS intended to similarly acknowledge the roles that Raj, Pet, and Centurion Quintus had played—with special medals minted for veterans of the MacFreithshire campaign.

Although Dame Honoria offered them lodging for the night, Uncle Ez loaded up Marko and Iris into his auto. They were following Bess Tippett back to her place, where they would spend the night. On the way, Uncle Ez was going to drop Basil and Professor

DeNimes off at the Blackfield station to catch the late train to Royalton. They were taking Edward Hastings—also known as Evvie, the late Lord Hurley of Evansham—home for a proper reunion with his younger brother and his mother.

Johnny promised to send Marko and Iris copies of the photos he had shot during their adventure. And he told Marko that if he ever needed a bodyguard again, he'd know whom to ask for.

"I realize that we got off on the wrong foot back there in Higgsmarket," Johnny said. "And that was maybe partly my fault, thinking that I always know best. But you have to admit that you did come on pretty strong."

Marko clapped him on the shoulder. "I suppose I did," he agreed. "But I didn't know much about you, except that you were some kind of star news photographer who was just twelve years old."

"Twelve and three-quarters," Johnny corrected him.

"Twelve and three-quarters, then," Marko repeated. "I wasn't about to let you go off half-cocked and get your head cut off. It was dangerous out there and we had to play it smart."

"I think the problem," Iris said, "comes down to two young male egos bashing into each other at full speed. Bound to be fireworks."

Nina was standing by Johnny and Mel. "Boys," she said, winking at Iris. "Who can figure them out?"

"In the end, Marko and Johnny made a fine team," Iris concluded. "All those kids from Bilbury Hall owe you two a big debt."

"And we owe you and Petunia, too," Mel said to Iris. "As soon as I get back home, I'm making three pairs of etheric goggles *pronto*. One for the king, one for Evvie's family, and another for you. So your mom can see Petunia whenever she wants to."

With that, Iris and Pet rushed to embrace Mel. Johnny figured the hug lasted a full minute.

By the time the guests had left, it was close to midnight. Weary and exhausted, everyone was about to head upstairs to bed when there came a loud knocking at Wickenham's front door. As if by magic, Gilligan the butler appeared out of nowhere, in his bathrobe. He opened the door and in marched Uncle Louie, suitcase in hand.

Johnny felt a new surge of energy and ran to greet his uncle.

"I'm never letting you kids out of my sight again," the big man said, giving them each a bear hug. He even gave Dame Honoria a quick squeeze, lifting her off the ground with a grunt.

It was another hour before Johnny's head finally hit the pillow. It was so good to be reunited with his family again. Another near disaster had been averted and everyone was safe. He knew he would sleep like a log tonight.

CHAPTER 46

THE VERY NEXT DAY, government officials insisted on debriefing everyone about the bog zombie uprising. So Johnny, Nina, Mel, and Dame Honoria were driven to a nearby army base, where they gave testimony to several severe-looking men and women in uniform.

The officers wanted to know every detail about Nina's attempted attack on his majesty the king. Nina was told that she could leave the country, if she wished. But she must return, in the event that they asked her to. Her word of honor was required, and she gave it. And Johnny knew that no one was more honest and trustworthy than Nina Bain.

But there was another reason why the four of them had been brought to the base. They were taken to a second grim room in another building. The home secretary himself was waiting there, along with Rex Ward. The two of them wanted to talk about Nina's ghost possession and what it might mean to the security of the Royal Kingdom.

Nina described her capture and subsequent captivity in a bedroom at Bilbury Hall. "While I was being kept there, Miss Worthington-Smythe asked me if I'd like a cup of cocoa. I felt kind of groggy after that. She drugged me, I guess."

"Did you feel anything strange while the ghost was inside your head?" the home secretary asked.

"Well, my right arm hurt. Guess that's because Mel had chopped off Checheg's arm back in Zenith. And I had an ache in my stomach, right where she got stabbed at Acme Ironworks. But I really didn't notice I was out of control until the night at Castle Henry. It's as if she waited until just the right moment to take over. I think that's why she didn't help the bad guys sooner. She was waiting for a big target."

"How Checheg managed to, well, *infect* Nina is a mystery to me," Dame Honoria said. "Until we have some idea of how the trick was pulled off, we won't know how to stop it from happening again."

"Or how to cure people who are infected," Mel added.

The home secretary's face turned slightly gray. "So no notion of the mechanism behind this phenomenon?"

"None whatsoever," sighed Dame Honoria.

"But if that knowledge becomes known to other ghosts, look out," Johnny said ominously.

"The living world would be turned upside down," Dame Honoria warned.

The home secretary shook his head. "Paranoia and fear everywhere. Who could be trusted anymore? Imagine if a possessed general started a war. Or an important banker with a ghost under his skull crashed a national economy."

Percy now had the power to cause huge disasters, Johnny realized. There was really no limit to what that crumb-bum could do, if he got away with this possession thing. He could change the face of the whole world.

"But we have a plan, Home Secretary," said Dame Honoria.

He looked at her hopefully. "Yes?"

"We may have some idea of where my son learned his new dark arts, and from whom. In two or so weeks, we plan to fly by aeroboat to Okkatek Island, mount an expedition, and find out all we can about the ghost shaman Morbrec. That is, of course, if he even existed."

BACK AT WICKENHAM THAT AFTERNOON,

Johnny joined everyone in the main-floor sitting room. They were all gathered around a cozy fireplace, ensconced in overstuffed chairs and on the big sofa, enjoying a pot of afternoon tea and biscuits.

Uncle Louie was talking about the weather, a favorite topic of pilots everywhere. He explained that the planes he had worked on during the last couple of weeks were rarely able to take off.

"The heavy ground clouds made it impossible. The pilots said they had never seen such peculiar weather. The fog was real thick, but it didn't seem to have any moisture in it. You couldn't see any dampness on the ground or on the windshields. It was like a weird kind of smoke."

"We've been thinking about that fog," Mel said. "We're worried that whatever Percy is up to, he might be causing some disruption in the ether."

"But what I still don't understand is why Percy kidnapped all those kids." Johnny said. "What did he plan to do with them?"

Dame Honoria's face darkened. "I fear that my son is plotting to do something bigger and more disastrous in the future. After all, when the children grow up, their bodies will make fine vessels for ghost warriors to inhabit."

"Or he could put them to other uses," Mel added. "Imagine a spy network of possessed children who are secret agents."

The idea made Johnny shudder. He'd always have to be suspicious of any kid he met.

"Whatever Percy's up to," Nina said, "we can't let him possess any more people. I know how it feels. It was impossible for me to stop Checheg from attacking the king. I had no control at all. I was seeing it unfold from inside my head, but I couldn't do a thing to stop it."

"That's why we have to end this madness before it can spread," Mel said, putting her teacup down on the table in front of her. "The trip to Okkatek is the only hope we have."

OVER THE NEXT COUPLE OF DAYS, Johnny helped Nina compose their news stories on Dame Honoria's typewriter. They decided to share the byline. Every article would say "By Nina Bain and Johnny Graphic." Mel also pitched in, and gave each story a close once-over, marking grammatical errors and typos with a red pencil. Their pieces on the train wreck, the destruction at St. Egbert's, the great escape at Bilbury Hall, the nerve-wracking flight in Thumper, and the Battle of Castle Henry all read like ripping adventure stories.

Johnny definitely saw more Newshawk awards in their future.

As soon as the stories were done, the three of them were driven by Dame Honoria's chauffeur to the Royalton office of the World Press Association, where they dropped off the stories and Johnny's pictures. Johnny had developed his many rolls of film in a darkroom that Gilligan the butler maintained at Wickenham.

Johnny was elated, knowing that Mr. Cargill would scoop everyone in the world, running the stories first in the *Zenith*

Clarion. The articles were published a day later in Royalton newspapers. Johnny loved seeing his pictures and the headlines.

The Great Ghost Battle of the Derailed Train

Daring Escape from Bilbury Hall: Watery Peril in a Culvert

Lost in Bog Country

The Attack on St. Egbert's

Government censors had changed a few things in the stories. Any mention of bog zombies was replaced with words like "ruffians," "hooligans," and "thugs." Dame Honoria had warned Johnny that might be the case—the government wanted calm to return to the country as quickly as possible.

The newspapers also gave him a chance to catch up on related developments. He especially looked for coverage of any attacks in Royalton, but was surprised to find no reports of any action there. Dame Honoria confirmed that, thankfully, nothing had occurred in the metropolis.

With the news assignments done, Johnny continued working on his photo essay about country life around Wickenham, hiking from one corner of the vast property to the other. He took hundreds of pictures, though he didn't plan to develop them until he got back to Zenith. He'd had enough of darkroom chemicals for a while. The harsh smell got in your clothes and up your nose. But it was a price you had to pay if you were a news lensman.

One afternoon he was in his bedroom at Wickenham, unloading the roll of film he had shot that lunch hour at the pub where Ozzie had been captured. He pulled it out of the Ritterflex, licked the glued tab at the end of the paper that covered the film, and sealed the roll shut. No chance now of it accidentally getting exposed to light and ruined. Tired, he stretched out on his bed and began to daydream.

In just a few days, they were all heading for Okkatek Island. Danny Kailolu, Mel's boyfriend, was going to fly the Zephyr Lines floatplane back to Rowestoft to pick them up. Johnny knew the reason for the trip was to find out where that rotten Percy had gotten his knowledge of zombification and possession of the living.

But Johnny had another goal, as well. Will and Lydia Graphic had disappeared on Okkatek. And it was his plan to go hunting for his parents there—all alone, if he had to. The zombie attack had delayed his and Mel's search plans. Johnny Graphic wouldn't be put off again. If he could get his folks back, he would never ask for another thing. *Ever.*

Still, even without parents in his life, Johnny was surrounded by people who cared for him. And he *knew* it. A great sister, a super uncle, the best friend and almost-cousin in the world, a remarkable godmother, a—

"Hey, Johnny…"

He had been daydreaming so hard, he hadn't noticed Nina come in through the open bedroom door.

"Yeah, Sparks, what's up?"

She had on her etheric goggles, and Johnny was surprised to realize that she was starting to look almost normal in them.

"Guess who stopped in to say hi?" She could hardly contain herself.

Curious, Johnny sat up on the edge of the bed. "No idea.

Who?"

"Basil Hastings. He's on his way to his new school, which is right here in Gilbeyshire. Evvie's with him. And his dad, Lord Hurley, who really wants to meet you."

"Well what are we waiting for?" Johnny hopped to his feet. Fretting about Percy Rathbone and the trip to Okkatek could wait. Right now Johnny intended to have some fun.

He and Nina raced out into the hallway and bounded down Wickenham's grand staircase.

EPILOG

PERCIVAL GORTON RATHBONE STOOD silently over the gaunt figure sleeping in the primitive jail cell, huddled beneath a ragged blanket. The prisoner—who had shaggy sandy hair, bushy beard, and freckles—dozed fitfully. Outside, an Okkatek blizzard howled like a mad demon, as it drove the biting snow through the bleak mountain pass.

Percy was well aware that, even for a ghost, he looked preposterous in his drenched parka, breeches, and mukluks. But he had, after all, tumbled into a frigid stream in the Okkatek wilderness and died quickly of hypothermia—basically soaked and chilled to death. Unfortunately, one was stuck with the clothing one died in. Better to be in winter gear, he supposed, than be some poor ghost who expired in the bathtub, and had to go through eternity dripping *and* naked.

The last time Percy had been inside a jail cell was back in Zenith, after the failure of the second etheric bomb. He had to waste a perfectly good body—albeit a dead body. Because escape had been impossible so long as he occupied it. So he surprised Burilgi by asking the Steppe Warrior to chop Percy's zombie head off. That worked like a charm. Once again a ghost, he was able to accompany his friend and co-conspirator Pamela Worthington-Smythe home to the Royal Kingdom.

There, all the preparations had been made for the war of the bog zombies. The corpses had been liberated and animated by ghosts willing to fight for their rights. That represented quite a bit of bog to dig up, but it was worth it.

They would have two initial missions. To raise havoc and sow anarchy in the sparsely populated northern shires, which would become their base of operation. And to capture schoolchildren who, when eventually possessed by ghosts, would operate as spies and saboteurs.

Percy had decided to test his bog army's battle strength by having them attack the king at Castle Henry. If things went well there, he would order a second assault on the centers of government in Royalton.

That they were ultimately defeated at Castle Henry was disappointing. But one does not take on a powerful government and win the first time out.

One keeps trying.

One does not give up.

One has another plan up one's sleeve—bigger even than the first two.

And what Percy intended to do tonight would set it all in motion.

Pamela had begged him not to. How could the effort go forward without Percy Rathbone personally at the helm? How could she lead those thousands of ghosts? How could she manage the secret, ghostly possession of hundreds of important men and women around the world?

Percy patiently explained that he had to go "under cover." He assured Pamela that he would join her and the others soon enough. And staying hidden inside this man's brain would give him plenty of time to ponder the mystery of the unnatural fog back in Mac-Freithshire. It was something he hadn't expected when he began his experiments.

Why had that strange, moistureless fog manifested itself when they made all those bog zombies? What did it mean? Was something happening in the ether? Percy had a scientific mind and he wanted to solve this puzzle. Perhaps the brain of the man lying before him could be useful in this task.

Percy was quite sure that Mummy had figured out his connection with Morbrec. His late night visit to Wickenham had been clumsy and stupid. But he hadn't been able to resist.

Just this morning his ghost agents had informed him that Mummy was flying here to the island with those infernal Graphic brats. Very soon. So, the time had come.

Continuing to stare down on the sleeping prisoner, Percy chuckled.

He began to shrink in size—from the stature of a man to that of a boy to that of a baby to that of a mouse.

He elongated his ghostly body.

And he flowed like a tiny snake toward Will Graphic's face.

The End

APPENDIX 1

THE TWO IMPOSSIBLE THINGS

The First Impossible Thing posits that no ghost may return to life in a physical body.

The Second Impossible Thing posits that no ghost may escape the ether and pass over to the great unknown that claims, upon their deaths, the vast majority of all living creatures.

APPENDIX 2

THE LAWS OF ETHERISTICS

1. Ghosts—also known as specters, wraiths, sprites, spirits, phantoms, phantasms, and spooks—are the sentient remains of deceased humans and animals.

2. Ghosts exist non-corporeally in the forms and with the perquisites in which and with which they died, in a non-material universe parallel but contingent to our own, called "The Ether."

3. Ghosts are creatures of free will.

4. Ghosts may exercise their free will by serving living humans and—thus endowed by living "effectuators"—assume a degree of corporeality required to perform the tasks requested of them in our material universe.

5. Ghosts' corporeality—including use of implements they may have utilized when alive—finds expression as it is needed and vanishes when it is not, often in the blink of an eye. The duration and efficacy of this phenomenon can vary, however, for reasons not yet understood.

6. Ghosts who are engaged corporeally in any activity that may harm living humans or animals are subject to the same injuries as the living—though they cannot be killed a second time.

7. Ghosts are free at any time to withdraw from their arrangements in service to practicing etherists, and others with the capacity to see and hear them, but thereby lose the benefits of corporeality.

8. Practicing etherists and others with the capacity to see and hear etherians are free to end arrangements with them, thereby terminating the ghosts' benefits of corporeality.

—Adopted this Sixth Day of May, 1896, by the Third World Congress of Consulting Etherists, gathered in Molderdam, Kingdom of the Low Countries. Anna De Waart, General Secretary, presiding.

ACKNOWLEDGEMENTS

It would have been impossible to write *Johnny Graphic and the Attack of the Zombies* without the help of several very talented people. Once again, Marlo Garnsworthy provided a highly insightful editorial review that improved the book in many respects. Kate Collins came up with a number of good ideas that I have implemented. Marie Joseph offered the perspective of a book-loving teacher, and caught quite a few typos, as well. Steve Thomas created both the original book cover and map, and the cover for the new revision. And most important, Sue Wichmann—dispenser of commas and slayer of long paragraphs—was the disciplinarian and Johnny Graphic expert who kept this sequel on track.

ABOUT THE AUTHOR

In addition to being the creator of the Johnny Graphic Adventures trilogy, D. R. Martin is the author of four Mary MacDougall historical mysteries and three King Harald canine cozy mysteries—written under his pen name, Richard Audry. He's also the author of the hardboiled PI mystery *Smoking Ruin*. You can follow D. R. at johnnygraphicadventures.com, drmartinbooks.com, and facebook.com/johnnygraphicadventures.

Don't miss the Rip-Roaring Conclusion of The Johnny Graphic Adventures...

Johnny Graphic and the Ghost of Doom

If you enjoyed *Johnny Graphic and the Etheric Bomb* and *Johnny Graphic and the Attack of the Zombies*, don't miss the trilogy's thrilling conclusion!

In *Johnny Graphic and the Ghost of Doom*, Johnny, Nina, and their companions fly to Okkatek Island to hunt for Johnny's lost parents. But an imminent volcanic eruption forces the group to change their plans. Johnny is determined to search for his mom and pop no matter what. Even if he has to take off on his own. Things go seriously off the rails, though, as he races across the island, only to face fiendish ghosts, giant ice wolves, tribesmen seeking human sacrifices, and the volcano itself.

Johnny Graphic and the Ghost of Doom is now available.